SCARLET NIGHT

DOROTHY SALISBURY DAVIS

SCARLET NIGHT

AVON
PUBLISHERS OF BARD, CAMELOT AND DISCUS BOOKS

For Sarah
at seventeen

AVON BOOKS
A division of
The Heart Corporation
959 Eighth Avenue
New York, New York 10019

Copyright © 1980 by Dorothy Salisbury Davis
Published by arrangement with Charles Scribner's Sons
Library of Congress Catalog Card Number: 79-28467
ISBN: 0-380-55128-2

First Avon Printing, May, 1981

AVON TRADEMARK REG. U.S. PAT. OFF. AND IN
OTHER COUNTRIES, MARCA REGISTRADA, HECHO EN
U.S.A.

Printed in the U.S.A.

ONE

While Jeff went downstairs again for the rest of the luggage Julie opened doors and windows. She had been gone a month—a month in Paris—but the feeling when she opened the folding doors to the living room was of a room closed up for years. And in a way it had been. With her husband away so much of the time, she rarely entered it, never sat in it when she was alone, and always hurried the cleaning of it. It was a Henry James kind of room, full of Victorian furniture, valuable bric-a-brac, and presences. The *objets d'art* suggested a collector who was at home abroad. And that was Jeff, a New York newspaper columnist with carte blanche to the world.

Julie opened the inside shutters, letting in the sunlight, and turned then as though drawn by an evil spirit to the one thing she truly hated in the room, the painting of Jeff over the mantel. It was the artistry of his first wife, Felicia, a tricky piece of work which Julie had once compared in her own mind to the crabbed "Judgment" card in her Tarot deck. Wherever you went in the room Jeff's eyes pursued you. Only they weren't Jeff's eyes, they were Felicia's Jeff's eyes.

The man himself came in, sniffed the dry muskiness, and took a long homecoming look around him. The smell, Julie thought, suggested elegant old ladies in taffeta shaking out lace handkerchiefs. What it was, actually, was the moth repellent exhaled by the vacuum cleaner.

"Don't you use this room when I'm not here, Julie?"

"Not much."

"Why not, for heaven's sake?"

"Ghosts," Julie said, not altogether flippant.

Jeff looked at her, an eyebrow raised.

"I'm kidding. No! I'm not . . . Jeff, are you passionate about Felicia's portrait of you?"

He looked at it from across the room as though he had forgotten it was there.

5

Having at long last brought up the subject, she plunged ahead: "It's spooky. It isn't you, really. Those eyes are nasty. You know what it's like? It's as though she wanted to paint a judge and used you for a model."

Jeff grinned. "That's very funny. Her father was a judge."

"Oh, boy."

He flinched. "I wish you'd stop saying that."

"I'll try. I will try."

He came and stood beneath the portrait and looked up at it.

"You're better looking than that," Julie said.

"I'd have to agree with you," he said dryly.

It was his distinguished air that Felicia had tried to catch. He had a strong face with wise dark eyes, and the tough mouth of someone who had to be shown. There were little pouches under his eyes that Felicia had overlooked. Or maybe they weren't there in her day. His hair was starting to gray now—at forty. He was a head taller than Julie, just under six feet, slight, but muscular, and fifteen years older. Which sometimes seemed a lot.

He took the picture from the wall and Julie thought of her psychotherapist and all the time they had spent on the subject of that painting until the doctor had finally said, "Couldn't you simply ask him to remove it?"

The mountain had turned out to be a molehill after all.

Jeff said: "We can take it up to the attic when we take the luggage and hide it there."

"Why don't we pack it up and send it to Felicia?"

He made a face of mock reproof. Felicia had recently remarried. "The question is, what do we do for a replacement?" The outline of where the painting had hung was plainly visible.

Julie almost said, "Move." But she didn't.

"We ought to look at pictures," Jeff said. "That's something we do nicely together."

Which confirmed her suspicion that he had been sorting out the days and nights ahead, his, hers, and theirs, now that he was to make New York his headquarters for a while.

"I wish I'd said something in Paris."

"We'll find something. I shouldn't want a reproduction. I'm sure you wouldn't either."

"Let's take our time," Julie said, which wasn't like

her. But whatever came in was going to have to make it among some pretty exalted company—a Rembrandt etching, an early Picasso, a Daumier drawing, two good Impressionists.

"I'm glad you feel that way," Jeff said, on his way to answer the first telephone call since their return.

Julie went to the window and looked down on the street traffic—light on Sunday: a few cars, more taxis. The apartment was the second floor through one of the last of the nineteenth-century townhouses left on Sixteenth Street. It faced a church and backed against the outer reaches of the garment industry, with a tired catalpa tree slouching in a garden where no flowers grew. But the house itself was well kept up. Jeff had lived there before his first marriage. In his and Julie's four years together it remained his in character. Not because he wanted it that way, but because Julie had not known how to change it. One thing she hadn't wanted to do was make a hash of the place just to prove that Julie as well as Geoffrey Hayes lived there. And now that Felicia's painting was going, she thought, she might not want to change it at all. Furthermore, she decided almost at the same instant, she was through with psychotherapy.

Until further notice.

They agreed that night, having coffee in the living room, that something had to be done soon about the bald spot over the mantel.

"What would you say to a good mirror if we can find the right style?" Jeff suggested.

"Not much." She wasn't fond of mirrors. But if Jeff wanted one . . . "Maybe," she added, trying to sound hearty.

"What we had better do," Jeff said, quite aware, "when either of us has an hour or two to spare is drop in on some of the better galleries—and if we see something we like, we can go back together and give ourselves time to consider it."

"Fine," Julie said. An hour or two to spare . . . that was Julie's whole problem: she had far too much time to spare and Jeff no time at all. The old floundering feeling and the depression that came with it began to descend. Do something, Julie.

She got up instantly and went to her desk in the bedroom. She looked up the phone number for Lieutenant Donleavy, Mid-Manhattan Homicide. He might or might not be on duty, Sunday night. He was there.

"This is Julie Hayes, Lieutenant. I don't know if you remember me . . ."

"The little fortune-teller. I'm not ever going to forget you, Mrs. Hayes. What can I do for you?"

Julie was chagrined at the description, the little fortune-teller. She had come close to serious trouble that spring—before she joined Jeff in Paris—by setting up as "Friend Julie, Reader and Advisor" in a shop on West Forty-fourth Street. She said, "I wondered if you could tell me what happened to Rita Morgan."

Rita Morgan was the prostitute she had mistaken for a child and tried to help.

"She's still under psychiatric observation, but I'll give you an educated guess as to what will happen."

"Please."

"Off the record, you understand. I don't think she'll ever come to trial."

Rita Morgan had murdered Julie's friend, Pete Mallory, who also had tried to help her.

"She'd be a great witness for the prosecution," Julie said. "I never knew of anybody so self-destructive."

"It's a pity she didn't do herself in, instead of Mallory," Donleavy said, going short on sympathy. "Do you want to see her?"

"I don't think so, and I don't think she'd want to see me. There's not much point."

"That's being sensible."

"Lieutenant, I've gone out of the fortune-telling business."

"I was teasing you. I don't think you were ever really in it. Were you now?"

"Not for long. It was a lark. You're right. Thank you, Lieutenant."

"Any time, Mrs. Hayes."

It was like a dream and more bizarre than most, Julie thought, sitting a moment after she put down the phone. She remembered very clearly leaving her therapist's office that April morning, angry and hurt because the doctor had said that until Julie was ready to find gainful employment and help herself, the therapy was a waste of Jeff's money. It didn't wash with Doctor Callahan that

Jeff liked "his little girl," his "child bride," his wife the dilettante. "Rubbish. He will like a woman better. And so will you, which is more important." She had known even then that Doctor was right, but she had felt abandoned, and when someone handed her a flyer on Fifth Avenue, advertising "Madame Tozares," like a mischievous child, she had decided to go into the business of reading the Tarot cards and advising.

Her rationalizations were numerous, of course. She had expected to meet, and God knows she had met, a lot of troubled people about whom she hoped to write someday. Of all the things she wanted to do, writing was foremost. But she lived in the shadow of a master whose work she had reverenced from the time he'd lectured on campus when she was in college, and the more he encouraged her, the less capable she felt. No, she decided, Forty-fourth Street had meant more to her than mere spite of Doctor Callahan: she had attempted to create an environment for herself among people who would not intimidate her intellectually. She had subsequently learned that the simplest people were by no means simple. And she had learned about herself that she functioned well in emergencies, even while pumping adrenaline. She had taken all her notes to Paris with her and Jeff had said he did not know an investigative reporter who could have done better at collecting material.

She went back to Jeff in the living room and told him what Donleavy had said about Rita Morgan, that she was probably incompetent to stand trial. "It's a sort of ending, isn't it?" she said.

"Or a beginning," Jeff said, looking at her over his reading glasses.

"Yeah."

Jeff took off his glasses and put them in his pocket. "Julie, keep the place on Forty-fourth Street for a while. I don't know how much I'll be at home, but you ought to have a place of your own to work in."

Julie's spirits took an upward leap. She said, "You're great, Jeff, absolutely great."

"Well, it's time there was a Geoffrey the Great," he said in mock seriousness. "There's been a Geoffrey the Handsome, a Geoffrey the Bastard—Archbishop of York, by the way—and a Geoffrey the Cat that I know about, but to my knowledge, I am the first Geoffrey the Great."

Julie's impulse was to throw herself into his lap, something she knew pleased him very much, but that was part of the "little girl" pattern, and the time had come to break it. She went around the back of his chair and hugged him. Straightening up, she faced the empty wall over the mantel. "Before anything, I'd like to find a picture," she said. "I'd like this room to be right, somehow. It's like starting a sentence and never finishing it."

"Then look. Go out and look at pictures. There must be a hundred gallery owners in New York waiting for you."

TWO

The gallery door stood open and a young man with a broom noticed Julie at about the same time she noticed him. "Come in if you want to."

Julie walked into the Maude Sloan Gallery. She had already seen too many paintings for one day, but the poster out front announcing the opening that afternoon described Ralph Abel's first American show as "Parisian fantasies." It wasn't so bad, only fourteen paintings when she got to counting them, with a lot of wall space and light around them. She strolled from one canvas to the next, not greatly impressed. They all had names, but so far as she could see, there was not much relationship between the name and the picture. Julie the art critic, she mocked herself. Except that once she had studied art . . . but then, what had she not studied at one time or other?

She had the feeling that the young man was painfully aware of her. He took plastic glasses from a box and lined them up alongside a punch bowl. Was he the artist? She felt that he was, although his attitude was uncharac-

teristic of any artist she knew. He put the box away and
went back to work with the broom.

"Hey!" Julie came up to a splash of city colors—or so
she saw them, a lot of red, blue, purple and black. Non-
objective. But she could sense the presence of the lurking
whores. She swung around to where the young man had
stopped in his tracks to stare at her. The color leaped to
his face. "Are you Mr. Abel?"

"Yes, I am." But he fled with the broom to the closet
at the back.

Julie read the legend beneath the frame: SCARLET
NIGHT.

"I'm going to have to close up for an hour, ma'am."
He really could not bear to be in the room alone with
someone looking at his paintings, not today anyway.

Ma'am, Julie thought, and wondered if there was a
Paris, Nebraska, or Iowa or Illinois. "I'll go peaceably.
No problem."

"I didn't mean to be impolite," he said, still blushing
to the roots of his corn-colored hair. It made his eyes
seem very blue. "It's nerves, that's all."

"I kind of like that," Julie said, indicating *Scarlet
Night*.

His smile was beatific. "I'm sorry the wine hasn't come
yet." He made a helpless gesture toward the empty bowl.

"Is everything here Paris? I've just got back from
there."

"No kidding? I'll tell you the truth, I painted most of
them in Naples. I couldn't get with Paris until I got away
from there. I guess that doesn't make much sense. . . ."

"You bet it does. I'd never make it in Paris alone."

"Funny. I thought at first you were a critic."

"No way. I don't even know why I like things."

"Do you think any of the critics will come? Do you live
in New York?"

"All my life—except for a month in Paris."

He was on a single track. "And you go to a lot of
openings. Right?"

"Not a lot."

"But you look like you do," he persisted. "The way
you dress, you know—a certain style, good material. My
father was a tailor."

Julie was beginning to feel the whole scene wasn't happening—not in SoHo, New York. "I usually wear sneakers and a raincoat."

"That wouldn't matter. I'd say the same thing. Even the bones in your face."

Julie turned her wide gray eyes upon him. "Look, I'm curious. This is your first exhibit, right?"

He nodded.

"What's the price on *Scarlet Night?*"

"I'm not allowed to talk prices. That's Mrs. Sloan's department."

"I didn't say I was buying. I'm just curious. I suppose it's rude of me, but I'm a very direct person." With some people; she had overstated the characteristic.

"It's not that, but Maude's been good to me. She said she'd give me a show after seeing a couple of transparencies and stuck to it when I got here with the rest, which I'm pretty sure she didn't like much."

"Oh, man. You need a larger dose of self-confidence than that. Don't *you* think they're good?"

"Yes, ma'am. I think they're beautiful."

"Then they are. Don't sell them short, for heaven's sake." Julie made a move toward the door.

"Don't go. . . . I mean please stay for the opening."

"I'll come back at five and join the crowd."

"What if nobody comes?" There was such a sweet, sad look about him. *Ah, Wilderness!* Julie thought, having played in it in college. Or *Our Town.* They ought to be sitting on two stools at a make-believe soda fountain.

"Don't you have any family?"

"Not real close. I have a cousin who bought out my father's shop from me when my father died. But he thinks I'm crazy."

"There are worse things—I mean than having a cousin think that. I have cousins with whom I pretend I'm crazy so they'll leave me alone. Not that I have to pretend all that hard. Where's the tailor shop?"

"Keokuk, Iowa."

"I like that."

"What's your name, if you don't mind my asking?"

"Julie Hayes."

"You're married, aren't you?" He pointed to her ring.

"Yes."

"I'll bet your husband is a professor. I'll bet he teaches electronic engineering or computer programming."

"You're way off. Jeff's a newspaperman."

"That's great. And you?"

"Well, let's say I'm a proletarian poet."

"I lived with the proletariat in Italy," he said, serious to the core. "I did a lot of life sketches, if you'd like to see them sometime."

"I would. I really would."

Julie had been edging toward the door. She came suddenly face to face with a sleek-looking woman on the far side of forty. She took one look at Julie and then ignored her. "Give me a hand with the wine, Ralphie. Why in the name of God didn't you turn on the air conditioning?"

Julie slipped out and away. She walked down Greene Street, wanting to urge everyone to come to Ralph Abel's opening. The street was a crazy mix of factories, businesses, and art galleries. There were remnant shops and garment shops, a thread mill, makers of brass fittings. The cobbled, potholed street supported tons of trash and pale-faced youngsters sorted through it for the stuff of their make-believe. New locks shone on rusty doors, and there were flowering plants and laundry hanging in the windows of the upper lofts. Among the ravaged storefronts, every third or so had entered on a new life, and the posters out front advertising the galleries deep inside were gay as poppy fields, noisy hawkers of tomorrow's Oldenburgs and Riverses.

At a quarter past five, having had an Italian ice on Wooster Street, Julie returned to the Maude Sloan Gallery. Wherever the people had come from, the place was jammed. Julie edged her way through to have another look at *Scarlet Night*. Nobody was talking to or about Ralph Abel. They were all talking about themselves. And the uptown galleries. And money. But Abel, his face flushed and streaming with honest sweat, didn't seem to notice that part. He wriggled around groups that ignored him until he reached Julie, smiling as though his face would burst.

"See," Julie said, "somebody came."

"How about that? I'd like you to meet Mrs. Sloan—if you still want to, that is."

"All right." Not that she had ever wanted to, but she allowed the tall, loose-jointed Abel to haul her to the desk. He had to lean over Mrs. Sloan to make himself heard.

Maude Sloan reached up and brushed a tassel of golden hair from his forehead. Her fingers were still moist from his sweat when she offered them to Julie. "Isn't it a marvelous show?"

"Great," Julie said.

Mrs. Sloan plucked a mimeographed sheet from a stack on the desk, a price list. "Perhaps you'd like one of these?"

"Thanks." Julie tried to think of something to say. It didn't matter.

Mrs. Sloan gave her a get-lost look and turned to her protégé. "You've got to mingle, Ralphie. It's important for you."

He looked out over the crowd, dubious.

Julie found a spot where she could look at the price list. *Scarlet Night* was down at five hundred dollars. Which could be a lot or a little. She went back and tried to see the canvas through Jeff's eyes. That didn't work very well. She thought she knew why she liked it, but she wasn't sure why Jeff wouldn't like it. Only fairly sure that he wouldn't. But suppose he said, "All right, Julie. If you like it, I'm quite willing to make a compromise. . . ." If Jeff said that, she knew as she stood before *Scarlet Night*, she would not want to buy it. Which probably had more to do with the psyche than with art. The picture was in a heavy but plain gilt frame that wouldn't quarrel with the Victorian setting. Nor would the painting quarrel . . . much. In any case, she was not going to buy a painting until Jeff saw it. Besides, it wouldn't cover the white spot, unless she hung it on its side.

Again she caught Ralph Abel watching her. He came over, bringing her a glass of punch.

"I can't afford to buy a painting, Mr. Abel. Besides, I've promised my husband . . ." Well, Julie thought, it's true.

"I understand. You both have to live with it."

"And each other."

"That price list isn't the last word," Abel said. "Maude would kill me for saying it, but I know. She says so herself."

"Look. I'll try and get Jeff to come down with me tomorrow and see it. Okay?"

"The next day. We're closed tomorrow. Mrs. Hayes,

I don't want you to buy it for my sake. I want you to buy it for you. Are you feeling sorry for me?"

"If I buy it, it will be for me. It has meaning for me, but whether it will also please my husband, I can't say. That's something we'll have to find out."

"But you do like it?" he persisted.

"Yes! I wouldn't be here if I didn't." A nice, forth-right lie.

"Please don't be mad. I was thinking: couldn't we put half a star on it? It wouldn't commit you to buy it, you know. But nobody else could buy it until you had a chance to think about it—and talk it over with your husband."

It was going to be a lot easier to put the star on than to take it off, she felt. But there was something in it for Ralph Abel too. To be sure, it was early, but nobody was running around looking for stars or even half stars. As a theatrical agent used to say to Julie when she was trying to make it as an actress, all you got to do is get that first olive out of the jar.

"Okay, let's do that," Julie said.

Maude Sloan was busy running the punch bowl, but Julie was sure the woman saw Ralph take the tiny star from a box and cut it in half. In fact she stretched her neck to see where Julie was. Julie avoided her eyes. It didn't help. She felt even more committed.

Abel returned and licked the half star, but before he got it on the title card, a hand caught his.

"Hold on, young fellow." With an air of boredom, the plump man held onto Abel's arm but spoke to Julie. "I'm sorry to disappoint you, miss, but I've made arrange-ments with Mrs. Sloan to buy this canvas." He let his eyes shift languidly toward Maude. With a message, Julie felt. Okay. Fine.

"Who are you?" Abel demanded, which was no way to speak to a customer.

"I doubt you would know if I told you."

"I'm sorry, sir, but I just promised this lady . . ."

Julie tugged on his arm. "It's all right." It was more than all right. "Hey, congratulations!"

It didn't work.

"It's not all right," the painter said. "I want you to have it."

"But I'm not even decided and this gentlemen *is*."

The gentleman, who Julie didn't feel sure was one, put his hand on Abel's shoulder, which was at about his eye level. "Let's have Mrs. Sloan settle it," he said, as though it was all too ridiculous.

Maude was waiting for them, smiling hard. It made all the wrinkles in her face get together. "What's the matter, Rubin?"

"Tell this young genius of yours that we just closed the deal on *Scarlet Night*."

"Aren't you proud, Ralphie" She didn't even bother with the intermediate step. "Mr. Rubinoff buys with excellent taste."

"And somebody else's money most of the time. You're going to a very distinguished collector, young man."

Abel was still glowering in spite of his good fortune. Julie had never felt more hung up. Or wiped out: that was closer. All she wanted now was to get out. "Well, it's been nice meeting everybody. Good luck, Mr. Abel." She offered him her hand.

He caught it and hung onto it fiercely while he appealed to Mrs. Sloan. "Don't I have anything to say about my own paintings?"

"Not at the moment," she said amiably, and finally threw a few words Julie's way: "Some of the other paintings are just as important, Mrs. Hayes. There's a lovely little circus theme, number eight . . ."

Julie shook her head. "I'll watch for your proletarian sketches, Mr. Abel," she said and got her hand away from him.

"I'm so sorry, Mrs. Hayes," Rubinoff said. "I know what it's like in this business when somebody outflanks you."

"I don't feel outflanked," Julie said and pushed her way through the crowd. She tried to hold back the tears until she could reach the street. Anger and frustration . . . and relief?

Her ardor for looking at pictures had cooled considerably. The next move was up to Jeff. When he had an hour or an hour and a half to spare.

THREE

Sean O'Grady was not supposed to be there. He was, in fact, supposed to be on the high seas. But blind trust did not come easy to O'Grady. He had been beggared by it more than once in his life. But in the few minutes before the painting was sold he had paid dearly for his curiosity. He had thought at first that the blond girl was to be his connection when the time came and that confused him: he had expected a man. Which was the way it turned out in the end, a man of sorts. While the squabble went on at the desk, O'Grady had looked in the guest book on the table by the door. He had noticed the slick, dark, pudgy fellow sign in with a flourish and wondered then if he wasn't the one: R. Rubinoff.

Who the girl was he had no idea: she had not signed the book. An innocent bystander. He was sure of it, her going out with tears in her eyes. There would never be tears in an operation contrived by Ginni. Nor surrender. He went outdoors after her, the sweat cold on his back, and watched how she carried herself going down the street. She knew how to walk, her head high and her limbs loose. Class. He was glad all the same that the fate of *Scarlet Night* was not in her hands. She hailed a cab at the corner.

He intended to go then. No one had noticed him. No one would have recognized him, for that matter, except Abel, who was blind at the moment with his own importance. O'Grady tried not to think him a fool. The lad was out of his element. So was Sean O'Grady, but in his case it didn't matter. He'd not be going this way again.

He crossed the street, proposing to find his way to the nearest subway, but he paused, seeing a white Porsche at the curb with the license RR: R. Rubinoff. Parked illegally, it squatted like a white toad with an eye in the top

17

of its head. He walked slowly around it trying to overcome a terrible temptation to do it some kind of violence
in return for the anxiety the man had caused him. He was
fortunate in the discovery of a beady-eyed youngster in
tattered jeans watching him.

"Hello, sweetheart," O'Grady said.

She turned her head away.

He stooped and looked into the car. Driving gloves.
Naturally. And a clutch of white strings hanging brazenly
from the side pocket to advertise a collection of sum-
monses. He caught the man's reflection in the car window
as he came prancing out of the gallery. O'Grady didn't
know whether to run or stand still.

"You, there, what are you doing?"

"Looking," O'Grady said and stood up to his full height,
six foot one. Then he thought, to hell with it: they were
going to meet later, why not sooner? "I'm O'Grady," he
said.

Rubinoff was short and soft, if not fat. He wore a blue
silk suit fresh from the cleaner's, but he looked a bit soiled
nonetheless. He stared up at O'Grady, furious, his dark,
protruding eyes slightly bloodshot. "What are you doing
here?"

"Wondering if you'd give me a ride uptown, if that's
where you're going."

"We were not to meet until I contacted you."

"I felt responsible for what's in there until your arrival."
O'Grady nodded toward the gallery.

"I don't like it. I don't like it at all."

"I didn't like what I seen in there, Mr. Rubinoff. You
came near to losing it to the young woman, didn't you?"

"What happened in there is none of your business."

The little street arab came and stood looking up at
them from one to the other, hoping no doubt they would
come to blows. And people had begun to come out of the
gallery.

"Get in," Rubinoff said.

O'Grady went around the car and when Rubinoff
opened the door to him he got in backside first and swung
his legs in, his knees just clearing the dashboard.

Rubinoff opened the roof vent. He started the motor,
revved it a time or two, and took off, bouncing from pothole to pothole. After a couple of blocks he pulled over
and stopped. He fastened his seat belt, easing it under his

belly. He seemed unable to bring himself to even ask O'Grady where he was going.

O'Grady didn't like him, but he was well aware that without the next step all that had gone before would be for naught. Or worse. "Look, man. We're in this together, no matter who's fore or who's aft. It's true, I wasn't supposed to be there, but it's a lonely business to be on the waiting end of a thing like this, and damned frightening to see how close it came to disaster."

"You simply do not know what you're talking about. If I had moved any sooner, there are people in that crowd who'd have said I was a shill for Maude Sloan, and that unfortunate young fool would not have sold another canvas."

"Are people buying them?"

Rubinoff ignored the question. "I have a reputation for taste. As it is now, Maude thinks I did her a favor. She knows the boy is an atrocious painter."

At least he was talking to him, O'Grady realized. He had never thought much of the pictures himself, but he put that down to his own ignorance. Rubinoff kept riling the motor: the Porsche sounded like a beast growling to be set loose. "I don't think Ginni had a very wide choice, Mr. Rubinoff. And it was to coax Ginni home that her mother agreed to give him the show."

"I know as much as I need to know," Rubinoff said. "I only hope your Ginni has not been too clever for her own good—for the good of all of us."

"Her calculations have worked till now."

"So it would seem." Rubinoff sighed and turned in his seat as though he could finally bear to look at him. "Sean O'Grady, is it?" He offered his hand, a wet sponge that O'Grady wrung lightly.

"Most people call me Johnny. Sean's my professional name."

Rubinoff put the car in motion. "Where do you want to go?"

"I'm going to McGowan's Bar and Grill on Forty-fifth and Ninth, but you can drop me anywhere midtown."

They turned north on Sixth Avenue.

"You're an actor?" Rubinoff asked, harking back to the professional name.

"I'm a merchant seaman, but I read a bit of poetry now

and then from the stage—you might say for political purposes."

Rubinoff threw him a furtive glance. You had to know that politics was not his game. An aging fag, O'Grady decided, which was sad. Except that he had money, at least a part of which had to be legitimate. Otherwise he would not have been all that persona grata among the crowd at the gallery. Or with Ginni. This was no caper for a common crook. An uncommon one maybe.

Rubinoff said, "I haven't seen Maude for years. She used to be a beautiful woman. Would you believe it?"

"I would, knowing the daughter."

"Do you know her *well?*" He trailed the word out in a way that you could not escape its meaning.

"Intimately." O'Grady laid it on heavier than he might have with another man.

"Oh, dear," Rubinoff said, as though he didn't approve of intimacy.

"This operation might never have come off otherwise, Mr. Rubinoff."

The man looked at him with amazement.

"Watch the road," O'Grady said and then went on defensively: "She knew who she was picking. It was no small matter, bumping another seaman from his berth at Naples in order to take his place. Otherwise, how would I have been on the docks here to get our boy through customs?"

"I'm sure I don't know." Rubinoff shook his head. Nor did he want to know.

But O'Grady was determined to rub his snooty nose in the dirty end of the business. "It was a good fight till the police broke it up. And in the end they did my work for me, giving the poor bastard a crack on the skull and carting him off to sober up before presenting him to the American Consul. By that time his boat was well out in the Mediterranean and me in his berth."

"Remarkable," Rubinoff murmured, patient now, as though deciding it was better that O'Grady unburden himself to him than to a stranger.

"Customs was the easy part. I've a friend, an inspector on the Brooklyn docks, see, and every time I'm overseas I bring him back a little vial of Rumanian pills for his mother's arthritis. All I had to say was I knew the boy, and him and his paintings sailed through without a question."

Rubinoff made a noise of approval.

Having told it all, O'Grady wished he hadn't. It didn't sound like much, laid out. "It'll be a trickier business, the return trip."

Rubinoff aimed the Porsche between a bus and a mail truck, both heading into the same lane. The Porsche shot out front like a spurt of toothpaste. Rubinoff drove like a teenager and he had to be fifty.

"You pulled that one off well," O'Grady said, grudging admiration.

"Tell me a little about Ginni," Rubinoff said.

"Have you not met her?"

"No."

"Ah, she's a wild, beautiful woman. Her father's a count or some such. He's well off."

"That I know."

"She plays him like a mandolin, coaxing money out of him for this artists' commune she's set up."

"Are they all as talented as Ralph Abel?"

O'Grady laughed. "Don't be too hard on the lad. Flattery makes fools of the best of us. Ginni's up to a number of things I don't think would interest you, Mr. Rubinoff."

"I dare say."

"She was on the other end of a commission I had once for an organization I belong to."

"Shall we leave it at that?"

"If you like, but they were great days," O'Grady said and lapsed into silence. All in all, they had been the best days in his life.

Johnny, or Sean as he signed himself, was the son of Irish immigrant parents who had nothing in common except their determination to make it to America. With that accomplished, and the seed that became Johnny implanted, the old man took off and thereafter showed up every year or so expecting a celebration of his return. Johnny's chief recollection of him was chasing Ma around the miserable West Side flat trying to get her into the bedroom. Ma generally made it to the kitchen where she kept the bread knife handy. It was a wonder to O'Grady himself that he had not grown up like Rubinoff. He learned his reading and writing from the nuns as well as a love of Irish song and poetry. Everything he knew that was practical he had learned on the streets. When his mother died, their parish priest had been instrumental in getting him the promise of a job on a deep-water vessel and hence his maritime papers.

O'Grady was thirty-three, handsome in a rough, sandy-haired way except for the cold blue eyes, a feature he could not abide in himself. That his voice was rich and warm was some compensation. From childhood he had been devoted to the cause of a united Ireland, and it was in service to the I.R.A. as a gun procurer that he had met Ginni. She was his Italian-Yugoslavian connection.

He had made two successful runs. The third ended in disaster, and he had had to dump the entire cache into the Galway Bay. He had told himself, answering Ginni's call in the present matter, that every cent he made on it would go to the Cause. And so it would. But deep down he knew that wasn't why he was in it. Ginni had set it up, and he was her pigeon.

Stopped at a red light, Rubinoff took a long look at O'Grady. "Now that you have satisfied yourself as to my competence, what do you propose to do for the next two weeks?"

O'Grady overlooked the sarcasm. "Does it have to be two weeks?"

"At least. The show doesn't close until a week from Sunday."

"I don't know. I'm damn near broke financing myself."

"You're not to go near the gallery again."

"I don't intend to."

"Nor to get in touch with me. When I'm ready I'll contact you. You ought not to be in the city at all."

"It's my home, man. Where else would I be landside?"

"I understood you would not be landside, as you call it, until afterwards." They moved ahead with the traffic. "That understanding was one of the conditions of my agreement."

"With who?" O'Grady said.

Rubinoff kept his eyes on the street. "With *whom*."

FOUR

Julie was out early in the morning. She bought a dozen golden daisies with rich brown eyes, and then, at Pierre's, two croissants which were still warm from the oven.

Jeff had dressed and made coffee by the time she got back; his valise was packed and standing at the door. She had either forgotten or not been told that he was catching the shuttle to Washington. She was sure it was the latter; he was sure he had told her, and both of them repeated that it didn't matter. He'd be gone overnight and, since they were to have dinner the following evening at the Alexanders', they arranged to meet there, Jeff not knowing at what hour he would get back.

Julie opened the shutters on the back windows after he had gone, and looked out over the straggly garden to where the machines were already humming in the factory across the way. A long row of dark Puerto Rican women worked on pieces of fabrics that would turn into some dress manufacturer's fall line. At lunchtime when the machines were off, you could hear their radios—salsa, calypso, and rock. You could hear their laughter and their harsh, excited voices. Julie thought about Mrs. Rodriguez over the shop on Forty-fourth Street where she planned to go later. She wondered if Juanita, the child with Orphan Annie eyes, would be out front to greet her.

The phone rang. It rang a lot oftener when Jeff was home.

"Mrs. Julie Hayes?"

"Speaking."

"This is Ralph Abel, the painter. Remember?"

"Of course." That was only yesterday.

"I mean I wasn't sure I had the right party. Geoffrey Hayes, the *New York Times* columnist. Right?"

"Yes," Julie said, but very softly. She was afraid of what might come next.

"I wanted to tell you, Mr. Rubinoff isn't taking that

painting. So if you'd like to take another look, come down this morning and I'll be here."

"I don't think so, Mr. Abel. . . . I'm sorry about Mr. Rubinoff, but . . ."

"To hell with Rubinoff. I'm sorry, ma'am. I didn't mean to say that."

"Of course you did and why not?"

"Look, I'm not trying to rush you, but if you could come down, I'd love to take you to lunch. Understand, I'm not trying to make out with you or anything."

Julie laughed.

"What?"

"You want to sell a painting, right?"

"It's more than that."

"But you've got to be realistic. I'm not a good prospect. My husband's in Washington today so that I can't bring him to see it. Maybe later in the week."

"Would you let me bring it to your house? You could just hang it and surprise him. Then . . . well, we could take it from there."

"We sure could," Julie said. "I'll come down in a couple of hours and we can have a bowl of soup or something and you might show me some of those sketches we talked about."

Not until she reached the door of the Maude Sloan Gallery and found it locked did she remember that Abel had said the gallery was closed on Tuesdays. While she hesitated, a youngster in shaggy pants came up and pushed the buzzer. She could hear the bray inside.

"Thanks," Julie said.

A shrug.

Abel opened the door. "I forgot to tell you to ring the bell."

"Your doorperson did it for me."

"That's 'Silly.' Her real name's Sylvia but everybody calls her 'Silly.' She hangs out on the street, runs errands . . ." Julie followed him inside. "It's pretty depressing in here today. It's like everything's done over in ocher from the cigarette smoke."

He looked pretty sallow himself; the look of boyish wonder was gone. And the one gold star stood out like a good deed in a naughty world. The room, empty of people and fetid with stale smoke, hung with paintings that had not sold—even the gold star was a false front—was bleak and lifeless, the light of day garish and cruel to man and pictures. "How come Mr. Rubinoff dropped his option?"

Actually, the man had said he'd bought the painting. Julie would have thought Mrs. Sloan could hold him to it. If she wanted to. But plainly she wasn't going to support herself or her gallery selling Ralph Abels. Or holding buyers with rich clients to bad bargains.

The painter moistened his lips. "It wasn't as though he was buying it for himself."

Julie walked over to *Scarlet Night*. The light couldn't hurt it, no more than light much changed the face of a whore. She could not escape that association. "I still like it."

"Bless you," Abel said fervently, and pinpoints of pleasure rekindled in his eyes. "Did you really mean it about wanting soup?"

"Why not?"

"Mushroom and barley?"

They talked over the soup and brown bread in a crowded resturant where you could also get hero sandwiches without meat. Abel kept talking about himself, saying he didn't mean to, apologizing, and going right back to the same subject. But not about himself the painter. He talked about growing up in the small town named after Indian Chief Keokuk who was buried in the park where they held band concerts on Sunday afternoons. In summers he had worked on the nearby farms, hoeing and husking corn . . .

Julie tried to slow him down, to get him to eat. He wasn't high exactly, but it was like that. Maybe he was trying to rise above disaster. Or was he going home, giving up the painter's dream? He told her about the Iowa State Fair and how he had reached the finals in the corn-husking contest. He stuck his hands out in front of her and they did look like the hands of a corn husker.

"Van Gogh," Julie said, whom she had always thought of as a farmer.

Abel's eyes filled with tears.

"Hey." Julie reached across the table and gave his hand a couple of reassuring pats.

"I've been thinking about Van Gogh all morning." Abel brushed his nose with the cuff of his denim shirt.

"He sold one painting, one painting in his whole life, and he wouldn't have sold that if it wasn't for his brother."

"Was he a farmer?"

Abel shook his head and before Julie knew how it happened, he was off on another talkathon. He had copied the Van Goghs in the Chicago Art Institute when he studied there, something his father had paid the bills for. "Like Van Gogh's brother, I mean the way he believed in me and worked so I could paint. Then he got sick and I went back and took over the store. Van Gogh wouldn't have done that. He was a selfish man. But you know, you've got to be. Otherwise, no concentration."

"What about Paris? How did you wind up there?"

"I sold the store and went when my father died. I couldn't have chosen a worse place. I tried to put it all in *Scarlet Night."*

"It's there," Julie said.

His smile was sweet; you had to call it that, gentle and sweet. He said, "I don't speak French very well and nobody thought I could paint worth a damn except the guy I studied with and he turned out to be a phony. Then this girl I'd met, Ginni, wrote me to come to Naples, and boy did I take off . . ." He fell silent and stirred up the barley at the bottom of the soup.

"Yes?"

He glanced at Julie and then down into the soup again. "I don't know how I feel about Ginni now, Mrs. Hayes. The whole thing went sour on me last night."

"Better call me Julie."

"Ginni was a kind of patron to a bunch of us. She's Maude's daughter, you see. Her father's an Italian count from a real distinguished family, and when Maude and he got divorced, Ginni decided she wanted to live with him. Anyway, I painted my head off and Ginni sent Maude a couple of transparencies, and the first thing I knew I was heading home to have my first American exhibit in SoHo. Ginni was supposed to be here for the opening. Now I don't think she ever meant to come. What I can't figure out . . . Julie . . . is why she did so much for me. It almost seems like she was making a present of me to Maude, something I sure fell in with. Or maybe she was just getting rid of me, period. Only I'm not all that hard to get rid of. You ask Maude this morning. She'll tell you."

"Eat," Julie said.

The girl at the next table smeared what was left of her butter on what was left of her bread and put it in a paper bag. She got up and sidled out between the tables. Abel looked grateful for her departure. Julie, in her place, would have nibbled at the bread and stayed to hear the rest of his story.

Abel moistened his lips and said: "Julie, do you have a hundred dollars?"

"Not with me."

"Don't you have a check you could cash or a bank card?"

"Yes."

"That's what it's going to cost you to take *Scarlet Night* home with you."

"I can't do that. It'd be taking advantage of you."

The veins were standing out at his temples. "Someday if you still feel that way and I'm still around, I'll take another hundred. Or you can give me two right now if that's how you feel."

"I'll loan you a hundred dollars," Julie said.

"No, ma'am. I don't borrow from ladies."

Julie was glad not to have been taken up on the impulse to loan Jeff's money. His being home was going to add a new dimension to her conscience when it came to spending money. "How about those proletarian sketches?"

"Why can't you take something you like?" He exploded. A direct hit.

"That is a very good question, my friend. You're not going to eat that soup, so let's go." When they reached the street she shook her hair away from the back of the neck. All the heat of the day seemed to have settled there. She had a number of questions, but the more she asked the more involved she got. "All right, a hundred dollars if we can find a Chemical Bank. Or shall I just make out a check to you?"

"I need the cash, Julie."

"What about Mrs. Sloan? Does she get a cut?"

"No."

"But what if you're not around when I come to get the painting?"

"It's going home with you today. That's part of the deal."

"That's crazy, Ralph. Does she know what you're doing?"

"Julie . . ." The veins popped up again. "Maude Sloan and I are through, bed, board, and gallery. Last night she told me what she really thought of me as a painter and I told her what she could do with her hospitality. Now do you understand?"

"It makes things a little clearer."

"There's a Chemical Bank on Broadway and Spring Street."

Julie looked at him but didn't say anything. They started walking. Then Abel burst out: "How else was I going to pay my own way?"

"Touché," Julie said, although it didn't quite fit.

She wrote the check for cash and countersigned it. She would have to cover it at her own bank with traveler's checks left over from Paris: they were in a different handbag. Money, money, money. It was wild. The more she spent, the further she got from earning it herself. Suppose she had a job now, nine to five, would she be in the present situation? It wasn't possible.

They walked back to Greene Street without much conversation. So many galleries with their signs of welcome out front. She wasn't sure for whom she felt sadder —Ralph Abel or herself: they'd both lost a little of their sheen in not much more than a day.

"Are you going back to Iowa?"

"Maybe. There're worse places."

Like SoHo, New York, the day after yesterday.

A station wagon was parked at the curb alongside the gallery. A man was waiting, his backside on the fender. He was burly and dour-looking with curly gray hair.

"Who's that?" Julie said under her breath.

"A guy who's waiting for me."

Which was pretty obvious. *"Nu?"* he said when they came abreast of him.

"Okay, okay," Abel said, and then to Julie as he touched her elbow with a kind of urgency. "Look, do you want me to get you a cab?"

"I'll get one and come back."

"You're sure?"

"I'm not going to back out now," she said, which wasn't much of a compliment, but stated the situation.

Was the hundred dollars to pay a debt? To the character waiting beside the wagon? She thought about how close they were to Mafia country. Which, in turn, reminded her of Sweets Romano, the gentleman-art-collecting gangster—the king of pornography—whom she had gone to see after Pete Mallory was murdered. It hit her that Romano might just dig Ralph Abel's painting; he might even dig Ralph Abel. Who probably knew how to take care of himself better than she'd thought. The question was if or how to make contact between them without getting herself involved. She didn't want ever to have to see Sweets Romano again. He was a scary man. Forget it, Julie. Give Abel the hundred bucks and run. In fact, go back and give him the hundred bucks and let the picture go. But she picked up a cab on Houston Street and told the driver to circle the block.

Abel was waiting at the door. He brought the painting and put it in at her feet, face forward. The back was reinforced with plywood and still bore the stamp of U.S. Customs as well as the clasps by which it had hung on the gallery track.

"Don't give it too much light," he said, and took the bank envelope from Julie's hand. Inside were five twenties.

They didn't even shake hands or wish each other luck. Nor did she look back. Not for anything would she have looked back.

FIVE

Julie knew before the cab turned into Sixteenth Street that she'd been kidding herself. *Scarlet Night* no more belonged in that living room than a bag lady. She kept the cab waiting while she ran upstairs and got the traveler's checks. And the keys to Forty-fourth Street. Back in the cab again, she wondered just how strong in her subconscious the association between the shop and the painting was. It was something she would have explored in therapy: the one sure thing her doctor would have made her fish for was the reason she had bought *Scarlet Night*. Jeff would ask the same question if she ever got around to telling him about it.

Because I like it. Okay. That would work with Jeff anyway.

"Welcome home," she said and set the painting against the chair in the front room of the shop. The floor was cluttered with junk mail beneath the letter drop. She scattered it with her foot but let it lie and went out again, having just time to make the bank before it closed. There was no sign of the child, Juanita, no mangled dolls in the hallway when she looked in. She hadn't thought she would miss her, but she did.

After straightening things out at the bank, she began to feel liberated. Or maybe the word was secure. Which, on Eighth Avenue, was crazy. The street was wretched, the whores and pimps and sex movies, porn shops, massage parlors, the debris on the sidewalk, buildings with their eyes smashed out. Yet in among it all were the hardware shops and delis, Greek restaurants and pizza stands, bars, pawn shops, clothiers, a pet shop . . . and Bourke's Electrical Shop, all of them run by decent human beings.

Mr. Bourke came out from behind the counter and shook her hand. "Oo, la, la," he said, which Julie figured had something to do with Paris. He looked about as healthy as skim milk.

"I went away without returning your spotlights," Julie said. Mr. Bourke had loaned her two spotlights for the front of her shop when Pete Mallory had decorated it for her. "I ought to pay you a rental on them."

"We can make some kind of arrangement. Or else I'll sell them to you at a good price."

"I don't expect to need them anymore, Mr. Bourke. I'm going out of the gypsy business. I mean, no more fortune-telling or advising."

Mr. Bourke approved. "It was not a very good business for such a lovely young lady. I hope you'll come back and see us now and then." He pushed his glasses back up his nose. They always seemed ready to dive off.

"I'm not moving out yet. Just closing the shop to the public."

"Your friends will like it that you're staying. Mrs. Ryan missed you something terrible." He mimicked the Irish voice. "And Fritzie, it seems, won't eat."

"It's worms," Julie said. Fritzie was Mrs. Ryan's long, low dog which wasn't entirely dachshund. "Fritzie loves Fritzie, and pro tem, whoever takes him for a walk."

Mr. Bourke laughed. Then: "It will be a sad day for her when he goes."

Their eyes met. He had spoken of the dog but both of them thought of Pete Mallory. Mr. Bourke had been very fond of him. "Look, I'll bring the lamps back and then we can decide what I owe you."

"Take your time." Mr. Bourke retreated behind the counter.

Julie started out, not wanting to see the tears she was pretty sure were in his eyes.

He called after her, "There's a Mass for Peter at St. Malachy's at five on Thursday."

"I'll try to make it." She was sure she wouldn't.

She bought some eyelets and picture wire before returning to the shop. The first thing she did when she returned to Forty-fourth Street was gather the junk mail. In among it was a folded piece of lined paper on which was written in a foreign but childlike hand:

Dear Julie
  Anyone looks for me I am back July 7. We go to Puerto Rico. Please.

                                            Rose Rodriguez

Julie crumpled the paper and put it into the plastic garbage bag. "Anyone" meant a trick, a john: Mrs. Rodriguez, her upstairs neighbor, presumably had a private practice which she conducted while her husband was at work. To date, happily, Julie had not encountered any of her customers. Today was July 7. Her final addition to the Glad trash bag was the window sign, *Friend Julie*. She braced the door open to let air in. Maybe the mold would crawl out under its own power. She took *Scarlet Night* into the back room.

Suddenly, through the doorway came Mrs. Ryan and Fritzie. Mrs. Ryan gave a great high croon of pleasure

that sent Fritzie into paroxysms of excitement. He yapped
and leaped and unintentionally peed on the floor. In the
hug between the two women, Mrs. Ryan's straw hat got
knocked askew with hairpins flying in all directions and
the gray hair tumbling.

"Everybody in the neighborhood's been asking after
you, people you wouldn't believe knew you were here.
Oh, dear. Look what Fritzie has done. His kidneys aren't
what they used to be. Poor boy, I know you didn't mean
it."

Julie got a paper towel. The unrepentant animal lath-
ered her face with smelly kisses when she got down to his
level.

"See? Even Fritzie missed you. You were in Europe.
Did you by any chance get to Ireland?"

"Only Paris," Julie said.

"For all this time? Oh, I dare say there's enough to see.
There was a play about Paris once in a theater where I
was usher. I saw it night after night, but I couldn't make
head nor tail of it. And it was about prostitutes. You
wouldn't think that would be so complicated, now would
you?"

Julie made a noise of agreement, stuffed the towel into
the trash bag, and went to the bathroom at the back of
the shop to wash her hands. She tried to open the small
window there, but it was stuck tight.

Mrs. Ryan followed her through the curtained partition
into the back room. "You'll need to air this place out. I
could loan you a fan. When old Mrs. Driscoll, down the
hall at the Willoughby, died, her son gave me her air conditioner. It's saved my life."

"I'll have to do something to get some air back here,"
Julie said.

"Will you be living here, dear?" Mrs. Ryan said hopefully.

"No. My husband came back with me. He'll be home
for a while now."

"I was going to ask about him," Mrs. Ryan said with
ill-concealed regret. "He works at home, does he?"

"Sometimes."

"Julie, are you married to the fellow who writes in the
New York Times?"

"Uh-huh." She had not advertised Jeff among her West
Side friends. She looked around in time to catch that

puckered shape Mrs. Ryan made of her mouth at something she did not altogether approve.

"I knew a lovely man once who wrote a column for the *Daily News*, an Irish name. I was hoping it might be him."

Julie said, "Jeff used to be a legman for Tony Alexander." It was a name well known to readers of the *News*.

"Did he?" Grudging admiration. "There's always something in that column worth reading." Making her tour of the room to see what if anything was new among Julie's possessions, Mrs. Ryan discovered the painting. Another of her high, crooning "ohs." Somehow, Julie thought, Mrs. Ryan had become more Irish in the past month. "Isn't that beautiful, whatever it is? They always tell you to make of it what you want. Did you bring it from Paris? It looks very Frenchie."

"It is," Julie said.

"Where are you going to hang it?"

"I haven't decided yet."

"It'd be very attractive on the wall in front with one of the spotlights perking it up."

"Yeah." Just what it needed, perking up.

Mrs. Ryan was looking at her carefully, making some calculation, Julie knew. "I suppose you have to go home and fix dinner for himself. Or do you have a cook?"

Julie laughed. It had not taken Mary Ryan long to fantasize the life of someone married to a *New York Times* columnist. "I don't have a cook, Mrs. Ryan, and as a matter of fact, Jeff's in Washington today."

"So you can have a bite with Sheila Brennan and me. We're going over to the Actors Forum afterwards. They're doing a play now with the public invited. I'm sure you could get in without a reservation."

There was no reason not to, really, and she did like to drop by the Forum now and then where she was still a member.

At dinner the conversation of the three women dealt largely with the unfortunate event that had brought them together, or at least had brought together Julie and the nurse, Sheila Brennan. But you couldn't talk long of Pete Mallory without mention of the New Irish Theatre where he had been working at the time of his death.

"There's another young man I'd love you to meet,

Julie," Mrs. Ryan said. "He reads beautifully. . . . Wouldn't she take to him, Sheila? The voice of a poet and the heart of a patriot."

Oh, boy.

Miss Brennan wiped away a small white mustache of beer foam. "I don't like his eyes," she said.

Mrs. Ryan gave her shoulders a shuffle. "You said that before. There's some people can't look at a person. He looks you straight in the eye."

"Oh, doesn't he? He nails you to where he's looking at you. I knew a priest like that once. He'd have you confessing sins you never committed just to get away from him."

Julie laughed.

"It wasn't a bit funny, let me tell you. I was a young girl then." Miss Brennan's pale blue eyes narrowed at the recollection. Her freckles had gone from red to brown with the summer sun. "And mind, it was through a screen where he shouldn't have been looking at you at all. The way he'd say, 'Ye-e-s?' you'd start making up things for fear there were some you'd forgotten and you taking up his valuable time."

"What are you talking about?" Mrs. Ryan said.

Julie understood perfectly what Miss Brennan was talking about. "He should have been a psychiatrist."

"Right on!" the nurse said, proud of herself for using a new phrase in her vocabulary that had gone out of Julie's before she left college.

"Isn't it nice," Mrs. Ryan said stiffly, "the two of you speak the same language."

To mollify her, Julie asked, "What's the poet-patriot's name, Mrs. Ryan?"

"Sean O'Grady. It has a wonderful sound in Gaelic. Do you remember it in Gaelic, Sheila?" Julie knew now where Mrs. Ryan had freshened her Irish.

"I wouldn't remember it in English if it wasn't for you. I'm not so taken with these I.R.A. people, Mary. If you worked in a hospital it'd chill your bones to see them come in as I have, even in this country, after a blast of some sort, with their eyes hanging out of the sockets, or their jaws blown off. There was a man walked into Emergency once and gave me his hand. He literally gave me his hand and then fell in a dead faint at my feet. . . ."

"Hush't before you spoil our appetites," Mrs. Ryan said.

The play was terrible. It went off in all directions and never came back. Julie stuck it out to the end. Never, never would Mary Ryan walk out on a play. As she said, it would be like leaving the Mass before the consecration. The only thing that cheered Julie was that it had been produced at all. Even if the playwright hadn't been able to pull it together, he'd laid it out. Right now she'd settle for that herself. You couldn't get *there* without a *here* to go from.

The next day Julie tried to get started on the story of Pete Mallory's murder. Most of the characters were going to work out all right: Peter Mallory, scenic designer for the Actors Forum and the New Irish Theatre; Rita Morgan, who had come to Friend Julie for advice on how to get out of The Life, soul-poisoned Rita, who took Pete's offer to marry her and take her home as the ultimate insult; Mack, Rita's pimp, whose disappearance after Pete's death was taken by Julie and the police to be the doings of Sweets Romano; Romano, "the king of porn," art collector, public benefactor, who had been in love with the same woman as Pete, the actress Laura Gibson.

In synopsis, Julie thought, it read distressingly like a soap opera. Only, soaps had more structure. Also, it was lacking its heroine, Julie Hayes, who was going to be even harder to write than Sweets Romano.

By the time Julie had to go home and dress for dinner at the Alexanders' she was convinced that she was a better detective than she was ever going to be a writer. But she didn't intend to stop trying.

SIX

O'Grady had spent Tuesday, the day after Rubinoff took over, putting together his next benefit for Irish victims of the British occupation. He had not set a date or a place for the reading, and try as he might, he was not able to work up his old fervor. He could read his head off and the Committee regale for a month of Sundays and between them not raise a tenth of the sum he'd soon be turning over to the Cause. It was a better thing to do, however, than lying on the daybed dreaming of glory. Or of Ginni.

He dressed Wednesday morning for a trip down to the maritime hiring hall. Not that he intended to throw in his card, but it gave him something to do among men who were familiar to him and a change of vision from the four walls of the apartment. The phone rang just as he was going out the door.

"O'Grady? This is Rubinoff. Something has gone wrong."

It came like a kick in the stomach. "I'm listening."

"That stupid boy has taken his pictures from the gallery walls and disappeared with them."

"All of them?"

"Of course, all of them. Why would I call otherwise? Mrs. Sloan telephoned me. She supposed he might have brought *Scarlet Night* to my office. He didn't."

"Holy God. What did he do with it?"

"You've got to find him. You've got to track him down and persuade him that this sort of thing isn't done. You don't walk out on a commitment made by your gallery no matter what your domestic relations with the owner. That's what this is all about. I told you I thought they were sleeping together."

"I don't remember your telling me that, Mr. Rubinoff."

"Perhaps I didn't, but it was my observation."

"Where am I supposed to look for him?"

36

"I have no idea. Neither does Maude Sloan, and worse, she doesn't care. It was only to keep on the right side of me that she called at all. We might not have known for two weeks."

"Unless we landed in jail before it."

"You're overreacting, my friend. I don't believe for a moment that all is lost. He may be in search of another patron. I suggest you inquire around the neighborhood. Someone must have seen him remove the paintings."

O'Grady thought at once of the youngster. She was all eyes. And maybe no tongue.

"When you find him," Rubinoff went on, "he shouldn't be hard to persuade. Maude says he has no money."

"Then he'd be bound to come around to you, wouldn't he? Unless he's decided to deliver it to the other customer."

A long silence and then, as though the words pained him, "We may have to consider that possibility. But I cannot believe he would throw away a solid sale for a promise to consider. That's all she was offering—unless a bed: he seems rather talented in that capacity."

"Not her," O'Grady said. "I'd take my oath on it."

"When you find him, Johnny, couldn't you suggest he bunk in with you for a while? Until he gets relocated, say?"

Johnny, he noted. "I'm supposed to be on the high seas, Mr. Rubinoff."

"But you're not, and as you said yourself, we're in this together. Let me give you my home telephone as well as the office."

"Wait till I get something to write on." He took down the numbers.

"The first name is Rubin, Rubin Rubinoff."

"I'll see what I can do, Rubin."

O'Grady glanced around the apartment as he went from the living room to the bedroom to get his pocket-knife. He liked to leave the place tidy as his mother had taught him. You never knew who you'd bring home with you when you went out or who'd bring you home if you couldn't make it on your own. He smiled at himself in the chiffonier mirror, rehearsing what he'd say to Abel if he found him. His teeth needed cleaning or it might be the mirror. His mother had cherished the old chiffonier because she liked the classy sound of the word, he thought:

even standing on tiptoe, she'd been able to see no more of
herself in the glass than the top of her head. He'd kept it
because he kept everything, the washstand and pitcher,
the chamber pot (although he now had a bathroom of
his own), the bed with lumps like cobblestones under the
faded cretonne spread. He slept in the living room on the
daybed where he had slept as a child. His button-eyed
bear still snuggled among the cushions unless someone
was coming into the house. Then it was banished under
the bed. The knife he took with him more for luck than
need. It was a gift from The Daughters of St. Patrick and
he cherished it.

He locked up and ran down the tenement steps, holding his breath all the way. The halls were perfumed with
cabbage and mice and mortality. On the street he took a
deep breath and headed toward the river. In spite of
what trouble might lie ahead, or perhaps because of it,
he felt exhilarated. There were great clouds in the sky
and the smell of the river in the air which his mother
used to say reminded her of dilce. She had grown up in
the bogs of Mayo, not far from the sea, a place where,
to this day when he visited, the cottagers came out to
welcome her son as though he were himself coming
home.

On Eleventh Avenue he got his battered red Volkswagen from a lot behind a diner where he parked it for
next to nothing. It was about as distinguished looking as
a tinker's donkey, but it had a sunnier disposition and a
vent in the roof.

He parked a few doors from the Maude Sloan Gallery
and sat in the car, watching and thinking. He was deciding on which of the nearby galleries to query first when
he saw the metal door open and the child come out.

O'Grady got out of the car and took a rag to it. It
wasn't long before the girl came over to watch. He ignored her.

Before he could get too far with the job, she said:
"Give me fifty cents, mister, and I'll do the whole car."

"Fifty cents." He folded his arms and looked down at
her. "It's not worth it."

She shrugged and turned away, the little witch.

"Hold on now if you're wanting fifty cents and I'll tell
you what I'm waiting here for. I'm waiting for somebody
to come by and tell if they saw my friend, Ralph Abel,

take his paintings out of the gallery there. Did you by any chance see that?"

She turned back, weighed the matter, and nodded her head.

She was not going to be easily primed, and she might be a little off in the head, having too wise a look for one her size. Of one thing he was sure: One false note and she'd be off and running. "Did he take them away by himself? There's a dollar in it for you if you can tell me where he went with them." He took the dollar from his pocket and stuck it under the windshield wiper. He didn't have many of them to give away.

"In a station wagon," the child said.

"All by himself?"

"Mr. Goldman's brother helped him."

"Ah-ha. And who is Mr. Goldman?"

"He runs a deli on Church Street."

"Could you point it out to me if we took the car?"

"Sure." She reached for the dollar.

"Take it," he said to mollify himself. She already had it.

She went around the car. He settled in and reached across to open the door for her.

"I'll tell you something else for fifty cents," she said.

"Get in and we'll negotiate."

But from somewhere nearby someone shrieked: "Sylvia!" and the youngster took to her heels.

O'Grady did too, so to speak, for he realized he'd come within inches of laying himself open to God knows what charges for coaxing a young person into his car.

There were not many delicatessens on Church Street. He found one called Benny's and sharing the ground floor of the building was a carpentry shop operated by Sam Goldman. O'Grady could not find a place to park until he had driven halfway around the block and discovered a devastation of rubble—urban renewal without the renewal. Far into the lot—it would be at the back of the deli and the carpenter shop—a station wagon was parked. O'Grady maneuvered the Volkswagen over its tracks and parked beside it. An acrid smell tainted the air which reminded him of when he was a kid and they burned old railway ties in the Pennsylvania Yards on Thirty-fourth Street. He went around to the front of the shops. It was high noon and Benny had a good custom.

O'Grady opened the door to the carpentry shop and
stepped in. A bell announced his presence, but no one
came. He moved toward the rear and called out: "Is
there anyone in?"

Not a sound. But there ahead of him, glittering among
the lumber and sawhorses and half-built cabinets, was a
stack of picture frames. Empty and bearing a terrible
resemblance to those he had shepherded into the country
surrounding the works of Ralph Abel. He tried to call
out again, but his voice was a croak; through the open
but barred window the smell he had noticed hanging
over the rubble floated in, and he wondered, sickly, if it
wasn't burned canvas and paint. It did not take much
looking around to find the plywood with which most of
the backs of Abel's pictures had been reinforced, and to
certify the catastrophe, the custom stamps were plain to
see. O'Grady stared at the frames, his legs watery. Then
he counted them. Thirteen. Out of fourteen. He counted
them again to be sure and had the strength after that to
go next door.

Both the Goldman brothers were working the noon-
hour rush, a line of customers reached halfway to the
door. Near the end of the line was Sylvia. "Beatcha," she
said.

When it came her turn she ordered two corned beefs
on rye with mustard and pickles to go. She was a familiar customer. She also told one of the Goldman brothers,
"Somebody's looking for Ralph."

"I am," O'Grady said, "but I'll wait till you're not so
busy." He'd have bought a sandwich himself if he could
have afforded it.

Sylvia got her order. "Seeya," she said and departed.

One of the brothers soon came from behind the counter and removed his apron. "I'm Sam Goldman," he said.
"What can I do for you?"

"I'm Sean O'Grady." They shook hands. "I helped
Ralph Abel settle in the Maude Sloan Gallery. What happened?"

"He wasn't so settled. They fell out. Come next door
where we can talk. You want some coffee?"

"That'd be grand."

They sat on boxes, the coffee containers on a nail keg
between them.

"I came in here first," O'Grady said.

"I saw you."

O'Grady looked around where Goldman indicated: a mirror hung on a bracket just outside the window. "I noticed the empty frames."

Goldman nodded. "He's given up on being the big *artiste*."

"And destroyed his pictures, if I'm not mistaken."

The older man grunted. It might have been a laugh by the little twist to his mouth. "He tried, but they wouldn't let him do a decent job of it. The police gave him a summons for polluting the atmosphere."

"The poor bastard."

"What am I going to do with the frames? I gave him a good price for them to help him out. It wasn't me he was friends with but my brother, Ben. He's the intellectual in our family. I don't care much for the SoHo crowd myself."

"Nor do I. I'm a working man."

"The whole experience isn't going to hurt the boy, only his pride for a while. His father was a tailor. Did you know that?"

"He did tell me that."

"Benny's and mine was too. We gave Ralph the old man's silver thimble for luck."

"Then he's gone home . . . Where was it he came from?" ,

"Keokuk, Iowa."

O'Grady repeated the name of the place. "Don't they have damnedest names for places in this country?"

Goldman shrugged. "Kiev: that's where my family came from."

"Well, when I stop to think about it, my mother came from a town called Ballina. It's what your ear is tuned to. *Did* he go home?"

"With that thimble in his pocket, he'll go home. You'll see. We knew what we were doing."

O'Grady finished the coffee and set the container back on the keg. "He did sell one of the pictures. What happened to it?"

"Don't worry. She came and got it before he cleared the place out."

"You're sure of that, Mr. Goldman?"

"I'm sure. I saw him put it in the taxi with her."

"She looked as though she could afford it," O'Grady said. "The good-looking blond girl?"

Goldman nodded.

"I'm glad to know that anyway. It's something."

A few minutes later O'Grady called Rubinoff from the nearest phone booth.

SEVEN

"Her name is Hayes," Rubinoff said. "I pay particular attention to names. Mrs. Hayes . . . I wonder if she signed the gallery book at the door."

"She didn't. I was watching."

"It's a common name, isn't it?"

"There'd be a few of them in the phone book," O'Grady said.

"We'd better have a look and see how many. Meanwhile, get on the phone and try to contact Abel himself."

"It doesn't make sense for me to do it, Rubin. It's you that's supposed to want the picture."

"I'm afraid you're right," he said after a moment, the arrogance down a peg or two. "Actually, it's Maude's responsibility, but it's too dangerous to press her in the matter. She's not a stupid woman."

"What could she do?"

"I don't know, but my instinct tells me not to go that route. I suspect that she already feels she's been taken. By Abel. Perhaps by Ginni, and I dare say not for the first time. For me to now demand that she deliver the canvas calls attention to all the circumstances . . . No, no, no. It's all wrong."

"Aye, but what's right?"

"I simply don't know at the moment. I assumed he would want to continue painting bad pictures and eventually find another gallery. I suppose if I were able to reach him by phone I could try flattery. But if it didn't

work—if he were to say, 'Go ahead, Rubinoff, sue me,'
then where would we be? I'm afraid we must find the
Hayes woman and persuade her that she has something
which doesn't belong to her. I'm looking in the phone
book, Johnny. There are not so many Hayeses . . . As-
suming, of course, she's in Manhattan."

"She must be. She travels by taxi."

"And eliminating those in the poorer neighborhoods.
After all five hundred dollars . . . You'd recognize her if
you saw her again, wouldn't you?"

"Wouldn't you, Rubin?"

"Yes, but she would also recognize me. It would seem
too much of a coincidence."

"It happens all the time," O'Grady said.

"I want to know something about her before I confront
her. Our last meeting was unfortunate."

"Wasn't it now?" O'Grady said with heavy sarcasm.

"Johnny, it will give you something to do: why don't
you copy a few of the addresses out of the phone book?
Stake them out, one at a time. See how it goes and we'll
confer again tomorrow."

"Holy God," O'Grady said, looking at the receiver
when he heard the click on the other end. He slammed it
onto the hook.

He went home and had a bowl of soup out of a can.
After that he copied the names and addresses of a dozen
Hayeses out of the phone book. His first approach, mid-
afternoon, was to a doorman in the East Sixties. "The
Mrs. Hayes in your building—I wonder—does she drive
a car?"

"That old lady? You must be kidding."

"Ah, then I have the wrong address."

One down and a legion to go. By suppertime he had
eliminated two more, a real-estate agent and a black Mrs.
Hayes. It was a hell of a tedious job and he felt in his
soul it would come to naught. He'd be better off putting in
his time on a novena to St. Anthony, who was great at
turning up things you'd lost. He decided to do a bit more
copying from the phone book after supper and let that
suffice for the day. He returned the Volkswagen to the lot
and stopped on his way home for a beer at McGowan's.

McGowan's was a cheerful place where the beer wasn't
perishing cold and where O'Grady had more than a modest fame. Many's the time he had seen the old man give a

jerk of his head in his direction and lean over the bar to confide in a customer that there was a fella down there who once ran guns for the I.R.A. They didn't hold it against him in McGowan's that he had lost a shipment. In fact, they very nearly put it down to his credit, for such a misfortune could only occur through the treachery of an informer, and at McGowan's they were dead nuts on informers.

"Billy . . . Sssst, Mr. McGowan?"

O'Grady looked around to where the woman stood in the doorway, a large, amiable presence, with the gray hair straggling out from under an enormous hat and a dog at her feet you could scrape your shoes on. McGowan came partway down the bar.

"Can I bring Fritzie in? He'll sit at my feet and nobody'll know he's there."

"Since when are you asking me, Mary? It's against the law. Come in and shut up."

"Thank you, Billy." She headed for the nearest empty stool, which was next to O'Grady, and in hoisting herself up, gave his shoulder a push with one bosom, then a shove with the other. "Mr. O'Grady! Isn't that interesting? I was telling a friend of mine about you only yesterday."

The dog yanked his leash out of her hand. The woman rocked on the stool like a staggered top trying to see where the animal was. "Is he all right, can you see?"

"He's fine." Fritzie had curled up like an eel under her stool.

"I'll have a lager when you get the time, Billy." She took off her hat and crowded it onto her lap. "That's better. I can't do a thing with my hair when I've washed it. I have a friend who used to do it for me, but she's gone out of the business and the prices they charge today . . . Drink up and let me buy you another."

"Thanks, but I've work to do," O'Grady said.

"Come on. I'm old enough to be your mother."

O'Grady grinned and downed his beer. He rarely had to buy his second at McGowan's. Or his third, although he tried: he'd say that for himself.

"Are you going to do another of your readings soon? I'd love to bring my young friend Julie, if she'd come. She's very fond of the Irish. You may have noticed her shop on Forty-fourth Street—Friend Julie, Reader and

Advisor? I was with her the day she bought the cards and crystal ball. It was all a lark, but she's very good, I'm told. . . ."

For just an instant O'Grady wondered about a look in the crystal ball.

"And one for Mr. O'Grady, Billy."

"Johnny," O'Grady said.

She waited until his refill arrived and then lifted her glass. "Cheers!"

"Slainte," O'Grady said. Gaelic.

"I was thinking after I saw her—you might know her father. He was an Irish diplomat, no less. But he did a queer thing: he took off before the child was born and had the marriage annulled. You'd wonder how he could do it, the Church being what it is in Ireland. Ach, I dare say you can do what you like when you get into his category."

O'Grady was thinking of his own father with his comings and goings. The last person he wanted to meet was another orphan like himself, and one who told fortunes at that. He attracted the damnedest people when you came down to it, widows and spinsters and a redheaded whore who sang hymns on Eighth Avenue . . . and the boys now and then. Ah, but there was Ginni with her green eyes and auburn hair, the one girl in his life who had made a man of him. A Dago Red, he called her, and she throwing back her head and laughing. What in the name of God was he doing here with this windy old bag and her string of a dog, and the treasure lost that would bind him to the fair Gianina?

"I'll buy us a round when next we meet," he said and emptied his glass. "I've to go now and do my work."

"I'll be waiting to hear when you're reading next. . . . I wouldn't care if it was the phone book, you've such a lovely voice."

EIGHT

Julie was late arriving at the Alexanders'. She had dressed carefully. A blue chiffon silk that suggested more bosom than could be proven.

Fran said at the door, "Jeff was worried about you."

"I don't believe it. I'm always having to tell people Jeff's going to be a little late."

"So that's what was worrying him—that he got here on time. Don't you look stunning!"

"Thank you." Julie could feel the color rise to her cheeks. Fran always looked stunning. She had a lot of style but it never got in the way of her being a real person. She was much younger than Tony, probably closer to Jeff's age. They were going to be like three generations at dinner. Fran ran a flower shop on Lexington Avenue where a lot of customers came in to drop off gossip they hoped might turn up in Tony's column in the *Daily News.*

"Here's our girl," Fran called out, leading the way through the living room out onto the terrace.

Tony heaved himself out of the chair. His dark shirt was sprinkled with ashes from his pipe. Jeff looked as though he had shaved and showered on arrival. He generally did look that way. Julie kissed him and then kissed Tony, just missing the sharp end of one white waxed mustachio.

"Orange juice and vodka, light on the vodka, right?" Tony said. The others were drinking martinis.

"You weren't really worried?" Julie said to Jeff.

"You're so rarely late I had to say something."

"Ha!"

They moved to the edge of the terrace. Manhattan south from the twenty-sixth floor on Fifty-sixth Street. A thousand million lights were coming on and the sun, wrapped in a golden haze, was going out for the night. "How was Washington?"

"Very Hebraic. I had an hour with the Israeli prime

minister this morning. I went back to the hotel afterwards and read the Book of Job—at his suggestion."

"Patience, right?"

Jeff nodded. "And with you?"

"I'd better read the Book of Job too."

Tony returned with the vodka and orange juice and the famous *Sauce Diable* on the side, and four plates with the little ivory forks that Jeff had brought from Africa. They had given them to the Alexanders for a wedding anniversary. Julie knew Jeff would have liked to keep them. Jeff collected, Julie gave away. She caught him looking at them covetously. Which made the gift more generous on his part.

Shrimps and orange juice weren't the greatest combination. They seemed to go fine with martinis.

"Steak and salad are all we're having," Fran said. The grill had been set up in the corner of the terrace.

Tony said, "Do I have a wine for you, my friend. I decanted it so you wouldn't see the label."

"But you saved the label," Jeff said.

"You're damned right. You're going to want it."

Fran smiled at Julie. "We'll go down later and have ice cream at Baskin-Robbins."

It wasn't meant that way at all, but it emphasized the difference in their ages—and everything else. She felt in no way the equal of a man who had spent an hour that morning with the Israeli prime minister. She chose this as the do-or-die moment, took a deep breath, and said something she had rehearsed all the way to the Alexanders': "Tony, what would I have to do to get a job with you—legwork maybe—like you gave Jeff when he was starting out?"

Tony scowled at her from under drawn shaggy brows. His hair was white, his mustache white, the brows black and ferocious. "First, you'd have to tell me why you want it."

"For one thing, I thing I'd be good at it, interviewing people, even writing about them, but I don't seem to be able to get started on my own. I need an apprenticeship."

"You're already apprenticed to a master," Tony said.

"That's part of my trouble."

"I understand what Julie's saying," Fran put in.

"So do I," Tony said. "I didn't think she was paying me the extreme compliment. I'm not in Jeff's class myself."

Jeff shifted uneasily in his chair and kept his eyes on the martini glass.

"But I like where I am," Tony growled.

"So do I," Julie said. "That's my whole point. This spring I met a lot of people, some pretty bizarre types—police, prostitutes, pimps, a priest . . ."

"A gangster or two, some theater originals," Tony added. Then, with a twinkle: "Don't think we haven't followed your career, Friend Julie."

"Oh, boy."

They all laughed, even Jeff.

"I must have twenty thousand index cards on bizarre types," Tony said. Then, turning to Jeff: "I was thinking the other day, I may have to destroy those files if the Supreme Court doesn't straighten out this First Amendment business."

The men fell to a discussion of the reporter and his notebooks at issue in a murder trial. Julie was glad to get offstage. Her heartbeat slowed to nearer normal. She sipped her drink. She wondered where Tony had learned about Friend Julie. Was it common knowledge among their friends? Jeff's kookie wife? Talk about bizarre types . . .

Tony wheeled around on her. "You were thinking of 'In the Spotlight.' Is that it?" Once a week he devoted most of the column to a profile, just short of actionable, on someone in the news. "I've got a deal for you, Mrs. Hayes: you do me an interview with Sweets Romano and I'll take you on."

NINE

"I understand perfectly," Jeff said later that night.

"It's not that I'm trying to compete with you. Ha! As though I could."

"Would that be so terrible?"

"I hate women who compete with their husbands. I'm not all that great a competitor with anybody."

"And yet, Julie, you've asked for a job in the most competitive field in journalism, the gossip column. Of all the people I know you're the least susceptible to gossip."

"But I'm curious. I'm a very curious person."

"You certainly are," Jeff said, grinning. He shook out his bathrobe and put it on.

"But Sweets Romano. That really threw me."

"Tell me about him. Why is he called Sweets?"

"Somebody told me it was because he looks that way—rather plump and immaculate and cherubic. And then I heard it was because he owned a piece of a chain of candy stores."

"That sounds more likely. But his main line is pornography?"

"That's how I got to him."

Jeff laughed aloud.

"It's true. Pete Mallory had made a porn film . . ."

"Acted in it?"

"Yeah. He was one of the principals. He needed money. It was when Laura Gibson, the actress, was dying and he was trying to take care of her. When I first went to see Mr. Romano, I thought it was Pete he was interested in. . . ."

"Is Romano homosexual?"

"Jeff, I don't know what he is. He told me he'd been in love with Laura Gibson for years. He called himself the ultimate voyeur. He makes a great thing of not having touched another human being in twenty years. And yet he has all this marvelous painting and sculpture, and the first thing he said to me when I was looking at one of the sculptures was, 'Do touch. It is the greatest tribute.' He speaks beautifully, Jeff. And it sounds natural. But natural he isn't."

Jeff grunted. "Are you afraid of him?"

"Well, I was pretty shaky when I got out of there."

"Concentration will help. It always does for me."

The idea of Jeff's ever being afraid hadn't occurred to Julie.

"Oh, yes," Jeff said, reading her eyes. Then: "Did he like you?"

"I think maybe he did, you know, the idea of my seeking him out and coming to see him about Pete on my own. And I really did admire his art collection."

"That might be it, don't you think," Jeff suggested gently, "a way in?"

"I'm not the greatest authority on art," Julie said, and thought of *Scarlet Night*. Something she had not yet told Jeff about. It didn't seem exactly relevant at the moment.

"Even if you were, you would want to defer to him under the circumstances. Do you know how to contact him?"

"I have his unlisted number at the shop."

"I have only one word of advice at the moment, Julie: don't wait too long. Make your contact."

TEN

Juanita was back in front of the shop when Julie arrived in the morning, trying to make her gallant band of crippled dolls shape up. Her mother was in the upstairs window, elbows to pillow to windowsill. "Hi, Mrs. Rodriguez. How was the vacation?"

"No good. My husband's brother—he wants us to bring the whole family to New York." A business catastrophe for Mrs. Rodriguez, Julie thought.

She spoke to the child. "Did you miss me?"

If Juanita had she wasn't saying. The only word in her vocabulary that Julie knew of was "bad." Someday she was going to break out in two languages and either tell Papa that Mama was a moonlight hustler or tell Mama what she *could* tell Papa if it seemed to her advantage. Blackmail: childhood's ultimate weapon. Juanita needed an ultimate weapon.

"Julie . . . ?" the mother crooned.

"No messages," Julie said and let herself into the shop.

She was glad when she heard Mrs. Rodriguez call the child upstairs. She could never quite overcome a feeling of responsibility when Juanita was hovering outside the shop door. She ought to have brought her something from

Paris, a doll, one more doll to tear the limbs from. What she might do was give her the Tarot cards and defy in herself that lingering superstition. But the cards had a certain beauty, worn though they were by perhaps a generation of gypsy hands. . . . Señora Cabrera, whom she knew only from Mrs. Rodriguez's description. She might mount the cards or make a collage of them and hang it alongside *Scarlet Night*. She glanced at the painting where she had hung it on the plasterboard partition between the front and the back of the shop. She had turned her desk sideways to that wall. If anything in the room looked temporary it was *Scarlet Night* with its bold heavy frame. The goose-neck lamp shone bleakly on the notebook, open to two empty pages. There were three director's chairs around the table she had cut down to knee height for reading the cards. On the table were the crystal ball through which the most she had ever seen was the magnified grain of wood in the table, and the collected poems of William Butler Yeats.

Sweets Romano. She dialed the unlisted number.

As had happened on the previous occasion, the man who answered took her name and number and promised to call right back.

She waited, her heartbeat noisier than the drip of the tap in the bathroom sink. Mrs. Ryan was right: the place needed more air and light. On the other hand, considering the things that came out from the walls to play, who wanted to see them?

The phone rang.

"Romano here, Mrs. Hayes."

"I don't know if you remember me, Mr. Romano. . . ."

"I do. Someone who cared what happened to Peter Mallory."

"I'd like to talk to you for a little while, Mr. Romano, if we could make an appointment."

"It would give me pleasure. Today? Tomorrow?"

"Tomorrow would be better for me."

"Come for lunch. My car will pick you up. Is it the same address?"

"Yes, but Mr. Romano, couldn't I just come on my own?"

A second or two of hesitation. "Very well. Alberto will be waiting for you in the lobby. Twelve-thirty."

One step at a time, Julie cautioned herself when she

hung up the phone. She had twenty-four hours for preparation. She wound up the cords on the spotlights in the front room, put the lights in a shopping bag, and went to see Mr. Bourke. It was he who had obtained Romano's phone number for her. He had given it with deep reluctance. In fact, her fear of Romano derived in large part from him.

Mr. Bourke had spent all his life in the neighborhood. He was one of those people whose age Julie could not begin to judge. Forty? Sixty? She could imagine him at seven, a myopic child with smudged glasses already taking root on his nose. He lived at the Willoughby when he wasn't at his electrical-equipment shop, which was most of the time. Mrs. Ryan had confided to Julie that he had once been in trouble: he liked young boys. Julie knew him as gentle, solicitous, street smart, and religious, but she had figured out early on that his "trouble" had made him vulnerable to pimps, police, and other assorted bullies. Mack, the pimp, who had once been Romano's bodyguard, had used the shop as a "cover" for his girls, including Rita.

Mr. Bourke would not take a cent from Julie for the rental of the two spotlights. "I don't think you operated at a profit. Did you?"

"I got a lot out of the experience," Julie said.

"Give a little something to St. Malachy's. They're about to convert the Actors' Chapel into a seniors' club."

They would do better, Julie thought, setting up a hostel for runaway girls. Maybe not. There were a lot of seniors—like Mrs. Ryan—hanging onto what was left of respectability in the neighborhood.

"Mr. Bourke, has Mack been around again?"

He shook his head, and pushed his glasses back into place. "Not since Peter's death. Even the police have stopped inquiring. And I must say I haven't missed him."

"Mr. Romano told me they wouldn't find him."

"He ought to know."

"Meaning?"

Mr. Bourke looked startled. "I said nothing, Julie. Nothing."

"What could he do to you?"

He was upset, but as he thought about the question, he calmed down. "I don't suppose anything—himself, and that's what you mean, isn't it?" Julie nodded. "I doubt if he knows I exist. It's the noncommissioned officers I have to deal with. From what I've heard, Romano is a perfect gentleman himself. And a very generous one. I don't know, Julie: I've never heard of a hospital or any other charity turning down his contributions. He disappeared himself from the streets several years ago, but men who call themselves his enforcers are still around. Oh, yes."

"Unless they're Mack," Julie said.

Mr. Bourke did not say anything.

"What else besides pornography, do you think?"

"Real estate, restaurants, nightclubs . . . Mind, it's all hearsay. And I wouldn't be surprised if most of it's legitimate. By now, Julie, some very nice homes and places of business in this crazy town are built in old stables somebody once cleaned out."

"Like the New Irish Theatre," Julie said. A building in the far-west Fifties familiar to them both.

Mr. Bourke nodded. "But on a warm day you still smell the horse manure."

Julie walked over to the newspaper branch of the public library and found it closed. Thursday. From there she went to the New York Times building, stopping for an Orange Julius and a pizza on the way. She spent the afternoon looking up assorted Romanos in the *Times* index. Not having a first name for him she could not be sure of her man until she found a *Sweets* in parentheses: A. A. Romano. In the end she found but one entry: he had contributed a hundred thousand dollars to Columbia University Medical School. All the news fit to print.

Since Jeff was not going to be home for dinner, she decided to go back to Forty-fourth Street. Then, remembering it was Thursday, the day of the memorial Mass for Pete, she decided to go on to St. Malachy's first.

Mrs. Ryan touched her shoulder with the back of her hand to move her further into the pew, bobbed toward the altar, and eased herself down next to Julie, settling her behind on the edge of the seat. Julie admired people who knelt up straight as saints. Her mind wandered off in search of the Judy Collins song she had liked so much when she was at Miss Page's school. . . . "The simple

life of heroes, the twisted life of saints . . ." It wasn't
that Julie was a Catholic. She wasn't anything. But she
sometimes wished she were.

On the church steps afterward, Mrs. Ryan voiced her
fury at the coming conversion of the chapel into a
Senior Citizen Center. "I wouldn't put my food in one of
them for the world, a community coffin. . . . Have you
time to go around to McGowan's with me and have a
glass of beer?"

"I'll walk over with you, Mrs. Ryan, but I won't stay."

"To be sure, your husband's at home."

Julie let it go at that.

"You don't mind stopping a minute at the Willoughby
till I get Fritzie? He loves the walk and Billy McGowan
never says a word when I tuck him in at my feet."

Waiting for Mrs. Ryan to fetch the dog, Julie thought
about how you always wound up going a little further
with her than you intended. She doubted she'd ever have
opened the shop if it hadn't been for Mrs. Ryan. Did she
love her? This beery, bigoted old soul? Yes. She even
had a certain affection for Fritzie who came out of the
building just then like a wobbly torpedo on his nonstop
aim for the fire hydrant.

Mrs. Ryan waited and then put on his leash, and the
three of them walked at Fritzie's option across Forty-
sixth Street toward Ninth Avenue.

ELEVEN

"It's a needle in a haystack, Rubin, and I'll spend no
more time scratching my way through the phone book."

"Softly, Johnny, softly. I'm inclined to agree with you,
but it did give you something to do, landside, for a day or
two, didn't it?"

"I've never been more at sea."

"I am trying to help," Rubinoff said. "There's a tailoring shop in Keokuk, Iowa, under the name Abel. But the news from there is not good. They gave me the last address they had for him—Paris. In other words, if he is going home, he has not informed the family."

O'Grady thought about it. "We'd better give him a day or two more, and wouldn't he get more of a welcome, arriving without notice—the prodigal son?"

"It's maddening. I should not have allowed myself to become involved in something like this. I may yet have to abort the whole operation."

"I wouldn't do that, Rubin."

"I may not have any choice."

"I'll find the woman," O'Grady said. He was at the window, staring down at the kids playing stickball between the rushes of traffic. There was one little devil going to get his arm broken, poking his stick at the wheels of the passing cars. "I'm going to hang up now. There's a youngster on the street who's going to get hurt if I don't give him a shout."

O'Grady opened the window as wide as it would go and leaned out, but the shout died in his throat. Coming down the street, like the empress of China under her hat, was the old lady with her dog, and alongside her, unless he was out of his mind, was the girl he'd been searching the city for. He grabbed his jacket and ran down the stairs where he stalled in the hallway to let them pass. It was the girl for sure. He crossed the street and followed them, no easy matter, traveling at the dog's pace. He couldn't remember the old lady's name but he could guess where she was going. At the back of his mind was the recollection of a girl she had told him about, the orphaned child of an Irish diplomat. She didn't look Irish especially, and she sure as hell didn't look like an orphan.

It was a long walk, the two short blocks from the corner to McGowan's. It gave him time to change his mind several times over on how to proceed. Should he meet her square on after Mrs. . . . Mary Ryan! He had it . . . after she introduced them? Didn't I see you in a SoHo, art gallery the other day? And what in hell would she think he was doing in a SoHo art gallery? Or should he pretend to nothing and let Mary Ryan do all the contriving to bring them together? As his mother used to say, if God had intended him for a thinker, He'd have given him the head for it.

Outside McGowan's the two women parted and
O'Grady followed the girl. Mary Ryan was safely put for
a while. He'd observed it before of the young woman:
she knew how to walk. It was a pleasure to keep pace
with her. A few doors short of the avenue she stopped
and spoke to a child with her thumb in her mouth. Then
she put a key in the door of one of those shops carved
out of the bottom story of a tenement building; she went
in and closed the door in the child's face.

People were parking their cars on that side of the
street. Six o'clock. O'Grady watched for a minute or two
and then crossed over, lingering near a car he could pretend was his if he had to, and took a long look at the
building. She couldn't be the one Mary Ryan said told
fortunes. Or could she? There was no sign on the place
and the windows were hung full-length with green curtains.
He could see a light shining through but nothing more.
The child had her nose to the glass to where there might
be a part in the curtains.

"Señor down there, hello!"

O'Grady looked up. From a second-story window
a woman was smiling at him, a glint of gold in her
smile and in the comb at the crown of dark hair, and
her cheeks as red as a bloody sunset. He had seen her
like in a hundred windows, the sailor's first welcome landing on perilous shores. Jesus.

"You are looking for someone, señor?"

"No, no one particular. I used to know someone who
lived in the neighborhood."

"A young girl?"

"No. An old lady. She must be dead by now."

"Señora Cabrera! She don't live here no more, but the
same arrangement is all right. I am Rose." She gave
a toss of her head that was supposed to fetch him up
the stairs.

"I'll keep it in mind," he said, edging away. "I've to
see a man now I've got an appointment with."

"Señor . . . Not after nine o'clock. Never. And not Sunday."

He circled the block before he returned to McGowan's
and eased his way into the bar next to Mrs. Ryan. "It
was on my mind that I owe you a drink."

"You don't owe me a thing, Johnny."

"Is the girl I just saw you with the one you were telling me about?"

"Why didn't you speak if you saw us?"

"I'm a shy fella when it comes to the girls." Not to say a sly one, Johnny.

TWELVE

"Julie . . ." The call was combined with a tap, tap, tap on the window out front, Mrs. Ryan's wedding ring.

Julie paused on her way to the door long enough to turn on the floor lamp in the front of the shop. She opened the door to Mrs. Ryan and a man who stood head and shoulders above her.

"I was afraid you were gone, dear. This is the lovely man I told you about who reads the poetry, Sean O'Grady. Meet Julie Hayes, Johnny." Mrs. Ryan stood back and looked from one to the other of them in triumph.

Julie saw at once what Nurse Brennan had meant about the eyes, their penetrating blue, as of a zealot priest. And yet the smile was warm. "Mrs. Hayes," he said, as though the name were a benediction.

Fritzie skittered into the shop trailing his leash over Julie's feet.

"May we come in?" Mrs. Ryan said.

"Of course." Julie wasn't sure why she hesitated. A feeling of . . . what? Not invasion exactly . . . of something being contrived to involve her.

"We won't stop long, Mrs. Hayes," he said, his voice deep and resonant. "I'm walking the two of them home on my way somewhere and Mary Ryan was determined you and I had to meet."

That was it, Julie thought: a Mary Ryan production.

Fritzie poked his head out beneath the curtain that partitioned the room, yapped, and vanished behind it again.

"Look at him, right at home," Mrs. Ryan said.

By the time Julie had closed the front door, O'Grady, no doubt so directed by Mrs. Ryan, was holding aside the curtain, and the older woman was sailing through. Julie followed but adjusted the curtain herself while the others hovered near the chairs. "Do sit down," she said. "Will you have a cup of tea? I'm afraid I don't have milk for it."

"Nothing at all, dear. It'd spoil our suppers." Mrs. Ryan gave O'Grady a nudge and pointed to the book on the table.

"The first thing I noticed," he said, "Willie Yeats."

Willie. All right.

Mrs. Ryan settled herself in a chair whose very joint squeaked. She removed her hat.

O'Grady waited for Julie to sit, and then seated himself, facing the door. He noticed the painting and let a small grunt escape. Mrs. Ryan turned to see what he was looking at.

"Isn't he the observant one?"

"It took me by surprise, the one picture in the room," he said. "It's a colorful thing."

Julie shot him a brief glance. He didn't seem able to quite control his lower lip—a sensual mouth, but hardly strong. She wondered if he might be an ex-priest, but that was the association with Miss Brennan. She had the feeling of having seen him before, which was easily possible in the neighborhood. "It is colorful," she said, utterly lost for small talk.

Mrs. Ryan said, "Julie brought it from Paris. She's just back a few days."

She might have told them the true story: it would have been something to talk about, but she doubted it would hold their interest. "It's a grand city, Paris," O'Grady said. "I've been there a time or two, but the prices are perishing."

"What do you do, Mr. O'Grady?"

"I'm a merchant seaman, but that's not how I got to Paris. It's the rare occasion you can ship out to where you'd want to go."

"And where would you want to go?"

He looked at her and away and back again while he mused, as though well aware that his eyes put people off.

"Well, now, I'm partial to the coast of Italy—you can name the ports—Genoa, where Columbus sailed from, but you know that without my telling you, Naples and around to Brindisi—the Isle of Corfu which is a gem set in an azure sea . . . and I'll go to Ireland, any port at all. I've business there now and then."

Julie could almost hear the singing heart of Mrs. Ryan, for his voice was indeed musical and he did have a way with words. And you knew from the way he narrowed his eyes what he meant when he said of Ireland: I've business there now and then. The I.R.A. He wanted you to know that.

"I was telling Johnny about your father, I hope you don't mind. None of the personal things, mind, only that you hadn't seen him since you were an infant and him having to do with the Irish government. Johnny is well connected over there. Was it the U.N. he was at, Julie?"

"It was not the U.N.," Julie said, furious with the old gossip. "And I do mind."

"Ah, I'm a blathering old woman. We'll say no more about it."

"Ireland wasn't admitted to the United Nations until 1955," O'Grady said, "with them holding her and Spain hostage you might say for countries the Russians wanted in. Have you ever been in Spain, Mrs. Hayes? There's a wild country for you. They've still got gypsies camping around."

"Are there none left in Ireland?" Mrs. Ryan wanted to know.

"A few in the west, but they're called travelers now. In my mother's day they were tinkers. If you call them that now they take grave offense. 'If ifs and ands were pots and pans, there'd be no use for tinkers' hands.' I used to wonder what the devil she meant by that."

"What did she mean?" Julie asked.

"The tinkers went around in their caravan from village to village mending the pots and pans."

"Oh."

"Shall we go, Mary Ryan? We're keeping the girl from whatever she was doing."

"There used to be a gypsy woman in this very shop before Julie and I discovered it empty. Do you remember the day, dear?"

"All too well."

Mrs. Ryan pursed her lips and lowered her eyes. She groped around her legs for the dog's leash. Julie almost regretted her sharpness. But not quite.

"When I grew up here on the West Side," O'Grady said, "it was nearly all Irish. You had to go to Harlem to find a Hispanic."

"I'd have thought you were born in Ireland, Mr. O'Grady."

He leaned forward and said, with a self-deprecating smile, "I'm a professional Irishman."

Julie had to laugh, something that cheered Mrs. Ryan considerably.

"I should never have taken off my hat, but I can't hear well with it on, and I didn't want to miss a thing you two would have to say to each other."

"You can only rehearse yourself, Mary Ryan, unless you're going to write a script."

"Isn't that the truth? You never know what people are going to say. But I'm glad you got on."

Had they got on? Mrs. Ryan was always a step ahead in her manipulation. A nice Doctor word. Julie got up before Mrs. Ryan could change her mind about going.

O'Grady gave a sharp whistle for the dog. He could have saved his whistle, for all the attention Fritzie paid it: he was a city dog, born and bred.

"If I invited you to one of my readings, would you come?" O'Grady said. "The New Irish Theatre probably, and there'd be some Yeats in it."

Déjà vu. Only it was Pete Mallory speaking. Julie said, "It will depend, I'm afraid, on whether my husband and I have an engagement that night."

He looked taken aback and Julie regretted saying what she had: it was full of air.

"I'm glad to have met you in any case, Mrs. Hayes."

"I didn't say just what I meant, Mr. O'Grady, and it sounded rude. But there are occasions when Jeff commits us far ahead. If I'm free, I'd love to come."

"Bring him along if you like. If his name is Hayes he can't be that far from the old sod."

"All right."

Mrs. Ryan looked as though she had bitten into a lemon. Obviously she had not mentioned the husband, much less ever thought of his joining them. "You need more lights in here, dear. It's terribly dreary."

"I like it," Julie said, at a loss for the moment for a stronger touch of venom.

"All you need, well," O'Grady said, nodding at the picture, "is the touch of color and a bag of poems."

THIRTEEN

O'Grady asked this question and that of Mary Ryan; then as soon as he got out of her sight went home as fast as his legs would take him. He called Rubinoff. "I found her, Rubin! By God, I found her. And I saw the picture with my own eyes hanging in her shop on Forty-fourth Street."

"I knew you could do it, Johnny. I never doubted for a moment."

"The queer thing is I could have met her before this." He told him about Mary Ryan and her conniving to bring them together.

"It's a small world," Rubinoff said.

"She's married to the columnist Geoffrey Hayes. Do you read the *Times?*"

"That's not very good news, Johnny. We shall have to be most circumspect. Did she wonder where she had seen you before?"

"I don't think she saw me at the gallery. It hit me like a flying fish, seeing the painting there. But I covered myself. It's a colorful bit of paint."

"Has she other paintings? What sort of a place is it?"

"It's a hole in the wall, the ground floor of a tenement with a practicing prostitute overhead. She must think it has atmosphere, the way Ginni does the working-class streets of Naples. To hear Ginni talk of the proletariat makes me roar with laughter."

"I asked about other paintings, Johnny."

"There are none. There's an electric plate, a typewriter,

and a crystal ball. Make something of them, if you will."

"Where does she live?"

"With her husband you mean? Down near the Village, the old lady says. It'd be in the book, I wouldn't wonder."

"Then what's the painting doing on Forty-fourth Street? I'd like to know what's between her and Abel. You don't buy a painting for five hundred dollars and hide it away with a hot plate."

"Maybe she's only keeping it for him. Maybe she's supposed to turn it over to you, Rubin. How about that?"

"That's brilliant of you, Johnny, if it's true. And it sounds right. As long as it's safe, let's give the matter some thought over the weekend."

"I don't like sitting around waiting, not after what I've been through."

"Look at it this way, Johnny: we are ten days ahead of schedule. There was never any thought of my taking possession until the show closed."

"But the show is closed, Rubin, and if you saw the place, you wouldn't be so damn sure the painting was safe."

"You're letting your nerves victimize you, Johnny."

"It's my stomach as well and the need to pay my rent while I've still got a roof over my head."

"Then you must find gainful employment, however temporary. Let me ask you a question: suppose I crashed up in the Porsche tomorrow, what would you do?"

"I'd be at your bedside praying that with your dying breath you'd tell me where the picture was going."

Rubinoff laughed. "Have a lovely weekend, Johnny."

"It's only Thursday, man," he said, but into a dead phone.

FOURTEEN

It began to rain as Julie stepped into a bus that would take her across the park. She had worn her raincoat. She always felt invulnerable in raincoat and sneakers. Someday it might not work, but on her present mission she enjoyed the feeling of security the outfit gave her. Except that she wasn't wearing sneakers. Sandals, and beneath her raincoat beige slacks and a blue tunic with a tasseled belt.

She tried to think of the questions she would ask him if she got the chance. Not a one came to mind. She had tried to do her homework as Jeff would have, but it didn't work for her. If Romano answered her with one syllable, she'd be stuck with one syllable. The great improviser. At least there was one thing about this assignment—she wasn't fantasizing the results, she wasn't dreaming of Julie Hayes, investigative reporter, she wasn't imagining Tony taking Jeff by the arm at the club and saying, "By God, the girl is good!" She wasn't hearing Jeff say, "I must admit, Julie, I hadn't expected . . ." She wasn't?

As soon as she gave her name to the doorman, a good-looking young man with sad dark eyes came to her and said, "Mr. Romano is expecting you, Mrs. Hayes."

They rode up in the elevator without a word. He wore a spotless white shirt, open at the throat, the cuffs turned up.

Romano himself opened the door of the penthouse apartment. He dismissed the younger man with a "Thank you, Alberto."

The blue eyes did not seem as remote as she had remembered them; the round soft face which looked freshly scrubbed and shaved *was* cherubic—like one of his porcelain sculptures come to life. He too was wearing blue silk, but ornamented with lizards. "How nice of you to come and see me again, Mrs. Hayes." He held his hands

63

high and limp, waiting to take her coat. They weren't out for the shaking, certainly. "May I?"

She couldn't very well keep it on through lunch although she would have liked to. "Thank you."

"You've been in Europe, I understand." An Actors Forum informant, probably.

"With my husband," Julie said.

"A distinguished member of the fourth estate."

There didn't seem to be anything to say to that. Julie looked around the foyer while he hung her coat. Some of the paintings she remembered, some she had forgotten, or more specifically, she'd forgotten where she had seen them.

"I have something I must show you," he said as they stepped down into the living room with its vast skylight on which the rain now fell with a soft patter. "You were kind enough to admire my Vuillard. Do you like Edvard Munch?"

They came up to a stark Munch woman, blacks and grays and only a little color, a whisper of red. Out of the depths.

"Oh, yes," Julie said with fervor. She did like it.

The little caesar beamed. "Isn't it splendid? I have been over five years acquiring it."

Just that brief escape from herself into the Munch and Julie felt more at ease.

"I wish I could understand suffering," Romano said.

Julie glanced at him: it seemed an odd thing to say.

"Does it seem strange to you, my curiosity?"

"A little."

"Think of all the *Pietàs* in the world. How do you think the artists prepared themselves?"

"By substitution maybe, the way an actor does?"

"Hurt for agony? A pinprick for the stigmata?"

"I think most of us have suffered a little more than pinpricks," Julie said.

"Ah-ha, you include yourself."

Julie felt herself blushing. "I was speaking generally, Mr. Romano. Actually, I was thinking of you."

"How intuitive of you. My life is one great substitute for living. Perhaps at this stage one might call it sublimation, but there is nothing sublime about it. Well, we've made an earnest start to our visit, haven't we?"

"I'd better tell you why I'm here, Mr. Romano. I'll feel a lot better."

He motioned her toward the same chair she had sat in before and drew the same one he had sat in at an angle to it and seated himself. The old man in the Vuillard painting looked down on them.

"I'd like to do an article about you for Tony Alexander's column in the *Daily News*."

He blinked his eyes. Nothing in his expression betrayed either pleasure or dismay. He sat quietly and folded one small plump hand into the other. "What would you like to know?"

"At this very minute? I'd like to know what happened twenty years ago that you haven't touched a human being since. You told me that yourself and I've thought a lot about it. I mean the way you touch sculpture—with love, like something alive. . . ."

He was looking at his hands, turning them palms upward. Then he looked at her. "This is information you would like to put in a column in the *Daily News?*"

The blood rushed to Julie's face again. "It isn't something I planned to ask you, Mr. Romano. But when you said, 'What would you like to know?' that's what came to the top. I'm not very tactful, maybe, but I am discreet. I don't think you'd have to worry about my saying something in print that you wouldn't want me to."

"But, my dear, those are the very things Tony Alexander would want to know—the source of my wealth, the number of people I've had rubbed out, to speak in the vernacular, where I stand in the Family hierarchy . . . and what ever happened to Mack the Pimp. Come now, can you tell me honestly that you have come here *not* wanting to know what happened to him?"

"I did wonder, it's true."

Romano folded his hands again and massaged them gently. "Shall I tell you he is alive and well in Costa Rica?"

"Okay."

"Alive, in any case. I didn't know you were a newspaper woman, Mrs. Hayes."

"Let's say I'm an apprentice. Tony is a friend of my husband's and I got up my courage the other day and asked him for a job. I've gotten to know some pretty colorful people lately."

"And do you think I'm colorful?"

"Yes. But I also think that Munch painting is colorful. A lot of people wouldn't say that."

"You are clever."

"What I thought we might hang the story on is your art collection."

"Is Mr. Alexander interested in art?"

"No. Collectors, yes, if they're famous."

"Or infamous. We must give the matter further thought."

"I won't have more than five hundred words," Julie said.

"Yes, but I shall want the last one, and I doubt Mr. Alexander would consent to that."

"He might—as long as he has the first ones, you know —things like Mr. Romano is the alleged . . . he is reported to be . . . things like that."

"Leaving you the second act in which to discourse on the part of Romano which bears public scrutiny." He glanced over his shoulder and Julie looked around to see Alberto in the doorway, now wearing a white coat. "Shall we have lunch and talk of old friends? I hope you like trout. They came out of the stream at dawn this morning."

Consommé with a thin lemon slice, the trout broiled just to the point where the skin was spotted with brown and cracked. Alberto showed them the fish and then boned them at the end of the table. Asparagus, an endive salad, and a cheese more delicate than brie. Espresso. Jeff would have approved. Julie resolved to open the article, if she ever got to write it, describing the luncheon, the silver, and the deeply polished, knife-scarred wood of the refectory table at which they sat. The wine was a Soave. Julie wished she liked wine better. Jeff wished it too and she kept trying.

Mostly they talked of Pete Mallory and Laura Gibson, the actress both men had loved, the Actors Forum, and theater as Romano remembered it. He was a lot older than he looked. His best memories were of the 1930s and 1940s, which made Julie wonder if he had got his start in the underworld during Prohibition. She hoped so. Nostalgia. She realized that he was saying things he did not mind her quoting, and for a few seconds when she realized this, anxiety took over and she missed part of what he was saying. He was talking about Shakespeare.

"I do believe," he said and paused, his hands folded on the table almost as though he were posing, "that I am among the few moderns who can accept *Othello* as completely believable."

Julie merely nodded.

"I thought you would understand," he said, and at that moment she was struck with what he might be telling her. Othello's problem was jealousy and he wound up strangling his wife. Killing her with his own hands anyway. . . . Surely not.

"Shall we go now and look at the paintings you've not seen before?"

He had a great American collection, people Julie especially liked—Levine and Sloan and Bellows. He had nonobjectives too, but you knew from where things were hanging which were his favorites. There were painters, too, unknown to Julie, so that she thought of Ralph Abel, but it was a long time before she said anything. They were looking at a Reginald Marsh, blousy women on the move. "Do you know an art dealer by the name of Rubinoff?" she asked.

"I've heard the name."

"I think he buys for collectors with a lot of money."

"It's a common practice. One rarely knows who buys at auction, for example, unless by association. And then there are people in the market, believe it or not, who don't trust their own tastes."

"That's very funny," Julie said. "I was just going to ask you if you'd look at a painting I bought. This Rubinoff wanted it, but I got it from the painter. It's in my shop on Forty-fourth Street. I like it, but . . ."

"You would like your taste confirmed."

"I would like your opinion. The artist is a friend of mine."

"You ought not to seek opinions on the work of friends, my dear, if you'll forgive the advice of an aging man."

"Well, you see, I'm hoping you'll like him."

"Ah-ha! I no longer leave this apartment, you know."

"I didn't know," Julie said.

"But if you would care to send it to me with my driver, I will look at it and be as frank with you as you have been with me. And by the time we talk again, I shall have decided whether you are to launch your career as a newspaperwoman on the revelations of Romano."

FIFTEEN

The driver, Michael, took Julie to the door under an umbrella and waited outside until she brought him *Scarlet Night*. He was a tough, thin little man with a limp, and with a scar on his cheek that made her wonder if he was a gang-war veteran. She had never had a good look at him until then. There was a lot of space between the front seat and the back seat of the limousine. If Romano never left his apartment, what did he need with a limousine and chauffeur?

She called Jeff and told him she thought the interview had gone well.

"How were the nerves?"

"Under control by lunchtime. And what a luncheon. I kept thinking of you. It was like dining with royalty."

"It probably was—of a sort. Shall we risk the weather and go out to Amagansett for the weekend? I may be away again for a few days next week."

"Let's do that," Julie said. The thought of waiting for Romano—or anyone else, for that matter—to call did not appeal to her, a one-time actress.

From Alberto to Michael: Julie wrote her account of the visit to Romano before leaving the shop. Then she went home and cleaned house: an anxiety ritual.

It was definitely time to tell Jeff about *Scarlet Night*, something she was reluctant to do: the reasons for which she had better clear up in her own mind. And while she was at it, she ought to understand just why she had asked Romano to look at it. Hoping for an opinion which would justify her having bought it? Romano's opinion before Jeff's? Be fair to yourself, Julie: there wasn't time . . . But how long would it take for him to say he didn't like it?

The rain came and went all weekend, so that Julie and Jeff spent a lot of time prowling the antique shops.

Maybe they weren't looking for one, but they came upon an oval mirror in a gilt frame festooned with husks, Adam style. Jeff proclaimed it a real find.

"All right," Julie said. And inwardly rejoiced.

SIXTEEN

O'Grady was no more able to stay away from the shop on Forty-fourth Street than he had been able to stay away from the Maude Sloan Gallery the day Ralph Abel's show opened. He had told Rubinoff then that he felt responsible. He still did. One of the things that kept going through his mind was the way old buildings were being destroyed by fire all over the city. His unemployment-insurance check came in the mail Saturday morning and he went by Billy McGowan's to see if Billy could cash it for him. McGowan gave him twenty dollars and promised him the rest by evening when he'd have enough money in the till. O'Grady meandered down Forty-fourth Street then, keeping his eye out so as not to bump into the old lady and her dog. It was cloudy and damp, but the rain had let up temporarily at least. The youngster was bringing her dolls out of the hallway alongside the shop and trying to make them sit up against the shop window.

O'Grady was inclined to speak to her. He was also inclined to visit the woman upstairs if she put in an appearance and renewed her invitation, for a scheme was beginning to take shape in his mind in case the situation became desperate . . . say if the Hayes girl refused under any circumstances to give up *Scarlet Night*.

"Anybody home in there?" he asked the child and when she shook her head he tapped on the glass as Mary Ryan had done when she brought him there. Not a sound from within.

But overhead Rose leaned out the window and smiled

at him. She motioned him up and spoke to the child in Spanish, a rattle of orders that made O'Grady queasy. He hadn't thought of them as mother and daughter till then. He went into the vestibule and waited for the buzzer, observing that there were four bells and four boxes, which meant that the flats ran all the way through the building. The buzzer sounded and he opened the door and went up the stairs. Rose was waiting for him on the landing, all smiles and perfumed to the navel. "I knew the señor would come. Señor . . . ?"

"Johnny." He gave her his hand before she went after it.

"You are a sailor. I can tell how you walk."

She drew him into the apartment. Clean and fancy, bric-a-brac and plastic covers on the furniture. He had to admit he'd been in worse places on a similar mission, although he did not care much for the picture of the Sacred Heart looking down on the transaction.

"What did you mean the other day, not to come after nine?"

"At twelve noon, you don't need to ask that, Johnny. I give you a nice glass of wine."

He wanted to say no extras, but he needed the time and the talk the extras might provide. He followed her through the dining room with the child's bedroom off it, and into the kitchen. The bathroom was off that, and was probably in the same place in all the apartments and in the shop downstairs. There was a large, curtained kitchen window.

When Rose turned her back, getting glasses, and the wine from the cupboard, O'Grady went to the window, parted the curtains, and looked out. The tenement opposite was maybe a hundred feet away, with a network of clotheslines passing between the buildings. He unlocked the window, opened it, and leaned out. The fire escape was a bed of geraniums, but he could see the outline below of the same window. In the distance, beyond the sea of broken glass and cans and other unspeakable rubbish, was a high wire fence and beyond it a parking lot.

Rose pulled him in by the shirttail, furious. "If I want to advertise, I put it in the newspaper. What are you, a cop? A fink?" She was a storm, the spittle flew into his face.

He caught her hand. "Don't be mad at me, Rose. Sweet Rose, don't be mad at me. You scared me saying not to come after nine."

She calmed down, closed the window and locked it, and drew the curtains. Then, after the fact, she thumbed her nose at the neighbors.

O'Grady, to further justify himself and to soothe her with the promise of a future visit, said, "You see, eight o'clock at night is the best time for me."

"Eight o'clock." She shook her head. Then as the thought further about it, she made a face suggesting that something could be worked out. She wasn't going to miss a trick. "We talk later, Johnny. Okay?"

She poured two small glasses of wine, Christian Brothers cream sherry, put the bottle back in the cupboard, and led him back through the dining room, squeezing past the large table which held a bowl of artificial fruit. Over the sideboard hung another sacred picture, Gethsemane. He hated to think what he would find in the bedroom.

By the time they reached the living room, her eyes had gone mushy as prunes. She touched her glass to his and said, "To love."

"To love," Johnny said and gulped down the wine.

She took a sip of hers and set the glass on the table. "Fifty dollars under the glass, please. I come back in a minute."

"Fifty? I'm a working man, for God's sake."

She looked around, halfway to the bedroom door. "How much?"

"Twenty. It's all I've got."

"Pffff," she said in disgust. Then: "Put it." She disappeared into the bedroom and returned in a few seconds with a huge, fluffy bath towel. "Now we take the bath."

"Both of us? I had one this morning. I'll wash if you like."

"I do it for you. Don't you want everything, Johnny?"

"Everything," he said with all the enthusiasm he could muster.

He took his clothes into the bathroom and dressed. When he came out she was waiting, all her treasures tucked away in a voluminous flowered housecoat. She put her hair up again while they talked. "You are a nice man,

Johnny. I teach you many things. When will you come back?"

"Soon." He wouldn't have minded.

"Maybe seven-thirty instead of eight. Juanita, you know?" She motioned toward the window overlooking the street. "When Señora Cabrera was downstairs, she took care of Juanita, but Julie's not like that. You know her?"

He assumed Rose might have seen him go into the shop with Mrs. Ryan. "She's a friend of a friend of mine."

"The lady with the dog."

"Mrs. Ryan. What about Julie? Is she there much?"

"She comes and goes. A whole month she was gone."

"Is she around at night?"

"Almost never. You don't have to worry. And she knows. She don't care for it herself but she knows. It would do her good, a nice man like yourself."

O'Grady was shocked. The boldness of the women today. And the sacred pictures all over the house. Or was it the Irish puritan in him? "I must go," he said, and looked at his watch as though it mattered.

She went to the door with him. "Always you ring the bell, Rodriguez, and wait till I come to the window. If I don't come, you go away. You enjoyed?"

"Oh, I did. You're the best. You're the Rose of Sharon and the Rose of Tralee all rolled up in one."

She smiled her golden smile. "Next time you bring more money."

SEVENTEEN

Jeff had an early meeting at the office Monday morning which he felt sure would result in his going to West Virginia: a strike in the coal mines. One of the awards hanging in his study was for his coverage many years before of a mine disaster. He wanted to go, no question. At breakfast he spoke of the recovery of the sick man of American energy which sounded like something out of a lead paragraph. Julie took his shorts and socks to the laundromat and picked up a paint chart at the hardware store. She proposed to paint the wall over the mantel herself.

The phone was ringing as she went up the stairs, but by the time she had managed to open the double lock it had stopped. She felt it was too soon for Romano to call, and yet . . . Ten minutes later the phone rang again.

"This is Alberto Scotti, Mrs. Hayes. Mr. Romano asks if you will permit him to reframe the painting. He feels that it shows to a disadvantage in so heavy a frame." It sounded like Romano speaking, the way the words were put together.

"Why not?" Julie said. "Okay."

She was disappointed, which was unreasonable. After all, he was looking at the picture, and therefore had in mind the story she had asked for.

Jeff called to say that he would have to leave at noon, which gave him very little time to get ready. He asked that she lay out his things for packing, among them a dozen shirts. He also suggested that now that he was home, they ought to have a telephone-answering service. Laying out twelve shirts and being home seemed like a contradiction.

The house seemed very quiet after Jeff had gone, a whispery quiet to which Julie was well accustomed. The mirror lay on its back on the living-room rug, and there it would remain until he returned and hung it. Meanwhile she could paint out the ghost of Felicia's portrait.

Shortly after noon a call came which she had certainly not expected. "This is Rubin Rubinoff, Mrs. Hayes. I understand you have the Ralph Abel painting we both were interested in."

Off balance, she took a moment to grasp what he had said.

"Am I right?"

"I do have it, yes."

"I assume you plan to deliver it to me at your convenience?"

Another snow job. "I don't plan to do that, Mr. Rubinoff. I bought and paid for it."

"But, my dear Mrs. Hayes, no one had the right to sell it to you."

"I understood you withdrew your offer."

"It was not an offer. It was a commitment, and I certainly did not back down on it. I couldn't have done that even if I had wanted to."

She had wondered at the time if Rubinoff could not be held to his purchase. It would seem Abel had lied to her. To spite Maude Sloan? For whatever reason.

"But look, no real harm's been done," Rubinoff went on smoothly. "One can sympathize with the young artist's emotional problems. I will pay you the five hundred dollars and pick up the painting at a time convenient to us both. I am sorry. Now you will be even more attached to it. But I am committed to my client. You can bring it to me if you like."

"I want to think about it, Mr. Rubinoff."

"There is not much to think about, I'm afraid. But I don't mind adding a hundred dollars to compensate you for your disappointment. Or you might find something in my gallery that you would like. Are you a collector?"

"My husband is," Julie said, throwing everything off-kilter, but she was using Jeff as a defensive weapon.

There was a beat of silence before Rubinoff said, "Then he will know how sacred these arrangements are among painter, gallery, and collector. Do you really want to involve him?"

Now that was odd. There was a lot of subtext Julie wasn't getting. She had a hunch what he meant was that *he* did not want to involve her husband. "Mr. Rubinoff, how did you know how to reach me?"

"Mr. Abel reached you, didn't he?"

"Then why don't you have Mr. Abel call me? If he wishes to have the painting back, let's do it that way. Okay?"

"Mrs. Hayes, I deal with galleries. I rarely talk with painters. I would advise you to do the same."

"That's fine, but I'll wait for Mr. Abel's call just the same."

"Let me give you my number meanwhile, in case you should change your mind."

Julie wrote down the number and, hanging up, sat and thought about the call. Let him have it! Get it back from Romano and give it to him. Call Romano now. And feel

like a fool: You see, Mr. Romano, I thought I'd bought
it, but . . . Five hundred dollars. Six hundred. And if Mr.
Rubinoff dealt only with galleries, why wasn't it Maude
Sloan who called her?

She went back to the paint on the mantel: for the right
mix she was going to need chalk white and a handful of
dust. If he had gotten her phone number or the name
under which it was listed from Ralph Abel, why not say so
directly? He'd been direct enough in saying she had no
right to the painting. She had the distinct feeling that he
was not in touch with Abel at all. And if that were the
case, how *did* he know to call Mrs. Geoffery Hayes?

She decided to pay Maude Sloan a visit.

EIGHTEEN

Julie rang the bell and tried the gallery door at the same
time. It wasn't locked. Maude Sloan was at her desk surrounded by empty walls. A week ago the scene had been
a lot different.

"Yes?" Mrs. Sloan watched her approach with a
look of trying to remember where she had seen her before.

"I came to the Ralph Abel opening," Julie said.

"Of course." She stopped sorting a stack of mail,
mostly bills.

"You introduced me to a Mr. Rubinoff."

"Yes—that unfortunate confusion. I'm afraid I've forgotten your name."

Which had to mean that Rubinoff had bypassed Mrs.
Sloan, ignoring his own advice.

"Mrs. Geoffrey Hayes," Julie said. It sounded rather
more dramatic than she had intended. But it scored.

Mrs. Sloan said, "I must apologize for the confusion.
It was unfortunate timing—a matter of a moment or two.
Won't you sit down?"

Julie said, "Mrs. Sloan, I have the painting, *Scarlet
Night*."

There was a slow, downward turn to that once hand-some face, and a shift away from Julie of the gray-green eyes. As though she had been dealt a blow. "Ralph wanted you to have it. . . . Or did you buy it from Rubinoff?" The latter possibility seemed to lift her spirits.

Julie sat in the chair alongside the desk. "Ralph called me the morning after the opening and said I could have *Scarlet Night*, that the other buyer had changed his mind."

"The morning after the show, yes. The gallery was closed. It seems a long time ago."

"I'm sorry the show went the way it did," Julie said, wanting to say something sympathetic.

"Are you?"

Julie decided she had better stick to her reason for coming. "You mean Mr. Rubinoff hadn't changed his mind at all."

"Not at that point. Today it might be different."

"Why? If you don't mind telling me."

"From what I know of Mr. Rubinoff, I'd say he often represents people who speculate in painting much as some men invest in the market—looking for growth stock."

"I get it. Ralph Abel's gone out of business."

"I don't know whether he has or not, but he's going to have trouble finding another gallery. I called Mr. Rubinoff when I discovered the paintings were gone. I supposed Ralph might deliver *Scarlet Night* to him."

"Mr. Rubinoff called me this morning and said I had no right to keep the painting. He gave me a high-minded lecture of ethics and commitments."

"Really," Maude Sloan murmured with a downward smile.

"He wound up saying we could settle the whole thing amicably: I was to give him the painting—for which he was willing to pay six hundred dollars."

"Isn't it interesting that he called *you?*"

"Instead of calling you, you mean?"

Mrs. Sloan nodded.

"I said that if Mr. Abel wanted his painting back he could have it. He didn't like that idea: he said he dealt with galleries, not painters, and advised me to do the same. So here I am."

Mrs. Sloan laughed dryly. "Somehow, I don't think he had me in mind."

"Do you suppose he went through the phone book till he found me?"

"You didn't sign the gallery book?"

Julie shook her head. "I'd mentioned to Mr. Abel that I was married to a newspaperman. That's how *he* found my number."

"Very curious behavior—everyone's." Mrs. Sloan gave a weary sigh.

"Do I have to give Mr. Rubinoff the painting?"

"Do you still like it? That's the first question."

"I do, I really do," she said, convincing herself at the same time. "I didn't like Mr. Rubinoff, but then I wasn't going to under those circumstances. I guess I ought to tell you too, all I paid Mr. Abel for it was a hundred dollars. He said that was all he wanted and that maybe someday —if he was around—I could give him another hundred."

"Then, if I were you, I would keep it. Until you hear from Ralph—if you do. Or until Rubinoff brings the matter to arbitration and involves me. I should be surprised, since he's gone this route, if he intends to do that."

"But if he did, would the painting belong to him?" Julie was immediately sorry she had asked that, remembering that at the time she was pretty sure Maude Sloan had opted for the whole star over the half star on the spur of the moment, something that might not stand up legally when push came to shove.

But she wasn't going to admit that. "I've never found it useful, Mrs. Hayes, to predict the outcome of arbitration."

"I was going to ask if you had an address for Mr. Abel."

"I do not. I suspect he's back in Iowa."

"Or Italy?"

Mrs. Sloan just looked at her. Julie shrugged. She felt that Iowa meant defeat for Ralph Abel the painter and Italy was where he'd had a lot of hope. She had not consciously made the association with Maude Sloan's daughter.

"I don't think he's in Italy. Did he tell you about my daughter?"

"He mentioned her as a kind of patron."

"A patron," she repeated. Then: "Ginni proposed to come over for the opening of his show. Now she proposes to come the day before it was scheduled to close."

"Oh, boy."

Mrs. Sloan was amused. "Exactly. I've decided to let

her come. I want very much to see her. She has asked for a party Saturday night and I'm going to give it. If you and your husband would like to come, you'd be most welcome."

"Thank you," Julie said. "I'll have to let you know after I've talked with Jeff." Who probably wouldn't be back from West Virginia or wouldn't be high on a SoHo party if he were.

"No need to call, just come. Drinks and buffet at eight." Mrs. Sloan took a card from the drawer and wrote the address.

"How nice," Julie said. Then: "Will Mr. Rubinoff be there?"

Mrs. Sloan spaced the words out with emphasis: "I . . . think . . . not."

NINETEEN

The answering service was hooked up Tuesday morning, freeing Julie to do . . . what? She was learning what Jeff meant when he said the hardest part of a newsman's job was the waiting. Her mind swiveled between Romano and Rubinoff and she wound up in the terrible position of racing the service for every phone call.

In the afternoon she got a number for the Abel Tailor Shop in Keokuk and dialed it.

"Mr. Abel?"

"There is no Mr. Abel, ma'am. My name is Amberg. Can I help you?"

"I'm trying to get in touch with Ralph Abel, Mr. Amberg, and I thought you might be able to help me."

"I have not heard from Ralph in over a year, ma'am. The last address I have is Paris, France, and I understand that's no longer any good. You're calling from New York, right?"

"Right. I bought a painting of his . . ."

"*Mazel tov*. Now he has sold two paintings I know of. But where he is, I cannot tell you. Why don't you leave your number and if he shows up here someday, I will tell him you called."

"Thank you," Julie said. "Did a Mr. Rubinoff call you?"

"Somebody called him twice in the last few days. No name. Just a number."

"My name is Julie Hayes." She gave him both numbers. "You're his cousin, aren't you?"

"Yes, ma'am, on his mother's side."

Julie couldn't think of anything else to say. "You've been very kind, thank you."

"Tell me something. Ralph is now an important artist? He can make a living at it?"

"He can make a living," Julie said carefully.

"Then how come you expected to find him back home?"

Julie cast about wildly for the answer to that one. "Roots," she said.

"Roots?" the man repeated. "He was pulling them up the last time I saw him."

"Good-bye, Mr. Amberg. Tell him I called—if he comes."

TWENTY

"You shouldn't feed the squirrels. They're vermin and you're contributing to their increase in population."

"How can you say they're vermin, Johnny? They're almost human." Rubinoff cracked open another peanut shell and held out the nut in the palm of his hand. The creature came right up to the park bench and took it from his hand.

What irritated O'Grady was not so much that he was feeding the squirrels as that he could afford to buy a sixty-cent bag of peanuts for that purpose while Johnny

O'Grady hadn't the nails to scratch himself. And a fortune awaiting their grasp.

"Ch-ch-ch-ch." Rubinoff puckered his lips to the creature. It gave a flick of its tail, turned its backside to him, and took off. He handed O'Grady the bag with the rest of the peanuts. "It was a mistake for me to have called her. At least until we were sure where Abel was."

"You can't back down on it now with her. Why don't you threaten to have the law on her? It's your property she's got sequestered there."

"Don't say things you don't mean, Johnny. It isn't helpful. If I did something that extreme, I can't be sure Maude would be entirely cooperative."

"Ah, now it comes out."

"And if I could reach Abel, what would he care, having burned his bridges? He might be more hindrance than help." Rubinoff looked at him, his eyes moist with melancholy. "If only you hadn't exposed yourself to the Hayes woman, you could go to her now and say you were Abel's friend and emissary."

"God almighty, man, I didn't expose myself to her. You make me sound like a pervert."

Rubinoff grinned. Very unpleasant: the teeth of a shark.

"If it wasn't for me you wouldn't know where the bloody thing was at all." O'Grady was shelling himself a handful of peanuts to eat all at once.

"Save one or two in case the little fellow comes back."

"He can eat the shells and improve his digestion. Rubin, I cased the place over the weekend. It mightn't be all that hard to get in a back window."

Rubinoff shook his head.

"I'm glad you feel that way, but I thought I'd better mention it."

After a moment Rubinoff said, "I wish you hadn't told me about it."

O'Grady thought that one over and took it to mean he'd approve if he wasn't consulted in advance.

Rubinoff too was considering. "She has a husband who is much in social demand, I'm sure."

"Aye, so she told me herself."

Rubinoff raised his eyebrows.

"I was inviting her to one of my readings. She has a certain sympathy with the Irish cause."

"My point was that she would be very unlikely to ever stay overnight on Forty-fourth Street."

"There's nothing even resembling a bed in the place."

"How observant you are," Rubinoff said nastily.

"I'm not all that observant, but when I see something that has to be done, I do it."

TWENTY-ONE

O'Grady sat in the car staring up Forty-fourth Street. There was hardly a soul to be seen between the avenues. He'd have given odds at that point that Rubinoff was not going to show up. Then, through the rear-view mirror, he saw the man come pattering along from the direction opposite to the one he had expected. O'Grady opened the door to him. He got in and complained of the lack of space in a Volkswagen.

"It's not a Porsche, sure. I thought you weren't coming."

"It's not much after twelve."

"There's things to be said. I'd like you inside with me, Rubin, if I can open the door to you."

"Under no circumstances."

"You've a woman's hands on you and that's what's needed!"

"I've given the matter some thought, Johnny. If you can open the door, I see no reason why we shouldn't leave it unlocked, take the picture out with us, and then bring it back when we've finished."

"Now you're talking, man," O'Grady said, enormously relieved. "I'm almost certain she had but the one lock, a bolt that opens from the inside and then one of them chain arrangements."

"You'd better go in prepared in case you can't open it."

"I have my knife. It has all the tools we'll need, save a wee hammer, and I have that in my inside pocket."

"And the tube, Johnny?"

"I have the tube. It cost me eighty-five cents, the robbers."

"Then go and good luck and try to hurry."

"Don't be rushing me. I don't want my nerves unraveled. This isn't common practice with me, you know."

"The night has a thousand eyes," Rubinoff said mournfully.

"Thanks." O'Grady got out and gave Rubinoff his wallet to put in the glove compartment. He took the eighteen-inch mailing tube from the back seat, checked his knife and the hammer. He started down the street toward the parking lot and had to turn back. He'd forgotten the crowbar. He took it from the trunk—Rubinoff's nose against the glass to see what he was after—and tucked it inside his jacket, the crook of it cold against his arm where he hooked it into the sleeve. He slammed the trunk door, an explosion in the stillness of the street. It was a damn shame, nobody felt safe on the streets at this hour, and it almost as bright as day with the high-intensity streetlights.

He had reconnoitered earlier, when the parking lot closed after theater hours. The fence was no problem, already broken through at one corner; but it was a trip for a cat from there to his destination. The back of every building was a hazard of a different sort—broken pottery, smashed bricks, crumbling cement partitions, and broken bottles by the carload.

The sky was a murky pink, sending down a faint glow, and there were lights peeping through the windows here and there, but no faces that he could observe. The rumble of traffic could be heard a long way off, and human screeches now and then that he calculated to be carrying all the way from Forty-second Street. The only consistent sound nearby was people coughing. It put him in mind of church on a cold, windy Sunday in Derry when you could hardly hear the priest for the hacking—the noise and the smell of disease. Even T.B. in this day and age, damn the oppressor.

He looked up at the clutter of flowerpots on Rose's fire escape. The kitchen was dark and he knew the bedroom to be at the front of the house. It gave him an uneasy feeling, thinking of the man sleeping innocent beside her. He made firm the wooden crate he had picked up on his first trip.

The crate creaked under his weight, but he was able to get the wedge end of the crowbar between the cement and the iron grill outside the small window. The cement started to crumble at once, seeping down like coarse sand into his sleeve. He hung onto the grill with one hand while he worked, his fingers twined through the interstices. Once started he never looked around. He could neither hide nor run. The best he could do was pray. The crate gave a shriek and went out from under him. He hung onto the grill but it also gave, and as he went down came on top of him bringing along an avalanche of dust and particles. It was out, well.

He crouched and waited, listening. Nothing. He set the crate up again; the window itself was child's play, the rotten wood yielding at once to his knife; the window swung open on hinges inside. He had no chance at all of hoisting himself up from below, the window no more than eighteen inches square and some ten feet from the ground, but he had taken that into his calculations. He threw the mailing tube in before it was crushed altogether, went down and moved the box to beneath the fire escape. Climbing up again, he was able to hook the crowbar into the ladder and bring it down. But it came down on the wrong side, far away from the gaping window, and that had not been in his calculation. He had to go up to Rose's garden and sidle along outside the railing. When he was over the window, he lowered himself till his feet touched the sill. By hooking the crowbar through the rail, he was able to support himself until his behind was secure on the windowsill.

He hung the crowbar on the swinging window, eased himself down and over on his belly. His jacket caught on the hook and something fell from the pocket making a clatter and a watery plunk below. It was his knife, and as soon as his foot touched the toilet seat he knew where it had fallen. His feet on the floor, he ran his hand over the wall looking for a switch. The light came on like a splash in the face. There was only the commode and a sink, no shower or tub. He rolled up his sleeve and groped. He reached as far as he could into a fixture as ancient as any he had seen in all his travels. Without success. He washed and wiped his hands on a paper towel, and cursing his luck, threw the towel into the bowl.

He picked up the mailing tube and left the bathroom. The bathroom light shone across the room. There stood the desk with the phone and the table with Yeats and the crystal ball. But the picture was gone from the wall. He turned from wall to empty wall, then ran to the room up front and turned on the lamp. Nowhere.

He turned out the lights, threw the crowbar down first, and went out the way he had come in, except that he almost knocked himself unconscious when he banged his head on the window frame and fell to the ground with a jolt that rattled every bone in his body.

When he reached the car he threw the tube and the crowbar into the back seat.

"Be careful," Rubinoff cried and reached for the tube.

"There's nothing in it to be careful of. The picture was gone from the wall."

"She's decided to keep it and has taken it home," Rubinoff said after a moment as though he had known all the time it would come out this way. "That's what comes of being impatient, Johnny. The mere fact of my calling about it has elevated its value in her mind. If her husband *is* a collector, he will soon disabuse her of the notion. Or else tolerate it to humor her."

"Put it in English for me, Rubin. I've had a rough night."

"Either she'll call me, pretending to concede that I'm the rightful owner, or we'll not hear from her at all. In which case, I must think carefully before committing myself further."

TWENTY-TWO

As soon as Julie opened the shop door in the morning she knew that someone had been there . . . or might still be there. She propped the door open with a chair. A cross-wind caught at the curtain between the front room and the back and she knew what it was that was different: the smell; the air was almost fresh. Juanita hovered in the doorway and for once Julie didn't send her away.

She pulled the curtain aside and from where she stood saw the open window in the bathroom, something she had not been able to achieve working from the inside. Her predecessor had nailed the larger window to the back room closed and Julie had covered it with heavy drapery and had all but forgotten it was there. Nothing was missing. There was nothing of value. The typewriter was so old it wouldn't bring five dollars at a pawn shop. She felt jittery, and although she had nothing personal in the shop, the violation of the place made the place itself suddenly abhorrent to her.

She went into the bathroom. A muddle of dirt surrounded the toilet bowl, the dust on the seat brushed off by the intruder. He might have tried to wipe away fingerprints, for there was a wad of paper toweling in the bowl. She flushed the toilet, then closed the window and latched it although she could see daylight through the frame where the burglar's tool had pried the latch open. She glanced down, then watched with dismay while the water rose to the top of the bowl, threatened to overflow, and then gradually receded. That too was a new development. She went out front, dispatched Juanita, closed the door, and thought about calling the police. The phone rang before she could make the call.

It was Alberto. "Mr. Romano would like to see you, Mrs. Hayes."

"Now?"

"I will send the car."

TWENTY-THREE

Alberto was waiting in the lobby. Grave, courteous, and utterly detached. Without a word to say. The elevator ride seemed to take forever and Julie had to fight a sudden feeling of panic. When they reached the penthouse Alberto moved ahead to open door after door for her, the foyer, the library, the gallery with American paintings. They came at last to a door where he knocked before opening.

Romano was at a desk in the center of an office, facing them. His desk was clear. He was simply sitting there waiting. Or in reverie. He did not speak or get up until she was well inside the room. He rose then and said, but without warmth, "It was good of you to come at once."

Alberto brought a chair for her and placed it beside the desk. The room beyond was a skylit studio. Julie could see an easel. Romano sat when she did. The office was full of books and papers, folios, and a lot of expensive-looking electronic equipment. A phone with several buttons was on a bracketed platform on the other side of the desk, but the desk itself was absolutely bare.

Romano nodded to Alberto and then said, "You must understand, Mrs. Hayes, I record everything. You may remember, I have many informants in the city, in many cities actually. I am a collector of more than paintings. I collect information on diverse subjects—and on people— and store it. Alberto speaks of my penthouse tapes."

Julie smiled a little but he had not intended to amuse her. He paused and seemed to compose himself before going on: something obviously was wrong. Alberto was waiting, his arms folded. The whole feeling of the room was of something about to happen.

Romano said, very quietly: "Why did you bring that picture to me?"

Julie tried to swallow her feeling of alarm. "When you come right down to it, Mr. Romano, I didn't bring the picture to you. I said I'd like you to see it; it was your idea to have Michael bring it here."

"That's quite true." He glanced at Alberto. Then: "So I must ask, why did you want me to see it?"

Julie's heartbeat wasn't helping matters, a thumping that made it difficult to speak. "It just happened. It was something I thought of off the top of my head. Maybe I thought if you liked it, you might do something for the artist. Now it turns out, I may not even own the picture. I wish I hadn't mentioned it to you."

"Who does own it, Mrs. Hayes?"

"Mr. Rubinoff thinks he does. Or whoever he was buying it for. He called me a couple of days ago. Ralph Abel told me he didn't want it, but he does. I went to see

Maude Sloan at the gallery and she suggests that I keep it—unless he decides to take it to arbitration. . . ."

Romano held up his hand to stop her. "How did you leave matters with Rubinoff?"

"I said that if he had Ralph Abel call me, I'd be willing to give the thing back to him and they could do whatever they liked about it."

Romano pushed himself away from the desk. "Shall we take a look at the thing, as you call it?"

The tension remained but what Julie now felt had been hostility eased off. Alberto even smiled. Behind Romano's back. She followed Romano into the studio and Alberto followed her. There was the smell of paint and wood, turpentine, and a mix of chemical smells she could not identify. Framing was done on the premises and other work as well. Romano approached the easel and motioned Julie to come where she could see. *Scarlet Night* was on the easel without any frame at all.

"Is it the painting you sent me, Mrs. Hayes?"

She nodded, but it did look strange, raw and naked.

He started to take hold if it and then drew back his hands and rubbed them together. He was pale and agitated. Alberto came and stood close by. Romano lifted the painting and turned it around on the easel.

Fastened to the back of the Abel canvas was a drawing of a running male nude. About sixteen by ten inches, it was very old, and Julie had to suppose, a master. She kept looking at it, feeling that something was wrong with the top of her head. It felt as thought somebody was trying to lift it off. And yet she could think: she was certain she had suspected. Or ought to have suspected: maybe that was it.

Romano hugged himself as he rocked back and forth, never taking his eyes from the drawing. "I would have given half a million dollars for such a treasure and here it is before me in my own domain."

TWENTY-FOUR

The one thing that was going to remain clear for Julie out of the next few seconds was the sudden, sickening horror of having gotten herself into something profoundly wrong. Alberto ran for a glass of water—for Romano. The little caesar sipped and gave back the glass. Julie didn't know at whom she was angry, only that it helped when the anger came.

"Let's wrap the whole thing up and get it out of here. I'll take it with me."

Romano looked at her, his eyes blinking rapidly. "And where will you take it?"

"To the nearest office of the F.B.I."

"And if you are intercepted on the way? Rubinoff must be a desperate man at this point."

"He is. My shop was broken into last night. Now it makes sense."

"Did you call the police?"

"Not yet. I had just gotten there when Alberto called."

Romano nodded. Then, of the drawing: "Do you know what it is?"

"Just what I can see—that it's old and—from what you said, it must be a master."

"Would you hazard a guess as to the artist?"

"I wouldn't—Leonardo da Vinci," Julie said in the one breath.

"You are right." Which surprised her. "Of course none is to be had at any price. . . . Put it away for now, Alberto. I am trying to control its environment. Somewhat futile under the circumstances. Five hundred years . . . I would rather die than see anything happen to it now."

"Do you know where it came from?" Julie asked.

"Yes. Alberto and I have made certain investigations."

Alberto carried the painting across the room to a display case, the glass top to which was open. He put *Scarlet Night* in on its face, closed the top, and was about to cover the whole with a black cloth.

"Shall we have another look?" Romano almost touched her in his eagerness. "Pen, and I think, bister—a so-called lake color that's supposed to be impermanent. Ha! Or what was it like originally? We must try to know sometime, Alberto. Cover it up."

He indicated the way back to the office. "Now we must talk, Miss Julie." She noted the switch from "Mrs. Hayes." He paused at the door and looked back at the studio. "Do you know our principal occupation here at the moment? It's a laboratory, really. We are trying to document the construction of the old pigments. The technique of certain masters, if you will. Alberto is the chemist. I am the provocateur."

A gentleman's gentleman, yeah.

In the office, he checked the tape deck before returning to his desk. "It is almost certainly the Leonardo stolen from the Institute of Art in Venice five months ago. Which is how I could identify it so positively, although like you, I did guess Leonardo."

"It really was a lucky guess on my part. I don't know that much."

"More than you realize, I think. You chose the best." He took a photocopy of a newspaper article from the middle drawer of the desk. "Here's the *Times* account of the theft at the time. Not one word about the drawing has appeared since."

Julie read:

VENICE. Mar. 8 (Special)—A priceless fifteenth-century drawing by Leonardo da Vinci was stolen from the Institute of Art here some time during the night of March 7. The case in which the drawing had been on display was pried open by the thieves who entered the gallery through the skylight. How they gained access to the roof of the three-story building is not known. A new alarm system is in the process of installation throughout the building. It is expected to be in use within three weeks.

Alberto rejoined them.

"Isn't it crazy," Julie said, "that I should have got my

hands on that particular painting . . . and then to have got it here? Just that impulse, you know?"

"Fate perhaps," Romano suggested.

Not entirely as guileless as she made it sound, Julie said: "I just realized something: You could have put the old frame back on *Scarlet Night*—or a new one—and sent it home with me. You could have kept the drawing."

"Believe me, Miss Julie, I contemplated the possibility. And there's something else you must realize: I might very well have got away with the acquisition. What jeopardy you would have been in under the circumstances is a matter we may want to think about. Bring a chair for yourself, Alberto. We must ask you many questions, Miss Julie—do you mind my calling you that? I find it less formidable than Mrs. Hayes. Is that an impertinence?"

"Just Julie would be fine."

He shook his head and went on: "I was going to say, you are right. Something must be done quickly."

"Not the F.B.I.?" Julie said.

"It is not my favorite law-enforcement agency."

"But you don't have to be involved at all."

He looked offended. "What would you tell them about the discovery? You don't even know how it came about, you might never have known."

"Mr. Romano, I just thought you might not want to mix with the F.B.I."

"The reverse is true, my dear girl. The F.B.I. may not wish to mix with Romano. Otherwise, would I be where I am today? Given what you think you know of me, would I?"

Julie held her peace. He was making a point, even putting her on a little. He wasn't really demanding an answer. "Did you know there was something—before you removed the frame?"

"I cannot say so. I keep asking myself. Alberto says I had nothing in mind but the bad taste of the Neapolitans, an opinion he doesn't share, by the way." He shot a mocking glance at the younger man.

Alberto threw up his hands. "My parents come from Naples, my whole family."

Romano shrugged. Julie realized he was enjoying himself. For the moment; he became serious again: "I did wonder, I must admit, what you—or for that matter, a Rubinoff—would see in the painting."

"Okay," Julie said.

"Don't be so sensitive. There is something to it, a certain, vulgar something, if you don't mind my using the word."

"That's what I saw in it too: Eighth Avenue, Place Pigalle in Paris."

Romano got a what's-a-nice-girl-like-you-doing look in his eyes. The king of porn. "I may as well tell you, Miss Julie, I wondered if perhaps your Mr. Abel had bought up old canvases and painted on the reverse side of something that might prove more interesting than *Scarlet Night.*"

"Poor Ralph," Julie said. Then: "I'm absolutely certain, Mr. Romano, he had no idea what was behind that painting."

"That was the question I was coming to. I wonder if you would mind telling us now—in your own words, as they say in the courts of law—how you came into possession . . . You may find it useful yourself to have a record of it."

Julie thought for a moment. "I'll take it from when I poked my head into the gallery before the opening, the Maude Sloan Gallery on Greene Street in SoHo."

Romano was great: he interrupted now and then with a question and made her repeat every mention of Ginni, but he always put her back on the track at the point at which he had taken her off. He was particular about dates.

"A beautiful operation, it would seem—until Rubinoff. There's more to it of course than we know. An appalling laxity at Customs, for example. But I wonder if the game could be improved upon—if it were possible to run it backwards." He glanced up at Alberto.

Alberto grinned, showing a beautiful set of teeth. It was pretty hard to find all that sorrow Julie had thought was in his eyes.

"Forgive me, Miss Julie. Alberto and I are at some small advantage. We were able to make inquiries yesterday, as you see. . . ." He indicated the newspaper clipping. "And more this morning. Consider the time difference between New York and Rome. . . . I gather you exonerate Maude Sloan as well as the misguided artist?"

"I think so . . . except for backing up Rubinoff's claim to prior purchase. I'm not sure about that."

"An understandable lapse of honor, given the frailty of her business."

"I figure she's trying to make up for it: she invited Jeff and me to a party for Ginni Saturday night. . . ."

Romano raised his eyebrows.

Julie began then to see enough of the smuggling operation to want to ask questions herself. "Is Ginni the boss?"

"Oh, yes. There's no question of that. But didn't you say she had backed down on on her promise to attend the opening?"

"Now she thinks she's coming before the closing. Or so she's told her mother."

"One wonders about that." Romano rubbed his hands together. "I must admit to being fascinated. If the looting of Italian treasure were not such a foul offense against the people of Italy, one might regret your interruption of the play, Miss Julie." He paused, watching for her reaction, his eyes very bright. "One might even consider letting it proceed—if one could be sure in the end of returning the Leonardo unimpaired to the Italian people."

Julie couldn't think of the right questions; what she was trying to do first was fix a line of demarcation between right and wrong. But certain vital qualifications were missing. If you could qualify right or wrong.

"Yes?"

"What I'm trying to figure out, Mr. Romano, is—why? I mean why would you let it proceed?"

"That is the question of the moment surely. You would not say I am an especially playful man, would you?"

"There are a lot of things I wouldn't say at this point, Mr. Romano."

He smiled broadly and looked up at the younger man. "Alberto, will you trust me to explain while you bring the sandwiches? We ought not to have wine. Clear heads. Iced tea or coffee. Or an orange something or other. Do you like orange, Miss Julie?"

"I do."

"There is an assumption we must make at the outset," Romano began when Alberto had left them. "The drawing was almost certainly stolen on consignment. In other words, the thieves knew what they wanted, where it was, and how much the consignee would be willing to pay for a work of art that would have to remain in the closet, so to speak, for very many years. We can learn a great deal, you, Alberto, and I, by working backwards from what we do know. And of course, such information as we are able to turn up can be made available to the F.B.I., Interpol, the Italian Police. The thieves and the smugglers might well be caught. I'm by no means sure that at this point a case could be made against Rubinoff . . . and, oh, my dear, the man—or possibly it was a woman—in whom I am interested is the collector for whom the Leonardo was stolen. That is the divine secret, known only to—whom?"

"Rubinoff."

"And possibly one other—his counterpart in Italy. There are ways, of course, to persuade Rubinoff, but they are crude for such an exquisite adventure, and you might find them offensive."

"You're putting me on," Julie said.

"Am I? Of course I am, but I am quite sincere in my conviction that it will be very difficult to get the name of the collector. I do wonder, however, if we three could not manage it."

"And then, in order to catch him," Julie said, "you'd have to deliver *Scarlet Night*."

"Rubinoff would have to deliver *Scarlet Night*—and the Leonardo. It would be safe, remember. It is destined for someone no less reverent than myself."

Julie nodded tentatively.

"You are wondering at what point we involve the police."

"Well, yes."

"It may be shocking to you, Miss Julie, but I want to point out to you the miserable record of the police, in this country as well as abroad, in the recovery of stolen art. In this case they would be dealing with an exceedingly wealthy person—possibly a resident alien—possibly a most highly respected person, a patron of the arts with an obsession that has tempted him to do something of which no one would ever think of accusing him. There would be the question of search warrants and their service, and suppose by that time the culprit had properly secreted his treasure and it was not found, wouldn't that be embarrassing?"

Alberto came, wheeling a service cart, and Romano got up and bounded across the room to help ease the cart over the doorstep. He inspected the open-face sandwiches. "Crabmeat, is it? And salmon. What are those?"

"Cucumber, which you always say clears the palate."

Romano approved and looked around at Julie. "Orange drink seems a bit odd, doesn't it?"

"Not by me," Julie said.

"Please," he said, indicating that Julie was to help herself to sandwiches.

Midway through lunch, he wiped his lips with his napkin and said: "Do you have a favorite charity, Miss Julie?"

"Well, yes."

"And you, Alberto?"

"My mother and my father."

Romano beamed. "Isn't he a good boy?"

Alberto blushed to the earlobes.

"What I feared was," Romano continued, "the money might be going to a bank in Switzerland or some other unsavory foreign cover. But with Ginni arriving here, I'm inclined to think there must be an American bag man."

"Mr. Romano . . ."

He interrupted: "Romano, plain Romano. Please?"

"I need to know what I seem to be agreeing to," Julie said.

"Why, to the most expedient return of an art treasure to the country from which it was stolen, and the furtherance of what we might call poetic justice. So far as Alberto and I are concerned, I think we should call it a counter-caper; you may find such a description compromising. But if you are to become a good newspaper woman, Miss Julie, it is the story of a lifetime. Believe me, it is much better than a profile of Romano. But I will give you both. There is one question, however, I think you should decide: to what extent are we to involve Geoffrey Hayes?"

"To no extent whatsoever," Julie said. "Absolutely not."

"You are misunderstanding. I don't wish to involve him. I did wonder how you could escape it if, for example, you are both going to Maude Sloan's party on Saturday night."

"We're not. Jeff is in West Virginia and he's not going to be home over the weekend."

"Then you must have an escort! Alberto is clean, well-mannered, and esteems every woman as though she were his sister. Have a slice of melon, Miss Julie. Then we must go to work."

TWENTY-FIVE

O'Grady awoke to a throbbing noise which seemed at first to be in his own head only; it came through stronger and he knew that someone was pounding on the door. If it was the police, sure, wouldn't they say it was the police?

He called out, "Who's there?" and got no answer, only a pause in the pounding and then its resumption, softer, as though the knocker was resting his knuckles and using the fat of his hand.

"Have you no tongue?" he shouted, trying to get his feet into his slacks. "Hold your bloody horses till a man gets his clothes on."

He unlocked the door and threw it open. There in her green-eyed, auburn-haired glory stood Ginni, laughing at him.

"Holy God, what are you doing here?"

"Hello, Johnny."

He retreated before her advance into the room. "Yes, well, hello."

"I got bored waiting. My God, you look awful. Were you in a brawl?"

"I had a bit of a tumble, an accident, never mind. I can't believe my own eyes."

She cast a critical look around the room. "Don't you even have a bedroom?"

"It was my mother's."

"But she's dead, isn't she?"

"Aye, but I don't like sleeping in there. It's . . . it's crowded. I still can't believe it. I'm going to wake up in a minute . . ."

"I hope so," Ginni said. "I feel about as welcome as a cockroach."

"Ah, love, give me a minute in the bathroom and I'll welcome you proper." He threw the coverlet over the daybed on his way to the bathroom, which was off the kitchen. Lucky he was to have one of his own. It wasn't the case with every family in the building. He paused at the kitchen door. "Have you seen your mother yet?"

"Why?"

She had the look of long-distance travel about her: the knit dress and the sandals, the elegant purse. She'd have perked up his neighbors coming up the steps. "I was wondering. She'll be surprised to see you, that's all."

"She knows I'm coming. You're the one that's surprised. Johnny, is anything wrong?" She was advancing again.

"Nothing fatal. I'm going in here or I'll bust. I'll be out in a minute."

It was going to take more than a minute to sort out the implications of her arrival—to say nothing of what she was to be told. She'd find out from her mother if he didn't tell her that *Scarlet Night* had gone astray, and it wouldn't bode well for him if she got it there first. Was he glad to see her? He wasn't sure. Something had retarded the customary leap of hot blood in his veins at the sight of her.

The look at himself in the mirror was a shock. He resembled a sick raccoon, his eyes in heavy circles from the bang on the back of his head. Which reminded him of where he had lost his pocketknife. He had always said the best days of his life were with Ginni, but he saw no way of making this day one of them.

He turned on the water in the fixture he had built for himself over the tub, and then called out, his mouth to the crack in the door: "I'm going to take a quick shower to wake myself up."

If she answered, he didn't hear her, and when he went out a few minutes later, there was no sign of her. "Are you playing games with me?" He went from room to room, all three of them. It wasn't as though there were closets or places to hide. He looked in the wardrobe and while there selected a shirt he could wear open. Ginni loved to twiddle with the hair on his chest. He opened the front windows and looked out. The air was muggy and getting hot. No sign of her below. His watch showed one o'clock. Rubinoff had said he would call him by noon.

O'Grady picked up the phone and started to dial. He put it down when he heard a clatter in the hall and giggling. His first thought was that she was moving in with him; his heart gave one leap and stopped dead, or so it seemed: if he couldn't sleep in his mother's bed, he certainly couldn't do anything else in it. Ginni, with her father's mansion and her mother's loft, and her goddamned love of the working class.

The door opened the width of a head. Ginni poked hers in, looking toward the kitchen. She murmured a word to someone behind her. The door opened wide. She saw O'Grady then, and he saw the two companions she was whispering with: they were young, good-looking, and male, dressed in flashy new suits and grinning at him. They dropped their suitcases inside the door and came forward to shake his hand while Ginni spouted to them in Italian and to him in English, introducing them as Tommy and Steph.

"Tommy and Steph," he said, looking at her after letting them shake his hand. He had a sick feeling that he already knew who they were.

"The whole bloody family," he said. Not only had she come over herself, she had brought the two who had made the museum snatch.

"Not quite. Only us kids," Ginni said. "When the circus closed for the season last week and they were looking for something to do, I thought, why not? They'd never been to America."

"Ginni, we're going to have to have a serious conversation, You and I."

"They don't speak English."

"I don't know whether that's bad or good."

"Don't just let them stand there, Johnny. Where's your Irish hospitality?"

"With O'Leary in the grave," he muttered blasphemously. Then: "Tell them to take off their coats. I'll see if there's anything cold in the kitchen."

"Oh, God, it's hot," Ginni said, following him. She ventilated herself by plucking at the see-through knit that clutched her breasts. Then in one swoop, she crossed her arms and pulled the top to her dress over her head. Top-less. Stark.

"Not in front of them, for God's sake. I'll get you one of my cotton shirts."

"They're in show business, Johnny. . . . You're such an old puritan." She followed him to the sink. "How's Ralph?"

"I'll tell you in a minute." He ran water over the tray of ice cubes to loosen them.

"Did he sell any pictures besides . . . ?"

"Will you wait a minute, damn it. There ought to be some easy way . . ."

"Mother has a refrigerator that just coughs them out. . . . I'll bet Ralph's living with her, right? She's al-ways been passionate about my rejects. The trouble was when I lived with her, she didn't wait for me to reject them."

"You shouldn't talk that way about your mother even if it's true." He filled the pitcher with water and plopped in the ice cubes. "Bring some glasses there."

The boys had not only removed their coats, they had hung them in the wardrobe. He put the pitcher on the ta-ble and got her one of his two professionally laundered shirts.

"If the show closes Sunday, how long do you think it'll be after that? The boys are terribly broke."

"Who isn't? Wouldn't it have been better for all of you to have waited over there the way we planned?"

"No. I'll tell you what happened, Johnny: I went with Papa to his bank one day, and I sat in the cage and watched them counting—American money, twenties, fif-ties, and one-hundred-dollar bills—and I realized a weak-ness in our plan. You could not possibly manage alone. And I thought of the horror, what if you had to sink some of it in the Bay of Naples?"

"That's not fair, casting up my one failure to me. It's to be safe money and I'd have converted some of it into larger denominations."

"You couldn't. Not over a hundred. They don't print them anymore and the banks are taking those left out of circulation. Isn't this so much easier? We'll spend what we need and buy what we want and have a simply marvel-ous time." She darted from one of the boys to the other, the shirttail flying behind her, and whatever it was she said in their language, the glisten of greed came into their eyes. It was plain to see she had grown out of the revolutionary stage of her development. "A few days, Johnny?"

"Something like that, but there's something you'd better stop and listen to right now, Ginni: That painter boy of yours was not the most reliable choice. He had a falling-out with your mother and pulled out on her the night after the show opened. He's probably ruined his chances for life and damn near ruined the rest of us. He took his pictures out of her gallery and burned them."

"What?"

For a few seconds, while he took a gulp of cold water himself, he enjoyed the shock that gave her. "All save the one."

"God damn you, John O'Grady, I'll cut out your heart if you ever do anything like that to me again."

He had to believe she could do it, too. "Yes, well, he decided without a by-your-leave from your mother to give *Scarlet Night* to a woman who'd tried to buy it at the show. We've been trying since to get it back from her."

"She still has it?"

He drew a deep breath. "Yes."

"And you dared say to me I should have stayed in Naples?" Her eyes were green flame, volcanic. "One step at a time, Johnny: how did it happen?"

The boys had gone pale at the sight of her wrath and O'Grady wondered if he hadn't as well. He could not bring himself in the end to tell her of the last night's misery, only that he had broken into the Hayes woman's shop to discover she had removed the painting, probably having taken it home with her.

"You don't know that," Ginni said.

"I don't. That's the truth."

She picked up the phone and handed it to him. "Get Rubinoff for me."

"You'd better watch yourself with him. He isn't starving like some of us, and it's his client, you know."

While he dialed she spoke to the boys, soothingly, as he had all but forgotten she once spoke to him. He'd have been better not to have put the shirt on her, for she left it open and it was a terrible thing watching them pop in and out and not be able to care. Rubinoff's secretary answered and said she would see if he could come to the phone.

The wonder of it: a normal day in the office of Rubin Rubinoff.

"Johnny, how are you?"

"I'm all right, well. Look, man . . ."

He got no further, Rubinoff interrupting. Ginni put her head next to O'Grady's to listen. "I can't talk to you now, Johnny. I'm flying to Buenos Aires with a client this afternoon. I'm sorry to tell you I've decided to let *Scarlet Night* go. I no longer consider it a viable operation."

"What does that mean?"

"I no longer believe the acquisition to be in the best interests of my client."

Ginni took the phone from O'Grady's hand. A clarion voice. "Mr. Rubinoff, this is Gianina Bordonelli. Will you please hold on for a moment while I get something from my purse?"

O'Grady began to look for the purse for her. She signaled him to forget it, but let another second or two pass. Then: "Here we are. Shall I read it in Italian or translate?"

He would have said to translate, for she began in English and carried on with the perfect intonation and hesitancy of the translator, and quite as though the message stood written in front of her: "I assure you there will be no defection at the top. I have myself authenticated three works I know to be in the cabinet of this same collector—which—if I were to correct my earlier attribution—would greatly weaken his collection and destroy his faith in our colleague." Then, "It's signed, of course, by Edmund Schoen."

TWENTY-SIX

"It will take all our powers of concentration, Miss Julie, all the technology available to us, and a degree of guile on your part I fear will not come easily."

"Don't count on that. I have a lot of guile."

Romano's gaze was solemn. "And you did study at the Actors Forum."

Alberto looked around from where he was going through one volume after another of the International Auction Records making notations. Romano, with a flick of his finger, directed the younger man to stay with his task.

"I am sure we are all qualified for what we must do. Our major problem is time. We must move quickly, but once we do move, we start the whole machination forward, and if we move before we are well enough prepared, we may lose everything. We must go back far enough to enable us to go forward, but not further; we must ask questions that will gain information without giving information. We must be extremely careful not to awaken the Italian government too soon. It is very complicated. But I will tell you what we have learned that makes me suppose we may well succeed. By sheer accident, I may have discovered the roots of the Ginni caper. I am almost certain the grand design was entirely hers.

"Here we go: among the unsolved art thefts which occurred in Italy in the past years is a fourteenth-century sculpture from the collection of Count Ricardo Guido Bordonelli."

"Ginni's father."

Romano nodded. "The count is a banker and a modest collector with two or three pieces of medieval art in his collection. Of questionable provenance, but valuable. The police in their investigation interviewed the guests who attended a dinner party at the Bordonelli villa a few days before the theft was discovered. Where the investigation went thereafter I have no idea. But early this morning, Alberto and I were able to obtain the names of those who attended the dinner party. Aside from the host and his daughter there were ten guests, only one of whom I think concerns us—an art dealer named Schoen who has offices in Rome and Zurich.

"Now, I have a marginal acquaintanceship with Edmund Schoen. There was a time I hoped to acquire a particular Guardi. I have since gone in a different direction. I was advised in a back-door manner that since my collection is more private than most, and since I am what is known as a patient collector—Mr. Schoen might be able to help me. I did not pursue the matter, but I understood that he would be arranging a purchase the export of which the Italian government would not allow, but which Mrs. Schoen could deliver nonetheless.

"I shall sketch quickly now, for much is speculation. I suggest that Schoen admired the sculpture, probably to Ginni, and may have mentioned a price he would pay for it, having in mind of course a likely customer or—as they call them in this business of gentlemen—a client. The theft—from her father's house—almost certainly was arranged by Ginni. Whatever occurred paved the way for the Leonardo job. She is a wild young thing, this girl, with some nasty political associations. One has to sympathize with her father."

Julie said a very quiet, "Yeah."

"In any case, there came the point when Schoen said, in effect, If you can deliver the Leonardo drawing that's in the Venice Institute of Art to a safe drop in the United States, it's worth, say, five hundred thousand.

"Now, whether the collector is Schoen's contact or simply Rubinoff's client on behalf of whom he was in touch with Schoen, I don't know. But I think it's safe to assume a longstanding relationship between Rubinoff and the collector. A great deal of trust has to go into such a commitment. This Rubinoff-collector relationship is very important to us. There are patterns in collecting. You must not think that because a man will pay an enormous amount of money for a stolen painting his collection contains other stolen art. It is much more likely that whatever the pattern of his collection, he feels it lacks only the Leonardo to become perfect. Do you see what I mean?"

"I think so," Julie said.

"Leonardos are simply not available: he is going the only possible route to obtain one. The question is, has Rubinoff bought for him before? Has he represented him at auctions? We must assume so.

"I am trying to put myself in the collector's place, Miss Julie. . . . Go back to work, Alberto. Alberto is checking Italian Renaissance drawings which have come to auction in the past three years. It is information we may not have time—or the means—to use, but we must prepare. A buyer rarely buys blind: almost always, his dealer will take him to the gallery to view the work coming to auction. You understand—all transactional information is confidential. The public learns where auctioned works are going only after they have arrived and *if* the collector chooses to give out the information. It becomes of course part of a work's provenance and must become public before the picture can be sold again. We cannot wait."

Julie said: "The police would not have any trouble getting this information, would they?"

Romano looked deeply offended. "Even they would have to know what they were looking for."

"I just want to understand things."

"I give you my word, if at any point the drawing itself is in jeopardy, I will withdraw and send you to the police. I have a feeling you would be more comfortable in collaboration with them."

"I am rather conventional," Julie said. "But wait. Wouldn't the same thing hold for something that was going to be stolen? Wouldn't the collector want to see that in advance, too?"

"I think we may assume he has seen it. Or something quite in its line. Leonardo is a class unto himself."

"I was wondering if he'd sign the visitor's book—if there is one—at the gallery in Venice."

Romano closed his eyes and thought about it. He sat, his hands folded over his belly. "There is one," he said, blinking, "but I cannot decide whether or not I'd have signed it if I were in his shoes. No, no. Of course not. But wait: suppose he was there before the suggestion of theft?"

"Alberto, let's have someone check the visitor's book for Rubinoff or Schoen—a two-year span before the theft. If their names appear, get those signing in immediately before and after. It would also be useful to follow the same procedure if there's a special sign-in arrangement for drawings. It's often the case."

"That's going to take time, Mr. Romano, unless we go to the police."

"No police at this stage."

"I don't have any relatives that I know about in Venice."

"Find some. We shall need the list by noon tomorrow."

Alberto whistled softly, marked his place in the book, and went from the room rubbing the back of his neck thoughtfully.

"How much time do we have: a question, isn't it?" Romano said. "When did Rubinoff call you?"

"Monday."

"And the shop was broken into last night. They are already impatient."

"Maybe because Ginni is coming."

"I don't suppose there's a chance that the break-in is coincidence and not related to the painting?"

"I don't think we ought to count on that, Mr. Romano, although I must admit, I don't see Rubinoff hoisting himself in through my bathroom window."

"I hadn't supposed that ever," Romano said. "There has to be at least one other working member of the gang on this side of the Atlantic. You did say Rubinoff phoned you at home? Then how many people knew the painting was at Forty-fourth Street?"

Julie thought of O'Grady instantly. Only two people had been in the shop since her return—and one dog. "I think I know the other member of the gang. I'm almost sure of it, an Irish-American merchant seaman, an I.R.A. man named Sean O'Grady. Mrs. Ryan brought him in. And of course! That's how Rubinoff could know I'm Mrs. Geoffrey Hayes!"

Romano watched her with a bemused expression as though he sensed the associations banging around in her head. Then: "Mrs. Ryan—do I need to know who she is?"

"I don't think so. But you *do* know: she lives at the Willoughby, where Laura Gibson lived. . . ." Julie stopped.

Romano lifted one finger to his lips. "I have her placed now," he said of Mrs. Ryan. "And may we suppose of this I.R.A. man that he is one of Ginni's radical political associates?"

"That figures."

"Then we must assume he is fanatical—and dangerous."

"He reads poetry."

"My dear, some of my best friends read bedtime stories to their children."

TWENTY-SEVEN

O'Grady kept looking down the street, watching every cab for Ginni's return. Hour climbed upon hour, and where he had been hurt at being left out of the meeting between her and Rubinoff, he was now getting angrier by the minute. "The boys" were settled in. It had taken them no time at all, given the signal by Ginni. She had gone in and snatched the coverlet from the double bed, and whatever she had said to them, the boys had crossed themselves, bowed their heads, and O'Grady supposed, said a prayer for the repose of Ma's soul. After that, they lugged their suitcases into the bedroom and began to unpack. After trying to convey something to him which he understood only after the fact, they removed his winter woolens from the bottom drawers of the chiffonier, replaced them with their clothes, and stored his in their suitcases which they then shoved under the bed. Stripped down to their shorts, they were as lean and muscled as young colts. He wondered if Ginni was sleeping with both of them, and maybe at the same time: there was nothing in that line he'd put past her.

O'Grady told himself over and over the one thing he should *not* do and finally did it: he called Rubinoff's office. The secretary told him Mr. Rubinoff was in conference.

"Ask him to call O'Grady."

"Mr. O'Grady, I have a message for you. Miss Bordonelli said to tell you she would call you later from her mother's house."

"And how was I to get the message, miss, if I hadn't called?"

"She said you would call."

He could have choked on his rage. Mostly because he *had* called. "Well, thank you," he managed. Then: "Miss? Do you mind telling me the hour of Mr. Rubinoff's flight?"

"The trip has been postponed."

He put the phone down gently, a kind of masochism, and turned to discover the boys hovering behind him, wanting to know, by sign or signal, what was happening.

"No comprenez!" he shouted at them.

TWENTY-EIGHT

"The time we are given, Miss Julie, depends entirely on their confidence in you. They must somehow be persuaded that you have the painting at home, that you in no way suspect what is between the canvases, and that you will surrender it to Rubinoff at a time satisfactory to everyone."

"That's a lot of persuasion," Julie said.

"I hate to spend time on this concern, but we must. The fact that your shop was broken into last night conveys their anxiety. It also tells us that they are unable to reach the artist, and are themselves pressed for time. We may be quite certain that Rubinoff will not confide this misfortune to his collector. But from their having broken into the shop and learned that the painting was not there, we must assume they may attempt a break-in of your home. And that, my dear, simply must not happen. It would be an utter tragedy if they were caught."

Julie laughed.

"Oh, I'm quite serious. They are doing badly enough with all their members. I should hate them to be deprived at this point. The whole mission might come apart."

Julie said, "Mr. Romano, I don't think they will attempt a break-in on Sixteenth Street. The shop was easy. And then there's Jeff to deal with, not just me. If only we could get a message to them accidentally."

"You may well be right," Romano said on reconsidering.

"I could probably get next to Sean O'Grady through Mrs. Ryan and the Irish patriot and poetry bit—but what would I say to him?"

"Nothing. I don't want you approaching him at all. I believe him to be dangerous. If he tries to see you in this period, I hope you will insist on this Mrs. Ryan's being present—or else meeting him in a public place."

It was curious, Julie thought, his feeling about O'Grady, and he had never seen him. "If I were going to pick out the dangerous one, I'd bet on Ginni. Hey, if she's coming over, they're not going to make another move till she gets here, not after last night."

"So, shall we also wait for Ginni?"

Julie nodded. "Or until they make another move."

Romano beamed. "This is going to be an absolutely stunning collaboration. Let us proceed and allow ourselves no more than two days to discover the name of the collector."

He took a folder from his desk which contained several pages from a legal pad covered with notations. "This is on tape, by the way, if you should want to refer to it. Alberto will help you until we have the tapes transcribed. I have someone coming to work on that tonight. Now:

"Starting from the Leonardo—male nude running. It is a study for a larger work, the Battle of Anghiari. Leonardo was under the influence of Michelangelo here. I mention this because it raises the question of why this particular Leonardo when Michelangelo who is at least somewhat available does the same thing—if not better, more dramatically. The question remains: is our collector interested simply in adding a Leonardo to his cabinet? Any Leonardo? Or something in this particular drawing?

"Is he interested in, One, Renaissance drawings—or, Two, Italian Renaissance drawings—or, Three, sketches or studies for masterpieces? Or possibly he collects on a theme: Four, the nude in art—or, Five, the male nude—or, Six, athletics, the athlete in art—or, Seven, war?

"If you can think of any category to add, please do. This is only a point of departure for us. It may turn out to be irrelevant."

"I like the number seven," Julie said. She had opened her notebook when he took the folder from his desk. She jotted down the themes.

"May I go on? You must forgive me if I repeat myself: there are few private collections of master drawings today. Most of them have gone to museums, and new collections are not being made simply because too many people are interested in art. The unattributed find that turns out to be a master is most rare. The bins in London, Rome, Paris conceal few treasures, and sadder still, there are very few scholars poking through them. They are waiting in comfortable offices for people to bring in their inheritances.

"It is natural, with this diminishing supply of available masters, that a watch within the marketplace be set up. An international gallery with whom I have had the good fortune to do a small business has a virtual network of informants on the whereabouts of art. If we can arrive at *one* likely work of art in the collection, I may be able to get a lead from them to the collector.

"There is information to be got from the practices and clientele of Edmund Schoen, but our quest is too diffuse to go there yet. . . .

"Our immediate and vital source has to be Rubinoff himself, and I have had someone working on that for several hours. He must call me by two o'clock no matter what his information." It was ten minutes before the hour.

"Mr. Romano, suppose this collector lives in Los Angeles or Las Vegas or Texas somewhere?"

"It could be managed, but without us. We must pray."

All right. But Julie didn't say anything.

Romano smiled wickedly. "The devil is permitted to quote scripture."

One of the extension buttons on the phone lit up. Romano wrote down the number given to him by the person monitoring his phone. It was eerie to watch the process from this end.

Before he started to dial, he bade Julie go to the phone in the studio. "We shall have it on tape, but better you hear it for yourself as it develops. The man is Andrew Davis. He is a dealer who hustles more than most of his colleagues would admit to approving. He knows more people's business than anyone else in the art arena. The information he gives me will be reliable and confidential."

He started to dial and Julie hurried.

After the amenities, the man said: "I'll answer your questions in the order you gave them to me, Mr. Romano. No, I don't know any of Rubinoff's clients, not even by name. Very close to the chest. His hobbies: he's gone in for sports in the last few years. . . ."

"What kind of sports, Andy? It may be important."

"Boxing, horse-racing, football."

"Spectator sports. Any personal performance?"

"He's homosexual."

"Go on to my next question, Andy."

"Any connection with the dealer Schoen: not that I've been able to ascertain. Like most of us he spends a good deal of time abroad, and it would be surprising if he didn't have contact with Schoen."

"Do you deal with Schoen?"

"No. Frankly, I'm scared of him. I have the feeling he sells what you want to buy: in other words he can fit a square peg into a round hole. Do you know what I mean?"

"I think so. He deals in attributions."

"Right."

"I want to go back to something you said earlier about Rubinoff. You said his interest in sports is recent. Is there any way you can fill that in for me? How do you know that? I'm not asking your source, Andy. What I want to know is with whom does he attend these spectaculars?"

"I'll try, Mr. Romano. You're outside the art game now."

"I know."

"You asked what his field was mainly. It used to be the Impressionists, and that ties in with your next question, his European connections. He took his master's at Columbia University, then he went abroad and studied in Amsterdam and London, but he wound up working for Jean Dufayard in Paris. Dufayard was an old man—he had known the great ones and bought some of them. For a while Rubinoff represented Dufayard in New York. Then the old man retired. About ten years ago Rubinoff went over and bought several things from him for a song. The old man died within the year and the Estate went after Rubinoff. They took him to court. You ought to be able to track down that story. If the paintings were legit, and they probably were, there'd have been a stink in the newspapers if they got out of France."

"You are a treasure, Andy."

"Mr. Romano, I may have a picture for you—a Harnett I've got a line on."

"Believe me, I am interested."

"Impeccable credentials."

"Any time. Let me ask you one more question, Andy. I am such a recluse. Do you entertain your clients, or do they entertain you?"

"They entertain me. I save my entertaining for the folks who can get me next to something I want to buy. Or who come to me on behalf of *their* clients."

"Andy, I'm going to buy the Harnett from you sight unseen. You must admit that's an act of faith."

"It won't be charity. It's going to come high, Mr. Romano."

"I understand, but I want you to do something underhanded, shall we call it. Whether you say yes or no, and whether or not you are able to do this favor for me, will not affect our Harnett transaction, I give you my word."

"You're a disarming bastard," the man said and laughed.

"You go to the auction galleries with some regularity?"

"Yes."

"Do you make an appointment?"

"Generally. Always, if I have a client going with me."

"Rubinoff would do the same. I want to run a check on a major auction gallery to find out when he was there. It should be in the appointment books. Understand, Andy, I'm not asking you to find out what he was interested in or whom he brought in, but if such information becomes available, it will be useful to me. Five auction seasons, let us say."

"Mr. Romano, why don't you hire a private detective? He could go in and say he's Internal Revenue, get next to one of the girls. Rubinoff's not the most popular dealer on the street."

"Andy, it's a lovely idea. Do you know such a detective?"

"It happens that I do."

"Front for me, Andy. I want the information not later than tomorrow afternoon."

TWENTY-NINE

"There's one great thing about trying out for a lot of different careers," Julie said. "You really get to know the New York Public Library." She had just phoned the Newspaper Annex on West Forty-third Street. *"Le Monde*—it's the only French paper that's indexed for the period. I'd better move. The library closes at five."

Romano trotted ahead of her through the apartment, opening doors. "You will keep Michael. I have no need for the car until later tonight."

"I don't think so, Mr. Romano. It's a very conspicuous vehicle, if you don't mind my saying so."

"You have all the information you need?"

"Jean Dufayard. I'll get a starting date from his obituary."

It was twenty minutes to five when Julie found the story she was looking for. A librarian was already disconnecting the microfilm and photocopying machines and tucking them under hoods for the night. There was time only for a rapid reading in her nonguaranteed French. She noted the pictures under question: Seurat, *Musicians* (painting); Picasso, *Child's Head* (litho); Maillol, *Blacksmith* (litho); Gauguin, *Breton Child* (drawing); Degas (attrib.), *Sketch of Young Athletes.*

At that point the librarian rewound the microfilm for her so that they could "get the show on the road."

Julie walked the few blocks to the shop, a kind of discipline because she would have preferred to go almost anywhere else. She supposed the only way she was going to overcome this distaste was to keep going to the shop until it wore off. Like getting back on a horse after it had thrown you. For once she was glad to see Juanita outside.

"What's new, little friend?"

She hadn't expected an answer, but Juanita had something to say. She pointed to a wet spot near the bottom of the door. "Dog."

"Fritzie?"

Juanita nodded and grinned. She'd lost a front tooth between smiles. "Bad dog."

Julie brushed the youngster's hair out of her eyes. "Don't be a tattletale."

Along with the throwaways beneath the mail slot was a white envelope with "Julie" written in a large, childlike hand. A lament no doubt from Mrs. Ryan. She stuck it in her purse until she'd made her phone call. She wondered, washing her hands, if Romano would follow the call-back routine this time. The water kept rising in the toilet bowl until this time it overflowed. Not much, but a damned nuisance. She stood for a few seconds trying to visualize the big Irishman squeezing through the small window; it was easy to see him throwing the paper towel into the bowl after he'd mopped up his fingerprints.

She dialed Romano. The same routine, instant call-back. She read the list slowly of the Dufayard paintings acquired by Rubinoff.

"If he obtained that lot for a song," Romano said, "the old man was in his dotage. No, no. Even buying at a bargain, he would have had to raise cash, even knowing where they were to go."

Julie said, "Let's not be too sure of this part till I get the whole story tomorrow, but I think this is how it went. By the time the Dufayard estate brought suit, Rubinoff had disposed of pictures and the courts refused to intervene. The French government permitted three of them to leave the country. The blow-up was over why the bureaucracy had been able to move so fast in this case."

"Which three?"

"I'm not dead sure, but I don't think the article said."

"You have done splendidly, Miss Julie. Now we must try to find out where they went, especially the three. I wonder if I shall have as good luck with the bureaucracy as Mr. Rubinoff. I too must wait till morning, but it will come six hours sooner, Paris time. I must say I find the

Degas most intriguing. I should suppose if it *is* Degas, it was done in preparation for his *Jeunes Filles Spartiates*, and think about that in terms of our seven subjects. Eh? Wouldn't it be lovely if it turned out that Schoen obligingly authenticated the sketch, and that it now resides in the collection of our Mr. X?"

"I can think of something even lovelier: suppose Mr. X loaned it for some exhibition and his name is in the catalogue."

"Oh, my dear girl!"

"I'll be going home in about an hour, Mr. Romano."

"Do not hesitate to call me at any hour. And if you are at all uneasy about your personal safety, I shall provide protection."

"I'm not really."

"What time will you come tomorrow? And do you want the limousine?"

"I don't, thank you. And I'll have to call you."

"Speak with Alberto if I'm not available, and tomorrow you must meet the rest of the staff."

The rest of the staff. She thought of a friend, a nightclub comic, who called Romano The Little King. He was right: that fit him better than "the little caesar." She had a feeling Romano wouldn't be caught dead with a cigar in his mouth.

It wasn't until she was in the deli on the way home waiting for them to wrap up a barbecued chicken that she remembered the letter from Mrs. Ryan. She opened it and read:

Dear Julie:

Mr. O'Grady asked me to find out if by any chance he left his pocket knife at your place that day we both stopped in. He can't remember having it since then. It is valuable for sentimental reasons. He thought he should ask before starting to question the pawn brokers in the neighborhood.

I miss you.

> *Love,*
> *Mary R. and Fritzie*

The phone call came a few minutes after seven.

"Mrs. Hayes? This is Ginni Bordonelli. I am Maude Sloan's daughter."

"Hello," Julie said. Very cheerful.

"I understand we are to meet at my mother's party Saturday. . . ."

Julie didn't say anything. She ought to have been prepared and maybe she was, but she didn't feel that way.

"I'm not sure I want to have the party after what happened to Ralph's paintings, but I suppose we might as well. It was going to be a celebration."

"What happened to Ralph's paintings?" Without a tremor.

"Didn't you know? He destroyed them all except for the one you have."

"That's pretty drastic," Julie said.

"Or did you decide to let that dealer have it?"

That dealer. "I haven't decided," Julie said. "In the end I may let him have it."

"Rubicoff, is it? Mother knows him. She always gets names wrong."

"Something like that," Julie said.

"I'm going to try to get Ralph to start over. I don't care what anybody says. I was his patron for a while. You and I agree, don't we, that he does have talent? You will come on Saturday?"

"I expect to," Julie said.

That voice of Ginni's: a half note higher and it would crack. But it gurgled with culture. "And your husband? Mother wanted to know."

"I can't ever be sure of Jeff. I hope he'll be able to make it."

"Do you suppose I could come by and have a quick look at *Scarlet Night?*"

"Why not?" Her own voice hit the top of its register, but she made it sound hospitable. She was dying to add qualifications, but something told her not to.

Ginni said, "The trouble is *when.* I want to see so many people while I'm in New York . . ."

"I'll tell you what," Julie said, "if I decide to let Mr. Rubinoff have it in the next few days, I'll give you a ring first and you can come by and we'll drink a farewell toast to it—or something like that. Okay?"

"Oh-kay," Ginni said heartily. "I'll see you Saturday if not before. You sound like someone I really want to meet."

"It's mutual, I'm sure."

Had she really said that? Julie wondered, hearing a kind of play-back when she'd hung up the phone. It was something her mother used to say, making fun of *her* mother who had said it in earnest.

THIRTY

By late afternoon, with no word from Ginni, O'Grady went out and provisioned his cupboard, begrudging every dollar he spent. The two boys ate as though they hadn't had food for a month. They left him with the dishes and stretched out, one on the daybed and the other on the only easy chair in the room. "Jet lag," Steph managed in English.

It was eight o'clock when Ginni called and the boys came wide awake at the mention of her name.

"Johnny, everything's fine," she crooned.

"Is it now?"

"How are the boys?"

"Oh, they're just grand. They're waiting for you to come and fetch them and take them out on the town."

"You take them, Johnny. They liked you the minute they saw you."

"They've changed their minds, shut up with me here."

"Take them to Little Italy. There's a festival. There's a band playing and crowds of people. They'll love it."

"And you, what are you doing?"

"I haven't seen Mother in over a year." Which didn't answer his question at all.

"Ginni, what did you mean, everything's fine? It's not as though I haven't contributed my share to this operation, you know."

"You're whining, Johnny. It's the worst thing in the world to do with me. It makes me furious."

"What a bloody shame to disturb that darling disposition of yours. What did you work out with Rubinoff? I want to know."

"Things will go on exactly the way they were planned. Mrs. Hayes has invited me to have a drink and see *Scarlet Night* one last time before she gives it to him."

"To Rubinoff?"

"Yes, Johnny, to Rubinoff. She's still making up her mind, but she'll give it to him."

"It wouldn't hurt you to tell me that without making me drag it out of you."

"You are a partner and you will get your share. I never promised you anything else."

"Christ! You'd think I was the one that mucked things up. You'd think I was the one running off to South America yesterday."

"Could you have stopped him?"

"That's beside the point."

"No, Johnny. It *is* the point. You were on the brink of disaster."

"Through no fault of mine, but to hell with that. Ginni, you're the only reason I'm in on the whole thing."

"I don't believe that. I really don't. Shape up! I've never felt so marvelous in my whole life and you should too. You're supposed to enjoy it."

He turned his back on the boys, whether or not they could understand his pleading. "Isn't that how we planned it, Ginni? All we were going to do, you and me, when I came . . . Remember the song I sang to you? 'Bring me back more money than both of us can haul . . . !'" He heard her sigh, a cruel sound, and yet he could not stop. "We were going to Paris, to the Riviera, though what in hell I'd do there I don't know."

"I've got to go. Someone's waiting for me."

"Who?"

She hesitated, then: "Really, Johnny."

"All right, forget I asked it."

"I'll call you tomorrow. Give the boys my love." And she was gone to whoever was waiting for her.

He stood a moment and tried to swallow the pain. Then he turned and roared at the two: "Put on your shirts and let's get the hell out of here!"

People were swarming like maggots around the booths and in doorways and around the bandstand where, without a doubt, the worst band he had heard in his life was playing the only way it could, loud. But the boys loved it she was right. They tried to buy clams with *lire* and of-

fered to open the shells themselves. O'Grady paid and
they'd eaten a dozen before he got his change. They
hugged and thanked him and a minute later gave the *lire*
to the statue of Our Lady where she was lit up and
shrouded with dollar bills. A soprano with a voice as big
as her bosom came to the mike and sang "O, dolce Na-
poli . . ."

The boys took off for the bandstand, O'Grady after
them. By the time they reached it, the whole street
seemed to be singing. All up and down Mulberry Street,
people hung out their windows or swayed on the fire es-
capes. People dangled among the banners like God's own
puppets. The confetti floated down and the smell of sau-
sage and garlic and sweat floated up. O'Grady's black
mood lifted.

People kept shouting new songs for the woman to sing
until she was hoarse. She tried to get off the bandstand,
throwing them kisses. The musicians left the stand and lit
cigarettes. Tommy and Steph seemed on the verge of
mounting the platform; someone beat them to it: a long-
haired lad with a harmonica. He was good and the singer
got off throwing kisses to him. But his playing wasn't
something the crowd could join in on and they began to
drift away. Before O'Grady could make up his mind
whether or not to try to stop them, Tommy and Steph
leaped up on the stand. The crowd gave them a hand.
Tommy mimed an organ grinder to keep the harmonica
player going and did a couple of twists and turns to advertise himself, while Steph moved chairs and music
stands out of the way. He and Tommy took off their shoes
and went to work, somersaults, leaps, and flips, things
O'Grady couldn't begin to name. The harmonica player
faded out and the crowd came back.

A plump, ruddy-faced man in a white suit and straw
hat came and stood alongside O'Grady. He puffed on a
cigar that fouled the air around him. He watched them for
a while, and out of the corner of his eye sized up
O'Grady as well. O'Grady wanted to move off but he was
afraid of losing the boys. As though he could.

The stranger took the cigar from his mouth. "Who are
they?"

O'Grady wasn't sure what to answer. The truth:
"They're circus performers here on a visit."

"Where from?"

He could be F.B.I. or Immigration—or Mafia. Or, considering where they were, a majordomo in the night's
celebration. "They're Italian," he said.

"Not you," the man said, looking at him with heavy
eyes.

"What difference does that make?"

The man shrugged. He put the cigar back into his
mouth and squinted at the boys through the smoke.
"They're good," he said then.

"They are."

"Friends of yours?"

"You might say." He didn't even know their last
names.

The man took the cigar from his mouth again and
pointed with it. "Come to the restaurant two blocks down,
Piccolo Paradiso. I want you to bring them. You will be
my guests. All right?"

"Thanks," O'Grady said. "I'll ask them."

The man laughed in his face. He threw the cigar into
the gutter and clapped his hands twice at the performers.
He spoke at the top of his voice in Italian, and whatever
he said, they stopped the act right there. When they came
down he shook hands with them and they all jabbered
away in the boys' native tongue. It was Tommy who introduced O'Grady to Tony Gatto.

Gatto led the way, shooing people from in front of
them with the hat. The vendors all knew him and hailed
him by name. The restaurant was festooned with great
paper flowers in all the colors of the rainbow. The diners
were mixed, some young and some older, a prosperous-
looking lot that worked more with their heads than their
hands, by O'Grady's guess. He doubted a man among
them lived in Little Italy, though some might have got
their start there. It was not McGowan's, sure.

Gatto set them down at the family table in back where
one of the waiters was having his own late dinner, a
round table with a fair sampling of the night's sauces
staining the cloth. He seated himself between O'Grady
and the boys and said he would order for all of them.
And order he did. O'Grady cursed himself for having
stuffed them with salami and spaghetti out of a can when
it could have been saved for the next day. Shrimp, ver-
micelli in butter and garlic, broiled chicken, and salad

soon arrived. The pitcher of wine was refilled every time
it went dry.

Gatto kept leaning back in his chair to where he could
look at the two of them. "Beautiful boys," he would say,
which conjured up all kinds of mischief in O'Grady's
mind. Then they would talk again: it was about the circus, he knew that. And Mama and Papa. Then he caught
the name "Ginni" and that turned him cold.

"Mr. Gatto," he interrupted, "would you do me a favor
and tell me what this is all about?"

Gatto, who had had only coffee, sat back and took a
cigar from his inside pocket. He went back for another
and offered it to O'Grady.

"Thank you, I'll save it." Billy McGowan loved a good
cigar.

"Do you know a club called The Guardian Angel?"

"I've heard of it."

"I'd like to book them in there for a week. We just lost
an act."

"Why in hell didn't you say so? Here I thought it was
white slavery or such."

Gatto gave a great booming laugh. He translated for
the boys.

A tough-looking little man with a limp took a place at
the table. Gatto greeted him, but made no introductions.
He turned back to O'Grady.

"Who is Ginni?"

"Well now," O'Grady said, drawing out the words, "to
the best of my knowledge, they must think her a kind of
fairy godmother." Christ! Who was Ginni? Had they no
sense, the two of them? "She collects all sorts of artists
and entertainers and does this and that for them."

The boys looked at him hopefully, expectantly. He
could feel the sweat cold on his back. Tommy spoke to
Gatto and Gatto translated: "They want you to call her
and ask her."

"Not me," O'Grady said. "They can give you an answer themselves tomorrow. They're visitors, man.
Wouldn't they need work permits?"

Gatto gave a great shrug. "A week—who would care?"

"Starting when?"

"By the weekend. Are you in show business? O'Grady,
is that the name?"

"It is. I've a good voice. I sing a song and read a bit of verse now and then."

Gatto looked at him with a mixture of pity and contempt and turned back to the boys. O'Grady hated himself for having yielded to a hope he had long tried to purge: he would have dearly loved to be an actor but never got beyond looking at himself in the mirror. The eyes of a mesmerist without the power to mesmerize . . . or a magician maybe, and him with a hand like a foot.

Gatto and the boys were at it in Italian again. O'Grady looked at the man across the table who was wiping his silverware with a napkin, something that made the Irishman feel a kinship with him. "My name is O'Grady," he said.

The man nodded and tied the napkin around his neck. Not the friendly sort. The waiter put a bowl of spaghetti in front of him.

Gatto rounded on O'Grady again and rested the dark, yellow-flecked eyes on him. "They say you're jealous. You're in love with Ginni and they are too. She must be quite a chick."

O'Grady ground his teeth, not knowing what to do or say, helpless and now angry besides, and feeling a little sick with all that food on top of a full stomach. "Tell them it's time we went home. You can give them your name and number. I'm much obliged to you for the meal." He pushed away from the table.

"You won't call her for them? There's a phone in back."

"I wouldn't know where to find her, and if I did I still wouldn't call her, not if the devil himself gave me a message for her. Tell them that. I'll wait for them out on the street."

Gatto turned back to the boys and shrugged. He took out his wallet and extracted a card from it which he gave to Tommy.

O'Grady went out the side door and waited. They weren't long coming out, preening themselves like peacocks. He caught Tommy by the shoulders and shook him, the way his mother had shaken him as a youngster until his teeth rattled. *"Stupido,"* he kept saying, *"stupido!"*

When he looked around, the lame man had left the table and was in the doorway watching him.

THIRTY-ONE

It was disconcerting to be able to track another person's lies even as they were being told. Julie could not get over that conversation with Ginni: she was such a stylish liar. She was probably a stylish thief and smuggler too.

She finished painting what could now be called the mirror wall in time to call Jeff at ten, the hour they had arranged. She went over his mail with him.

"The more things change, the more they are the same," Jeff said of the situation with the coal miners. "The rhetoric and the wretchedness. The only new ingredient is ecology. How are you doing with the gentleman gangster?"

"I'm going to have a great story, Jeff. Not at all what I started out after. I want to tell you the whole thing, but not until it's over."

"You be the judge," he murmured.

"It's wild. . . . Jeff, do you know when you'll be home?"

"No. Does it matter?"

"I just don't want to involve you in any way in case something goes wrong."

"That sounds rather sinister. Are you in any danger, Julie?"

"I don't really think so."

"I doubt if I'll be home until this time next week. Call Tony if you need advice and don't want to involve me, as you say."

"I might do that. Jeff, you'll understand when I tell you."

"I expect I will. I just hope you know what you're doing."

"I do. Wish me luck."

Afterward she thought about how her mother used to say that: I hope you know what you're doing. Which, with her mother, implied that she didn't know but would do it anyway and it would be disastrous.

121

THIRTY-TWO

Julie would have preferred not to go to Forty-fourth Street in the morning at all, but one flush of the toilet when she got there told her that the less things changed the more they were the same: this time it really overflowed. Following Mrs. Rodriguez's directions, she tracked down the building superintendent, whose name was Orlie, in a tenement across the street. It was one of several in the neighborhood he serviced—if you could call his services servicing. She used her best Miss Page diction on him and put across the idea of a pot of gold if he could get things moving again.

A few minutes later he showed up with what he called his root-toot-tooter, a huge plunger, several wrenches, something that looked like a car jack, and something else that looked like an old bedspring. He was equipped to tackle the whole Manhattan sewage system. Cheerfully. Julie was not prepared to have confidence in anybody that cheerful about that kind of job. He reassured her with an account of his problems upstairs. Juanità was in the habit of drowning a doll every week or so, presumably a naughty one. Or maybe it was euthanasia.

After a half-hour of bellowing and Spanish blasphemy, he gave a cry of triumph. He would not allow Julie to come near until he had washed the offending object thoroughly in a basinful of Woolite. He came out drying the pockknife on his shirttail, its blade, screwdriver, scissors, corkscrew, etcetera, wide open. O'Grady's pocketknife had turned up after all.

"Yours?" Orlie said proudly.

"Well, not exactly." She should have made it a simple "Yes."

"I keep it then."

"No. It belongs to somebody I know. How long do you think it's been down there?"

Orlie shrugged. "It don't got no rusty. A couple days maybe?"

"Yeah." Julie went into the bathroom and tiptoed through the tools to where she could stand up on the bowl lid. She unlatched and opened the window. The knife marks were plainly visible. She looked out the window and down to where the iron grill lay on the ground below.

Orlie was making noises of distress. When Julie gave way, he climbed up and looked down. He pulled his head in. "You go to the police?"

The phone was ringing and Julie let his question hang for the time being. She'd have a lot of trouble explaining why she hadn't gone to them sooner.

It was Alberto. "Mr. Romano wants to know how soon you can come. You don't have to go back to the library. We have information."

"A half-hour?"

"Shall I send Michael?"

"No thanks. I'll run."

Alberto laughed, a nice sound.

To Orlie she said, "I've got to go out now. I'll decide later about the police."

Orlie hauled his tools out the front door. "I don't tell if you don't tell," he said, "and I fix the window real good." He pointed upstairs. "The señora, she don't like it when the police come."

"I'll bet. I'll need the knife, Orlie."

He surrendered it reluctantly, but no more reluctantly than Julie took it from him.

"It's clean. No shit." He grinned at her.

Julie wrapped it in a paper towel and put it into a drawer. She brought her pen and a ten-dollar American Express check from her purse. "Okay if I write your name on one of these and you can cash it?"

He was still grinning. "I don't leave home without it."

"My dear Miss Julie, I do believe things are falling into place."

"They sure are," she said. They certainly were falling into place at Forty-fourth Street.

"Yes?" Romano was very alert. He looked scrubbed and polished and wore pale blue slacks and a matching shirt. "Has something more happened? I've just awak-

ened from a nap. I was up at three. Too early, it turned
out, for the French. I had to wait an hour. We are fortunate it's not yet August. I'd have had to wait a month.
What's your news?"

"I told you last night about the note from Mrs. Ryan—
O'Grady's pocketknife?"

"That gentleman seems to be going to pieces," Romano
said when he had heard the rest of it. "We may as well
start with him. Shall we have some orange juice first?
Come along."

They went through the foyer and the dining room into
the kitchen, at the sight of which Julie could not repress
an "Oh, boy." There was an island in the middle of the
room with a six-burner stove, two ovens, and a grill. A
variety of skillets hung overhead and the polished copper
pots gleamed on a wide stretch of white wall. A chef in
costume except for his hat, which hung on a peg between
a string of onions and a mesh bag of shallots, was chop-
ping vegetables.

"May I present Monsieur André, Mrs. Hayes?"

The man was tall and skinny and looked more like a
dentist than a cook. He bowed formally and showed no
sign whatever of being glad to meet her. He probably
wasn't. She didn't look like an eater.

"We won't disturb you," Romano said as he took a
surreptitious look at what was in preparation. He padded
across to the refrigerator and took out a half-dozen oranges. He put them through an electric juicer and then
started to take the washable components to the sink.

"Leave them, monsieur. Please."

Romano raised his hands—a plea for peace—and he
and Julie, taking their glasses, went out of the kitchen—
not on tiptoe, but softly. They settled in operational headquarters, the office.

"Let us now consider Mr. O'Grady," Romano said. "I
do want to say it sounds as though you handled Ginni
beautifully."

"That's how she thinks she handled me."

"Exactly as it should be. She would seem to have arrived and taken over at once. I find that reassuring. But
would you believe, she has brought with her two Italian
members of the circus, two acrobats?"

It took Julie only a beat. "The ones who broke into the
gallery in Venice?"

"Isn't it marvelous, the sheer bravura of it? She has housed them with O'Grady, and last night those three gentlemen cut quite a caper on Mulberry Street. You may wonder how I know . . ."

Julie was away ahead of him, but it would have been impolite to say so.

"You will remember in our concern over Peter Mallory I was aware of your conversation with a brash young comic at The Guardian Angel?"

Julie nodded.

"Another of my interests is a restaurant, Piccolo Paradiso."

"I know."

"Ah, of course you do. I'd forgotten. But what I want you to understand about my curiosity, Miss Julie: I do not violate people's privacy. I merely share in it."

All right. Julie didn't say anything. This was the Romano she had first come to see. In trepidation.

"Each night Michael makes the rounds of the establishments where I have interests, and brings back such information as my people think warrant my attention. I shall play part of a tape for you in a moment and you will be astonished at how interwoven our paths are with those of the conspirators we are conspiring against.

"There is a festival in Little Italy at which the two young acrobats from Italy volunteered their talent. I have a man named Tony Gatto who coordinates certain of my enterprises. Entirely without my knowledge, he proposed last night to book these young men into The Guardian Angel for a week. Needless to say, he will change his mind today. But last night he took them to Piccolo Paradiso. . . ." Romano started the machine. "I shall translate where necessary."

Julie listened hard, for there was the clatter of dishes and a murmur of peripheral conversation throughout. About all she heard in English for a while was the repeated, "Beautiful boys." Romano watched her face, smiling at the mention of Ginni. Then: "Mr. Gatto, would you do me a favor and tell me what this is all about?"

"That's O'Grady!" Julie cried.

The tape played on. Julie shook her head in sad sympathy with O'Grady when he said, "I've a good voice. I sing a song and read a bit of verse now and then."

Romano played the segment of tape through, cutting it

off when O'Grady left the restaurant to wait for his companions in the street.

"Now, we've spent enough time on that unhappy Irishman—unless we have use for him."

"That's what I was wondering," Julie said. "If we need him, it might be possible to convert him."

"He's anticipating a considerable amount of money for his part in their undertaking."

"Acquiring money isn't exactly an Irish thing, Mr. Romano."

The Little King raised his eyebrows. "That is folklore, my dear. It isn't an Italian thing either. Some of us simply happen to be good at it."

"Right," Julie said and knew she was blushing. "Nevertheless, most of them aren't good at it."

"He is a member of the I.R.A.?"

"According to Mrs. Ryan. I imagine that's what he'd want the money for."

"Then I don't see how he could be diverted. That's my point."

"It would have to be a conversion. We'd have to put it to him in some patriotic disguise—you know, like saying what if somebody stole the Book of Kells? That might work."

"But think if it didn't work." Romano remained doubtful. "And then there's the Irish antipathy toward informing. It seems to me their whole dramatic literature dwells on the informer."

"Yeah, but it wouldn't be that way if there weren't any informers," Julie said.

"Impeccable logic."

Julie smiled broadly. That certainly had never been attributed to her before.

Alberto had come in with an armful of books, auction catalogues. He said they had to be returned by afternoon.

Romano said: "There's something at the back of my mind about the theft of a painting from the National Gallery in London some years ago. Or it might have been the National Portrait Gallery. The thief was an Irishman—I think an I.R.A. man—but the reason I remember: there was a great outcry over the painting's having been first stolen—in effect, not actually—from the Irish National Gallery in Dublin, a gallery wanting in so many areas while the British were storing things they hadn't room to show."

"We've got to find that story," Julie said. "I think I know how to use it. And I'd like to have O'Grady on our side—on account of Mrs. Ryan. I know it's sentimental, but I would. She's very fond of him."

Romano nodded sympathetically. "Do you suppose he has the usual Irish bonhomie with members of the police force?"

"I wouldn't be at all surprised."

THIRTY-THREE

"Please join us, Alberto. We need all three heads to put to this business. Now: Concerning the paintings which were allowed to leave France: the Picasso went to a British collector; where the alleged Degas went is not known. It seems probable that Rubinoff kept it. At the time, at least. Which is in itself interesting, since he disposed of the other four he had purchased from Dufayard almost at once.

"But here is the treasure, my dears: Seurat's *Musicians* was the most valuable of the lot, and to whom did it go? A Zurich dealer by the name of Edmund Schoen."

"Neat," Julie said.

"Provocative, not yet neat, I'm afraid. Schoen sold it almost at once, along with two other paintings, to a collector named Peyton Wade in Dallas."

"Dallas, Texas?"

"All is not lost. Forgive me if I ask that neither of you interrupt for a few minutes. I want to put this together as quickly and accurately as I can."

Alberto had not said a word.

"We know something about Peyton Wade: he collects works of art concerning music and musicians. One thing that is immediately apparent is that if our Leonardo nude is a musician he is well disguised. No, I feel sure we can assume Peyton Wade is not our collector. But the fact that

Schoen sold him three paintings, including Rubinoff's Seurat, is significant. There are collectors who simply will not buy single paintings. The famous Hirshhorn was one. Schoen may have bankrolled Rubinoff's purchase from Dufayard. He was probably waiting for the Seurat to complete his sale to Wade. In which case, Rubinoff did him a great favor in obtaining it and passing it along.

"I have a peculiar hunch—which may turn out to be as suspect as your comment on the Irish and money, Miss Julie—but I think this business of collecting on themes smacks of new money: it suggests ignorance and laziness. Yes! How much thought or study goes into it? Why not collect beer cans or license plates?

"Alberto, have Eloise bring us in *Who's Who*." To Julie: "Eloise is my secretary. She has an office in that part of the house." He motioned to wherever *that* was.

Romano went on while Alberto spoke softly into the phone. "I want to remind you that although we've thought of seven categories into which the Leonardo might fit, and because we are certain that it was stolen on consignment, this does not necessarily say that *our* collector follows a theme. We simply don't know enough about him yet.

"For the time, let us set aside all consideration of the two paintings from Dufayard which stayed in France. We can also eliminate the Picasso, for it remains in the cabinet of the Englishman who bought it from Rubinoff.

"And that brings us to the alleged Degas—and our little dream, Miss Julie, of its authentication. I have consulted at length with a curator who knows a great deal about Degas. Nothing with the Dufayard name in its provenance is in the catalogue of Degas's works, and there has been an addition to the catalogue within the year. So it is possible even today to come on something the artist never intended to leave to posterity. My curator friend raised a pertinent question: Why in the world would a collector of any stature buy a possible fake Degas or an inferior one when there are numerous authentic and excellent works coming up for sale regularly? The answer that seems most logical to me is that he had complete faith in his dealer, and possibly but not necessarily, a limited trust in his own judgment.

"An interesting aside—Degas spent many months on several occasions in Naples. His father had been a Neapolitan and he had family there. Furthermore, *The Young*

Spartans dates from that period and it is known from his journals that he made many sketches. Wouldn't it be curious . . ." He interrupted himself and shook his head. "I must not take us any further afield with speculations that are too remote. For the time being we must assume that the alleged Degas sketch remains with Rubinoff."

"That doesn't sound right, Mr. Romano."

"I agree, but it is the safest place for us to leave it for now."

Romano looked at his watch. "I regret to say I have a business and luncheon meeting of my own Board here at eleven-thirty."

Julie said: "I think I should take *Scarlet Night* home with me, don't you? I mean suppose Ginni gets jittery and does come by to make sure . . . ?"

There was an instant chill in the room, a complete change in atmosphere.

"If you think so," he said distantly.

"No, it's a matter of us all thinking so. Maybe it's just that *I'm* getting jittery in case she does come."

"It is ready to go now. It had to be put together again right away to be sure that every nail was accurate, everything an exact fit. I am sure Miss Bordonelli has a microscopic eye. It may well have been photographed. Will you bring it, Alberto?" The chill was unmistakable.

Alberto went into the studio and returned with the painting neatly wrapped in brown paper and tied with a strong white cord. His eyes refused to meet Julie's. She felt she had broken a code, but she didn't know what to do about it. It wasn't as though she wanted the picture home at all. But she knew, getting up from Romano's desk, that no matter how she protested, nothing would prevent the picture's leaving with her now.

A middle-aged woman, well dressed and competent, came in with a volume of *Who's Who in America*. "Leave it on the desk, Eloise."

No introduction.

The woman asked: "Do you want me to take minutes during the meeting, Mr. Romano?"

"I think not. There may be language."

"I know how to spell those words, Mr. Romano."

"Thank you, but we'll use the tape." To Alberto he said: "See that Miss Julie gets into a cab—a reliable cab company."

"What time am I to come back?" Julie said. "If ever."

Romano looked at her carefully, as though wondering whether he had made a mistake. He decided in his own favor. "I shall be available at three."

On the way down in the elevator, Alberto carrying the picture for her, Julie said: "What have I done wrong? It's not as though I want the responsibility of the picture again."

Alberto glanced at her and away. His eyes were sad again. "Mr. Romano is very sensitive."

"So am I!"

Alberto smiled wistfully.

There hadn't been any suggestion of using the limousine this time and Julie was about to tote that up on the negative side when, just as she was getting into the cab, she saw the big car pulling up to the building. She glanced back, her cab stopped on the corner for a light. The passengers were piling out, Michael holding the door. They waited and then went indoors in a body. Like pallbearers. Then, out of the corner of her eye, as the cab moved forward, she saw Alberto get into another cab. She could be only reasonably sure that he followed her until, from behind the curtain in the vestibule door on Sixteenth Street, she watched and saw him pass. His face was drawn back out of sight, but the checked shirt he was wearing was not to be concealed.

If he was following to protect her—or to protect the picture—why not say so? It had to be that Romano was making sure she hadn't gone to the F.B.I. with it. It was something to remember about him: the habit of mistrust ran deep.

THIRTY-FOUR

Julie knew she had to call Mrs. Ryan about her note, whether or not she admitted to her that the pocketknife had turned up at the shop. She decided against that. After all, the knife could have lain harmless at the bottom of the catch basin or whatever, at least so far as O'Grady would know—for some time.

"I'll look around again just to be sure," Julie said.

"The man is beside himself with some kind of worry," Mrs. Ryan said. "I suppose it's the politics over there. I often meet him at McGowan's, and I was thinking if I see him today I might invite him to come to supper and fix him a bit of steak. He needs cheering up."

Oh, boy. Mrs. Ryan didn't have any kitchen—just an electric plate on a board over the tub in the bathroom. She cooked potatoes in an electric coffeepot.

"It's very comfortable now with the air conditioner and the blower clears the smoke in no time. You wouldn't be free yourself, would you, Julie?"

"I'm not sure, Mrs. Ryan. I won't know until about five-thirty. Is that too late to call you?"

"Just come if you can and we'll make do. I might be out with Fritzie when you called. I've been saving that fan I promised you and Johnny could carry it over for you afterward. He's as strong as a horse."

THIRTY-FIVE

"I hung it in the dining alcove. It's not exactly the right place for it, but it's on the wall at least."

"And you do think she may turn up?" Romano wanted to know.

"Yes! I do think it's possible—after she's talked with Rubinoff and O'Grady maybe. And if she did come—where would I say it was? They know it's not at Forty-fourth Street."

"I understand your anxiety. And if she brings Rubinoff with her? And if he suggests taking it with him? That must not happen until we're ready."

"Mr. Romano, why didn't you say that when I first made the suggestion?"

"Because, frankly, I thought you were using it as a pretext to confide the whole disposal to the F.B.I."

"That's crazy."

Romano leaned back and laughed. "Alberto, have you ever heard anyone say that to Romano before?"

"No, sir."

"If he did insist, I'd say, 'No way. Now if you want it, go ahead and sue me.' I'll bet he'd back off then."

"I'm sorry if it offends you that I mistrusted you, Miss Julie. I suspect it was a variety of transference, to use psychiatric patois. I was distracted from our issue by issues to be discussed with my associates who were about to arrive. They are not always in agreement with my methods of doing business. I apologize."

"No need to," Julie said.

"Thank you. There are some splendid developments." He pulled the open *Who's Who* across his desk and referred to it as he said: "Peyton Marcus Wade is an oil-company executive. He's—let me see, he would be forty-three years old. Divorced. Lives in Dallas, but he is on the Board of the Houston Museum, a member of the Mid-Texas Tennis Association, and a director in several

firms—one of which might interest us: Campbell Drilling
Equipment, now owned by A. M. and M., which is a con-
glomerate." He closed the book. "Your turn, Alberto.
What do you have for us from Venice?"

Alberto referred to a note pad. "The information
comes from last year's registration of visitors to an exhibit of master drawings at the Institute of Art. On Sep-
tember seventeenth, E. Schoen signed in, an address in
Rome. The persons signing the book ahead of him were
apparently with a Swedish tour, but the names that follow
are . . ."

Romano interrupted: "In this order, note."

". . . G. T. Campbell, New York, and Peyton Wade,
Dallas, Texas."

"Well?" Romano was impatient for Julie to react.

"Is Campbell our man?"

"A distinct possibility."

"He lives in New York," Julie said.

"That does make him more lovable," Romano said.
"He is not in the phone book. Nor am I, for that matter.
He has been in the news in recent years. Eloise is checking that for us. I rather think it has to do with a stock-
holders fight in Campbell Equipment. It will have been
in the *Wall Street Journal* if not the *Times*."

Which reminded Julie of her brief search in the early
afternoon for the story of the I.R.A. man's theft at the
National Gallery in London. "It's going to take time to
find it," Julie said, "and I may be coming up against
Mr. O'Grady soon."

"Then make it up—as it may turn out I did with much
of the story. It's possible—unless his only dedication is
to violence—that he'll be able to give you the correct
version."

Julie let her eyes rest on Romano, two thoughts collid-
ing: his distaste for physical violence and his quick prag-
matism.

"Yes?"

She shook her head and averted her eyes. "I was thinking that you know a lot."

"Rather more than is so, perhaps, and certainly more
than I understand. When do you expect to see O'Grady?
I'm by no means easy about him."

"Mrs Ryan wants to have both of us to supper tonight."

"Oh, dear, and we are having blanquette of veal, one of André's specialties."

Julie burst out laughing, thinking of André in his kitchen and Mrs. Ryan in hers.

"What?"

Julie did not get to answer, for the house phone rang and Alberto went downstairs to bring up Andrew Davis, the dealer whom Romano had charged with hiring the detective. Romano set about changing and marking tapes. "Auction Gallery information," he murmured.

Not one man but two came in with Alberto, and while Romano was polite, Julie knew he was annoyed at the penetration of his tower by an unexpected person. Davis was tall and tanned and there was a tinge of yellow to his gray hair. He had coached the man he brought with him, for when he introduced him to Romano, Dave Schweitzer, private detective, made no move to shake hands. A small man, he wore a conservative business suit and looked as much as anything like an investigator for the Internal Revenue Service. Romano made formal introductions. Everybody was going to know his place during this interview.

"Since you said time was of the essence," Davis said, starting to explain.

"Say no more."

"I've got to say something more, if you don't mind. I had to give Dave a rundown on values, procedures, and so forth, and since I'd done that so that he could get you extra information if it was there to get, I thought he ought to be here for you to question."

"Just so."

"I'm a quick study, Mr. Romano," the detective started, his accent pure New York, "but I don't understand the ins and outs of the art game. I didn't get to the gallery till noon. I had to work on my credentials, you know what I mean."

"Precisely. What gallery?" Schweitzer's homework did not interest him.

"Bristol's. Mr. Davis figured we might as well hit the biggest."

Romano nodded.

"I figured the boss might be out for lunch. He sure was."

"He will be away until October," Romano suggested.

"Almost. Anyway, I got six dates for you—and I took down the auction dates as long as I was at it—about a week's difference every time between Rubinoff's visit and the auction coming up. I'd made up photocopies of phony bank records which I was pretending to check against. I can tell you what three of the pictures Rubinoff and his client wanted to see."

A quiver of excitement played at the corner of Romano's mouth. It was more than he had expected.

"A drawing of an oarsman by Thomas Eakins." He pronounced it EEkins. "Tin-tor-etto's *Swimmers* . . . and there was a Michelangelo there that almost blew it for me. I was supposed to know that was big money, the commission on that baby. So I pretended to think I had something on Rubinoff—that he hadn't reported it, see. But what it turned out to be—nothing secret about it. He didn't get it. It went to a museum in Kentucky that immediately advertised it was their bid that won it. But here's the inside information, Mr. Romano. This gal that was helping me said he mustn't've really wanted it because when Rubinoff wanted something for that client, he got it. Money's no problem."

The little detective sat facing Romano, his notes written in block letters on a large index card.

Romano put out his hand for the card. "May I?" He looked for the date the Michelangelo had sold. "January of this year. Perhaps he was saving the money for something more pertinent to his client's collection."

"When you get more pertinent than Michelangelo, Mr. Romano, you're talking astronomy," Andy Davis said.

"Would I be interested otherwise?" He turned to the detective. "May I keep this?"

"It's what you're paying for," Schweitzer said. "The private previews are in the first column, the dates of the auction in the second."

"Admirable."

"I took Miss D'Arcy to lunch, and I said I'd treat her information confidential, so that's what I'm doing, right? It's confidential information. She wanted to know if I thought Rubinoff was in trouble. I said it could be and that seemed fine with her."

"You will of course add the luncheon to your bill."

"The whole thing comes to about three hundred dollars,

Mr. Romano. I don't mind taking cash if you got it around."

"I pay nothing without a record, sir. I have no wish to complicate the audits of the Internal Revenue Service."

"Whatever you say, Mr. Romano." The detective was crestfallen. "If I can ever be of any service to you, I'd like to leave you my card."

"By all means. And your statement."

Andy Davis said: "I have a little something for you myself, Mr. Romano."

Romano held up a finger to silence him temporarily. "Alberto, why don't you take Mr. Schweitzer into the business office? Perhaps he would like his check now."

"I can always use a buck," Schweitzer said.

"We must remember that."

When Alberto and the detective had gone off, Davis said: "I wouldn't be surprised if you found a sketch for Courbet's *Wrestlers* on that list. I remember it coming up in the last few months. Looks like they're collecting athletes, wouldn't you say?"

"It does seem to be going that way."

"Want me to make a guess who he is?"

"You're certainly entitled to, Andy."

Davis glanced at Julie.

Romano said: "We are as one in this voyage of discovery."

"G. T. Campbell. He's an aging playboy who keeps from going to seed by pretending he's a Rockefeller when it comes to art. He made a lot of money when he got squeezed out of his father's business in Texas. Since then he's come up north and gone into race courses, gambling, sports events. He owns a string of health clubs. His good deeds always have to do with athletic scholarships. I've got one more lead for you, if you want further confirmation: Leonard Kliegman. You know who I'm talking about?"

"It would be hard not to," Romano said. He glanced at Julie.

She nodded, knowing that Kliegman was one of the most popular figures in the current art scene—he painted sporting events, jazz musicians, circus scenes, all the action stuff.

"I'll bet you twenty-five cents he's done a portrait of Campbell."

Romano laughed softly. "Would you believe it, he has done that pen-and-wash thing—very effective, I must say —of certain members of the family? We all have interests in common, it would seem."

Davis ran his tongue between his lips. "Never sat for him yourself?"

"No, but perhaps I should. Andy, have you any idea where this G. T. Campbell lives?"

"I don't know his Manhattan address, but I know he's got a place about fifteen miles up the Hudson. Ever hear of Maiden's End?"

"No, but it's a provocative idea. Forgive me, Miss Julie."

She shrugged. She seemed to remember that Maiden was a proper name. She had been there a couple of times with Jeff. Several broadcast journalists lived there.

"He bought an estate up there a few years ago, proposing to race outboards on the river. He didn't have them in the water when they outzoned him for noise pollution."

"Oh, boy," Julie said. "I've met him. At a dinner party once. He switched over to sailboats and sponsors a regatta every summer, right?"

"That's the gentleman."

Romano was making a steeple of his fingertips. "Does he have a family?"

"I don't remember," Julie said. "I mean I don't think there was a wife that night." What she remembered most about Campbell was that while he was dressed pretty normally, shirt, jacket, an ascot, he wasn't wearing socks— just loafers on his bare feet.

Romano got up from his desk, a signal that seemed to work in moving people out. "When am I to see my Harnett, Andy?"

"Now he wants to see it. Yesterday it was sight unseen."

"Dear friend, my trust in you is limitless. I am simply eager."

Alberto took the two men downstairs, a custom of the house. Romano picked up the phone and said, "I'm glad you're still here, Eloise. I want you to call the Metcalfe Gallery and find out if Leonard Kliegman is in town. You may say who it is that's calling. If it can be arranged, I should like to have him to lunch tomorrow to discuss doing a portrait of me. Then come in and meet Miss Julie."

Julie took the detective's information to the desk where Alberto had stacked the auction records and began a search of the latest volume. Romano hummed softly as he removed and marked the tape of the conversation with Davis and Schweitzer.

Alberto returned just as Julie found what she was looking for. "I've got it!"

"The Michelangelo?" Romano said.

"Right. 'Athlete—drawing.' Four hundred and seventy thousand dollars. Wow."

"He will pay more for the Leonardo. Even in legitimacy, it would have been so, a lesser drawing by a greater artist. Pause and think of the scene that must take place—at Maiden's End, I shouldn't wonder now—Rubinoff's arrival with Scarlet Night . . ."

"Something like what happened here?" Julie said. She wasn't ever going to forget it.

Romano nodded. "But just suppose Campbell had already acquired the Michelangelo, a much more macho figure—so characteristic of him—it would be only human for him to be disappointed in the Leonardo. Rubinoff was wise to let the Michelangelo go.

"Just to keep things tidy, Alberto, see if you can discover from the dates what other auctioned works he may have been interested in at Bristol's. We must have every documentation available to us. It would be too terrible if we had the wrong man."

Julie looked up G. T. Campbell in Who's Who and read the entry aloud. Andy Davis had paraphrased it.

Romano chortled. "So that's where he got his information, from Who's Who. What an accomplished fraud he is!"

Very soon Eloise came in with her shorthand pad in hand—filled with loops and lopes and squiggles. Julie envied her the skill. Romano introduced them and apologized for his morning distraction.

"Mr. Kliegman is in East Hampton for the summer," the secretary said, "but they will try to reach him and call us back. Do you want the information on the Campbell Company now?"

She read from her shorthand in a singsong voice the story of a fight for proxy votes and the ultimate con-

glomerate takeover. Julie did not understand a lot of
what was in between, but Romano listened carefully,
nodding now and then at something he found significant.
When she had finished, he said: "It sounds to me as
though he wanted out of the business all along. I'm sure
that's what it means, but he was advised to hold out until
A. M. and M. raised its offer. He was probably so advised by someone in consultation with A. M. and M. His
holding out upped the market price of a very weak stock
to everyone's satisfaction. But he's not a fighter, that boy.
Andy was right."

Eloise offered to work late transcribing the tapes.

"Perhaps you'd better, and have dinner here. I've promised André at least three appetites at table. Now, Miss
Julie: that embattled Irishman—are you sure it's worth
the risk? Michael has a number of former colleagues
among whom we might recruit more reliable assis-
tance. . . ."

Julie's eyes must have conveyed her instant assessment
of Michael's former colleagues, for Romano backed
down: "Mmmm. Perhaps we can manage with less professional skill, but I beg of you, weigh matters well before
giving your trust. I must admit there is no zeal like that of
the convert, but I should hate to have him jump aboard
and sink us."

THIRTY-SIX

O'Grady arrived at the Willoughby early. He was glad
to get out of the house where the boys were sour and sul-
len. He was sure they blamed him because Tony Gatto
had changed his mind about hiring them. That Ginni
would have changed theirs about taking the job was un-
provable. She had not called. Nor would he call her. He
was resolved never again to crawl to her like a snake to a
charmer. What he longed for, arriving early, was com-

pany of his own kind, a woman of simple faith like Mary
Ryan. As for Julie Hayes, he wished he could make up
to her in some way for his violent intrusion upon her
premises. His mood was penitential, a feeling by no
means unfamiliar, aware as he was of his strong inclination to sin.

His first thought when Mrs. Ryan called out to him to
come in where the door was open was how three people
were going to stand up in the place, never mind sit down
to their suppers.

Strictly speaking, Mrs. Ryan did not have an apartment. She had managed to keep the room and bath, into
which she had jammed almost forty years of living, while
the Willoughby converted to larger and more expensive
units all around. Her walls were hung with photographs—
many of them inscribed—of actors and actresses who had
themselves faded even more than Mrs. Ryan's pictures of
them.

"Before you sit down, Johnny, would you take Fritzie
for a short walk? I was meaning to, but I didn't have the
time."

O'Grady gave over the half pint of whiskey he had
brought as a gift and took the leash from her hand.

"You shouldn't have done that, Johnny," she said of
the whiskey, "but it'll give us an appetite."

Fritzie, much as he favored a walk, showed little inclination to go with O'Grady. As soon as the man reached
for him, he scuttled under the daybed.

"Aw, Fritzie," Mrs. Ryan crooned, and then to
O'Grady, a lament: "He's not used to men. That's the
late Mr. Ryan there on the dresser." She took back the
leash and got down on her knees at the side of the bed
while O'Grady edged around the armchair and television
to get to the dresser: a sickly young face under a hat two
sizes too big for him.

"Take it to the light," Mrs. Ryan said.

"A fine-looking man," O'Grady said heartily.

"It's hard for me to believe that if he had lived he'd be
seventy-six years old. To me he'll be twenty-nine until
the day I die." She lifted the skirt of the quilted spread
and peered under the bed. "Come out from there, you
villain."

O'Grady was thinking as he put the photograph back
in its place that if there was, as he'd been taught to be-

lieve, the resurrection of the body, there'd be a conspicuous discrepancy between them when that time came. But
then, you couldn't have resurrection in any case without
a certain amount of restoration. He returned to the door
where it stood open. The bed ran alongside that wall.
With his feet in the hallway, he knelt and spoke to the
dog who, from what O'Grady could see, was behind a
barricade of books, old shoes, and pocketbooks. "Do you
want to go out or don't you? You'll have a long
wait otherwise."

Fritzie surrendered to Mrs. Ryan, who snapped his
leash onto his collar. In the hall, with all the stubbornness
of the dachshund side of him, he made a last stand and
turned the whites of his eyes to O'Grady. O'Grady took a
step back and lifted his foot. He had no need to plant it:
Fritzie trotted to the elevator like a little gentleman.

They were at the first fireplug outside the Willoughby
when O'Grady spotted Julie swinging briskly down the
street. He had admired her walk the first time he laid
eyes on her. He did not know how he felt about seeing
her now. She would know her shop had been broken into,
but if the knife hadn't turned up yet, it might never turn
up, and the lies he'd composed could go untold. He *was*
glad to see her. There was a freshness about her that you
could almost say came from the soul, unlike the tinseled
beauty of some he knew.

"Hello, Mr. O'Grady," Julie said.

"It's much too crowded in her nest up there to be calling me Mr. O'Grady. How are you, well?" He shifted the
leash and offered his hand.

The dog was trying to dance on his back legs. "Yes,
yes, Fritzie. You're a good dog," Julie said.

"If you don't come with us a ways, I'll have to carry
him," O'Grady said.

"Come on, you spoiled beast," Julie said. And when
they were under way: "Isn't it nice tonight? The humid-
ity's gone down."

"There'll be a grand sunset, and I see by the paper,
near a full moon."

"Do you always look in the paper for the phases of the
moon?"

"I do, though I never thought about it till now."
O'Grady was struck with what seemed like a wonderful
idea. "It'll rise early tonight. I've a small car, and while

it's short on all other luxuries, it has a window on the sky. I was going to suggest when we go up that we all take a ride after supper. We might go along the river on one side as far as the Tappan Zee bridge and come down the other."

Julie cast him a sidelong glance. It was wild, his making that suggestion—a ride that would bring them within a half mile of Campbell's estate. Or could that be what he had in mind for reasons of his own? Did he know *Scarlet Night* was to go to Campbell? The strange blue eyes turned on her and then skittered away.

"All right," Julie said.

He smiled broadly. "I was afraid you were going to say I could drop you home on the way."

"It's a beautiful drive," Julie said, and went on calculatedly, "I've sometimes visited Maiden's End. We have friends who live there."

"Have you ever gone up on the river itself?"

"No." The mention of the hamlet seemed not to have meant a thing to him.

"I've shipped out a couple of times from Albany and you come down in the morning mists and see all sorts of things—the heathen redskins whooping it up by the campfires. I mustn't call them that anymore, must I? . . . You can see Benedict Arnold sneaking off and leaving West Point to the British . . . and George Washington himself going ashore with his men . . ."

"That was at Maiden's End," Julie said.

"I suppose Maiden was somebody in those days," he said thoughtfully.

"Exactly." By which Julie meant that O'Grady had not made the common mistake of taking the name for a condition. "The Maidens were Tories."

"Aye. It's them that has the money."

"There's the both of you!" Mrs. Ryan called at the top of her voice, having come out at the sound of the elevator's stopping. "I was afraid you were lost, Johnny. I understand now."

Don't understand too much, old lady, O'Grady thought. You'll kill the plant before it's borne a seed. The girl was removing the dog's leash. With any luck the creature would bury himself for the duration under the bed.

It might have been a fine seating arrangement, their

supper table, if he'd been a horse wearing blinkers. The card table was hard against the doorframe with Julie sitting on the foot of the bed, Mrs. Ryan on the inside free to fetch and take, and O'Grady astride a folding chair, elbows in the room, his head fading in and fading out and his arse in the hallway. But they laughed a great deal and got along fine and there was no traffic to speak of at that end of the hall. They finished the whiskey among them, even Julie taking a thimbleful to respond to O'Grady's toast to a united Ireland.

"Do you consider violence the only way, Johnny?" She had finally broken down and used his first name.

He smiled with the pleasure of that and then said, "If you'll show me the country otherwise free, I'll give it consideration."

"Canada," Julie suggested.

"They'd have been better off having to fight. They'd have wound up knowing who they were at least. And when they've sorted out the Frenchies from among them, maybe that'll do it. But whether that's going to come about peaceable . . ." He shook his head doubtfully.

Julie, as she had several times through the evening, thought of Jeff. The only way she could see him at this table was if it were in a remote part of the world, sort of a native compound.

"Are you partial to the French, Julie?" O'Grady asked, for she had said nothing.

"I do like France, and Jeff's there a lot." Having no intention of saying his name, she'd said it.

Mrs. Ryan had that funny little pinched look that generally appeared at the mention of Jeff. She said: "I must get the dessert before it runs down the sink."

"I'd be willing to help if you hadn't exiled me out here," O'Grady said.

Julie said, "We should have used paper plates, Mrs. Ryan."

"It never tastes the same."

"It was delicious."

"You don't have much of an appetite, do you?" O'Grady said.

"I'm rather unconventional in what I like."

"You're an uncommon person altogether."

Julie looked at him.

"Well, damn it, you are," he said and averted his eyes.
Julie laughed.

Mrs. Ryan came with three saucers of ice cream. "It'll
be soup if we don't eat it."

"Soup, beautiful soup," Julie said.

"Where have you gone to, Sean O'Grady?" Mrs. Ryan
said, seeing him stare into space. "It isn't fair not to take
us along with you." To Julie: "He's been all over the
world."

"And none of it home," he said with a sigh.

"I feel that way too sometimes," Julie said.

Their eyes did meet then, but his real show of sensitiv-
ity was in his mouth.

Mrs. Ryan said, her hand on Julie's: "If only you'd
known your father, it would have made all the difference."
She was back on that tack again.

"I knew mine," O'Grady said, "and if I'd had the
strength I'd have killed him."

Silence. Except for the gnawing under the bed of
Fritzie on the steak bone.

Mrs. Ryan said: "I should never have given him that
bone. He won't have a tooth left in his head by the time
he's done with it."

O'Grady said: "I shouldn't drink whiskey. It depresses
the hell out of me. I apologize to you both."

"You're not reneging on that drive to the Tappan Zee?"
Julie said.

"I've never reneged on a promise in my life . . . though
I've failed to keep one or two."

He was serious. Julie didn't laugh. She pushed back
from the table and pulled her knees up to swing her
legs off the bed. "Let's do the dishes and go."

"We'll leave the dishes," Mrs. Ryan said. "I won't be
taking a bath until tomorrow."

Mrs. Ryan and Fritzie rode in the back of the Volkswagen, Julie beside O'Grady. As they drove up the West
Side Highway, Mrs. Ryan leaned forward and said of
the George Washington Bridge in the distance: "Will you
look at the lights the way they're strung out like a rosary."

O'Grady asked Julie: "Do you drive a car?"

"I've driven," she said, and then laughed at herself.
"In a case of extreme emergency. But I can sail a boat."
Which really was wicked of her: she could sail a boat

about as well as she could drive a car, and no one would consider himself lucky to be her passenger in either.

"Ah, there's something I'd love to be able to do," O'Grady said. "You'd think being an able seaman, I'd know the water like the palm of my hand, and all manner of boats, but it's not like that at all. There's times I might as well be working in the subway. You do what you're told to do and live for the time you're landside. And when you go ashore, the first thing you want is a drink, and maybe it's the last thing. It's a terrible life when you come down to it, seven months out of the year employment and you long since broke with nothing left but pious resolutions."

"I know," Julie said. "I've read Eugene O'Neill."

"Aye. It hasn't changed much."

"And you're not married?"

"I'm not. I've not been especially blessed in the women I'd have chosen. The blessing, I suppose is, they wouldn't have me."

As they crossed the river on the George Washington Bridge, O'Grady said, over his shoulder: "Look back now, Mary Ryan. There's your city in all its glory. There's no sight like it in the world, a fairyland of glittering towers, a passion of lights."

"Holy Mother of God," Mrs. Ryan said reverently.

They stopped at Rockefeller Lookout on the Palisades Parkway and got out of the car. A fat oval moon splashed a long reflection across the river. A few miles ahead lay Maiden's End.

"Could we go down to the river's edge at Maiden's End?" Julie asked.

"If you know the way."

"I do." With luck. All that she really knew was that the river was there at the end of a winding road. Say a prayer, Julie. The nonpraying member of the caravan.

"We'll go off the next exit," O'Grady said. "We must be getting near Maiden's End."

"I'm not the greatest navigator you ever sailed with," Julie said.

"If we get lost, does it matter? Aren't there people?" She nodded.

At the exit they turned toward Nyack and when after a few miles they passed the Geological Observatory, Julie knew they were almost there. She remembered the traffic light and the sign that pointed toward the community church. There was also a sign that said the road had no outlet. The white church with its steep, graceful roof stood in a flood of light.

There was not a car to be seen as they started down the winding road Washington was said to have followed with his men on the way to rendezvous with Lafayette. "There are some great houses," Julie said, "some of them from before the Revolution. I wish we could see them."

"We'll come back in the daylight," O'Grady said.

He drove very slowly, and the closer they came to the river the nearer to the road were some of the houses. Lamps shone within them, and their shutters and gingerbread trim were visible in the moonlight.

"Some have names," Julie said. "Like there's a Captain Somebody's House and a Bell House and a Ferry House. Some pretty famous people have lived here." She named a few of the theater stars who had at one time or another lived at Maiden's End.

"Oh, is that where we are?" Mrs. Ryan said with awe. "Now I remember the name."

She'd have been almost as impressed, Julie thought, to hear the name of the television correspondent she and Jeff had visited.

The river lay dead ahead with only a railing between it and the end of the road. "Now what do we do?" O'Grady wanted to know.

"There's enough room to turn around," Julie said. "Park for a minute and turn off the motor."

Julie rolled her window all the way down. The only sound was the rhythmic splash of the water against the sea wall.

O'Grady said softly: " 'I will arise and go now, for always night and day/I hear lake water lapping with low sounds by the shore . . .' "

"I can't hear," Mrs. Ryan wailed, having heard just enough to know she was missing something. She pulled herself forward, hanging onto the back of Julie's seat.

O'Grady raised his voice: " 'While I stand on the roadway, or on the pavements gray . . .' "

Julie joined her voice to his on the last line, for she knew it well: " 'I hear it in the deep heart's core.' "

Mrs. Ryan sighed and sat back when O'Grady started the motor. They drove slowly up the hill. After a moment she said, as though surprised: "The houses are not all that grand."

"There isn't a one I wouldn't settle for," O'Grady said.

"You know what I mean, Johnny."

Julie turned, as though to speak particularly to Mrs. Ryan; she wanted to watch O'Grady without his knowing. "There's one place I suppose you'd really call an estate: it belongs to a man named Campbell."

There was not a quiver in O'Grady's face. She would swear the name meant nothing to him.

"He sponsors a sailboat regatta in the summer and he's supposed to have a great art collection." Just a little twitch to O'Grady's nose and a slight lift of the shaggy brows, but a response.

For O'Grady it was a moment of surprise, hearing her speak of an art collection. He felt as though something had been slipped in on him. Ginni was great at such tricks, committing him to something before he even knew what she was talking about.

"Do you know whose place it used to be?" Julie said, and named an actress whose fame was only remotely known to O'Grady.

But Mary Ryan was beside herself. "She was one of the nicest human beings ever stepped on the stage. Could we drive past the place, Johnny?"

"Could we, well?" he said, looking at Julie. He put his suspicions down to his imagination. Who with money didn't have an art collection of some sort?

"We can go up to the gate anyway," Julie said, "but Mrs. Ryan won't see much."

"She'll feel, never mind. She's a great one for feeling."

You couldn't go far astray in Maiden's End: there were not many roads and the only way out was the road you had come in on. At Julie's suggestion they drove between two stone pillars marked Private. She had once walked this way. Within a quarter mile they came to the wrought-iron gate. Julie bade him stop a few feet before it, the snout of the VW just short of the post with the electronic eye and the intercom through which, presumably, a watchman would speak.

"We're as far as we can go," Julie said, "except for a lovely walk that skirts the fence and goes on through the woods into the park system."

"It'd be a grand night to explore it," O'Grady said.

"We can't leave the car here. There's a park entrance on the highway. The time I was here before we came out that way."

"Shall we go find it?" He swung the car around and drove back between the stone pillars.

Julie turned in her seat. "Are you all right, Mrs. Ryan?"

"I've been sitting here thinking about *The Barretts of Wimpole Street*. There's nothing at all like it on the stage today. I cried every night. I was an usher in those days. An usherette."

On the highway, they soon came to a driving range. It was doing a thriving business. Julie remembered the park entrance was opposite. A barricade closed the path to vehicular traffic. "It's a fair walk."

Mrs. Ryan was leaning forward. "Why don't you park the car where Fritzie and I can sit and watch the golfers while you two go on? The night air's a little sharp for my chest."

THIRTY-SEVEN

"She's a devil, that old lady is, sending us off into the woods alone."

"She'll count every minute we're gone," Julie said. They crossed the highway and went around the park barrier—a single pole locked between two posts. "What's crazy is that she's the one that wanted to see the place."

"I have a certain amount of curiosity myself," O'Grady said.

"Oh?"

"I don't like fences. I suppose I'm a poacher at heart. Do you know what that means?"

"Taking illegal fish or game."

"Well, it depends on how you define legal—or more to the point, who makes the laws. I've never had salmon in

Ireland that wasn't poached. They were in litigation for years over whether the rights to fish in the Carib River belonged to an Englishman living in France or to the Irish people. How can you have any respect for a government that would take that long to consolidate their national resources?"

"And yet you want a united Ireland."

"Yes, but I'd want a few other changes as well. For example, there's got to be something done outside the Church to civilize the Protestants of the North."

Julie laughed.

"You've always heard it the other way round, is it? The Catholic savages?"

Julie made a noise of assent.

"British propaganda."

She though about Romano's story of the painting stolen from the National Gallery. Not quite a non sequitur, but not much of a sequitur either. The sound of the cars on the road behind them gradually faded into the distance so that the hum and wheeze of insects became audible.

O'Grady took an occasional slap at a mosquito. "I'd forgot about them, well."

Their footfalls made a soft, plopping noise in the damp mixture of last year's leaves and this year's grass. "What are the silvery trees?" Julie wondered aloud.

"You're asking a foreigner. Would they be ash?"

"They're like ghosts among the others. Why do you live in the city, Johnny?"

"It's where I was born and bred."

"You don't sound like it."

"That's from my mother. She was a country woman, County Mayo. I wish I'd been born over there. I have a notion I might have been a poet or such in Ireland."

"Then why don't you go and live there?"

"I might find out for sure that I wasn't."

They walked in silence for a moment. Then Julie said, "Shall we go on until we catch sight of the river and then turn back?"

"Don't you want to see the fence?"

"All right." It was odd that he was the one to say it, when she had led them to Maiden's End for the very purpose of scouting the estate. It had to be well after ten o'clock. The moon was almost directly over where she supposed the Campbell property was. When they reached a fork in the path they turned toward the Campbell estate and crossed a stream by way of a viaduct.

"You could drive through here if they'd let you."

"I think park vehicles do come this way. They'd have to in case of fire."

"Look," he said and touched her arm. They had come to a clearing where the grass was tall but such trees as there were were only seedlings and no higher than the grass. It was as though a road had been started years before and then abandoned. Beyond lay the river jeweled with the lights of water craft, and beyond that, the Westchester shoreline with two trains approaching each other along the water's edge. "Watch out!" O'Grady said as the engines raced toward one another. They passed, a few seconds of strobed light, and continued on and out of sight.

A road angled into the woods on the far side of the clearing, much more pronounced than the footpath, which was all that was left from there on of the trail on which they had come.

"Would this be a service road to the estate, would you say?"

"I doubt it," Julie said. It showed little sign of use.

"For emergencies maybe. Come on."

Julie followed along, ashamed of her inclination to hang back. What impelled him? Did he know something by intuition? Or was it a lark—like a small boy's daring on Halloween?

"I was right," he whispered. "Can you see the fence on either side? And the lights of the house, can you see them now?"

"Yes."

They were considerably closer to the house than they had been when outside the front gate.

The back gate, matching the cyclone fence, was chained and padlocked. O'Grady called her attention to the barbed wire which was strung along both gate and fence. "The barbarian," he said with contempt. He reached up and touched the wire. "I'm surprised it isn't electrified."

"It's not?" Julie said, wanting to be sure. She wanted such information as she could take back to Romano to be accurate.

"I'd have found out soon enough if it was. Suppose I

could find a gap in the fence—or a place we could go over without tearing ourselves to shreds, would you be game?"

Julie hesitated, much as she wanted to take up the challenge. "I can't, Johnny. I can't take the chance of our being caught."

"I suppose not, but it's a pity."

She didn't say anything.

"It's a handicap, isn't it, being married to a man of fame?"

"In this case, yes. Jeff has colleagues who live in Maiden's End."

"Well, do we go back now or what?" He was irked at having to abandon his tilt with the fence.

"I'd be willing to go down to the shore by way of the clearing if it goes that far."

They returned to the broad stretch open to the sky. The long grass bent toward them as though combed by the wind, with a narrow path beaten down to one side. They walked single file, Julie ahead. She paused and tested his mood: "What's golden by day and silver by night?"

"I give up."

"A wheat field. I remember a poem with something like that in it. Then it goes, '. . . As if a thousand girls with golden hair might rise from where they slept and go away.'"

They came to a narrow plateau, a huge flat rock. Beyond it the ground cover became a mass of twisted scrub and bramble among the rocks which had been tumbled ahead by bulldozers when the clearing was opened.

"Isn't it curious," Julie said, "that they stopped here?"

"It's where all those girls with golden hair got up and went away. Look down there now. See the lights shimmering in the water?"

"And the boat," Julie said. "It's a cabin cruiser with people aboard. See the dinghies?"

"We could have roamed the place at our leisure and not been discovered at all."

"You're bolder than I am, Johnny."

"But not bold enough."

They stood for a moment. Muffled laughter and the sound of voices wafted up from the anchored boat.

"Is he as much older than you as the old lady says he is?"

He was speaking of Jeff, Julie realized. "He's fifteen years older. It's not so much."

"It's a fair difference. Why did you marry him?"

"Because I loved him."

"That's a good reason." Then: "Do you still love him?"

"Yes."

"Then we'd better turn back now. I'm only flesh and blood and you're a very attractive woman."

"Thank you," Julie said and started up the hill at once.

THIRTY-EIGHT

It was almost midnight when they got back to the Willoughby. Julie waited in the car while O'Grady went upstairs with Mrs. Ryan and brought down the fan.

"There'll be more noise than air circulating from this," he said, maneuvering the fan into the back seat.

"It must go back to before air conditioning."

"Before the windmill."

The place where O'Grady was able to park on Fortyfourth Street was almost identical to where he had left Rubinoff while he broke into the shop. He dreaded going in there again, much as he was drawn to the company of the girl, and much as he loathed the thought of going home. "Will you have a beer with me afterwards at McGowan's? It's a family place."

Julie laughed and said, "We'll see." She laughed, but she was on tenterhooks herself. She opened the door and lit the way through while he brought the fan. He closed the door behind him with his heel.

"In here on the desk, for now," Julie said.

"It's better on the floor tilting up. And you must never touch it while it's running."

"Any place," Julie said.

He set it on the floor alongside the desk. He was caught then looking at the wall where the picture had hung. "You've moved the painting."

Julie nodded. She opened the chest drawer and brought his knife to him.

"It showed up after all," he said.

Julie wiped her hands in the towel before throwing it in the wastebasket, a gesture not lost on him. He could begin the lies now and swear the knife must have been stolen, and commiserate with her if she told him the place had been broken into. But she knew. He could tell from her eyes when she caught him looking at the empty wall. He did not want to demean himself, telling lies she would know were lies. But how much did she know? Ginni had said she was having a drink with her to see the painting before she gave it up. He longed to be free of the whole thing, aye, even the money. And especially Ginni. But he had a tiger by the tail.

Instead of pocketing the knife, he set it down on the coffee table, and sat down himself, his hands between his legs, and just looked at it.

"Shall I put on some water and make a cup of tea?" Julie said.

"That would be a great kindness."

He turned his chair where he could watch her. He began to feel that she knew everything, just the calmness of her, and maybe the kindness. But she couldn't: a woman like her, and with a husband in the position hers was, would have long since gone to the F.B.I. What she knew was derogatory only of Johnny O'Grady. A tremor of anger. With himself for not knowing false in a woman from true. And if he didn't know that, how did he know she hadn't already gone to the F.B.I. and was maybe now working in concert with them? When she went to the desk and twisted the neck of the lamp to focus it as though about to begin an inquisition, fear sent a cold chill over him.

But Julie turned the lamp to where it would not shine in either of their faces, and sat down across the table from him. "Johnny, I wonder if you know the story of a painting that was stolen from the National Gallery in London by an Irishman many years ago. I think he was a member of the I.R.A. He wanted to take it back to Ireland where he believed it belonged."

"You've got it wrong," he said, and had to pause to overcome that instant of fear. He took a deep breath and then dredged his memory for the incident she was talking about. "He got into the gallery all right, but they caught him before he got out. And the painting's still there, for all the agitation there was to make them restore it to the Irish people. It's a story I heard a long time ago and I may have it wrong myself, but that's the gist of it. You might trust me to remember the derogatory part."

She gave him a little twist of a smile. "Is the Dublin museum called the National Gallery of Ireland?"

"It is. A lovely old building. I remember the white staircases going up and around."

"And the collection?"

"What would I know about the collection, Julie? I was there for a patriotic occasion. What are you getting at, girl?"

"The same thing as the I.R.A. man—how rich the London Gallery was in comparison. *Is* in comparison."

"There can't be much comparison. Ireland's a poor country altogether."

They sat in silence, looking at one another and then away, until Julie said, "Shall we talk about your knife and how it got here and why?"

"I'd rather not." Then, after a second or two: "Is the place bugged?"

Julie shook her head. "Not to my knowledge."

"They wouldn't tell you, well."

By *they* she assumed he meant the F.B.I. He was so close to an admission. Or was he? A wrong word now would be disastrous. But she was so far out on the tightrope, she could not now get safely back either. "Or about Ginni? We could talk about Ginni. She called me. I'm invited to the party at her mother's on Saturday night. I intend to go. She's very clever."

"Too clever by far." His eyes narrowed.

"I'd hate to have her for an enemy," Julie said. "I'm not smart in the way she is."

"You know, I've never seen her in the company of another woman."

Julie's hands were moist with the tension. He had admitted knowing Ginni. The building was very quiet. Somewhere overhead a toilet flushed. O'Grady's eyes, starting at the ceiling, seemed to follow the sound to where it finally died in the depths beneath her own bathroom. Julie looked around at the kettle as it came to life on the electric plate.

O'Grady, too, looked around. "My mother used to say, 'Johnny, will you go and see if the kettle has started to sing?' "

Julie was halfway across the room when she swung back. "Suppose the National Gallery of Ireland had a very important work of art which was stolen and smuggled out of the country to someone willing to pay a lot of money just to have it for himself. And suppose you found out about it, what would you do?"

He ran his tongue over dry lips, only there was no spittle in his mouth either. "Give us the tea, girl, for Christ's dear sake."

"What would you do?"

"If it was in my power I'd see that it went back safe."

Julie poured the water over the teabags in the two mugs and brought them to the table.

"And I'd want to punish the perpetrators."

"Skip that part," Julie said.

He plunged the bag up and down in the mug. Julie took the bag from him and threw it along with her own into the wastebasket. O'Grady took a mouthful of the scalding tea. He set the mug down carefully. "Are we talking about this fellow at Maiden's End—Campbell?"

"Are we?"

He shrugged. "You know more than I do, I shouldn't wonder."

"Johnny, if we could get the drawing back safely to where it came from—listen to me carefully now—and if we could get the money as well—I'd be willing to give my share to the National Gallery of Ireland—anonymously. Oh, boy. I do mean anonymously. But if we could do that, would you be willing to help?"

"Do you mind saying that whole thing over again?"

Julie repeated the proposal in much the same way.

"Who is *we?*"

"I can't tell you that, but I give you my word it is not the police or the F.B.I. It's not any law-enforcement agency at all."

"Aren't you taking a bit of a chance, telling me this?"

"You bet. But you've been taking chances too."

"Haven't I? And mucking up on one or two."

"I know."

"Then why take chances with a *gobeen* like me?"

"I'm not sure myself," Julie said. "We'll figure that out later."

"After all I went through getting the bloody thing out of one country and into this," he said thoughtfully. "I've never done anything like it before—except for the guns and that was different—and won't ever again, to be sure, if I get out of this alive."

"How come this time?"

"Well, I told myself it was for one thing, the money for Ireland, but it wasn't altogether that by any means. I don't think I want to be naming names. I'd feel queer about that. And I've two hulking lads in the house with me now I never seen before. They're over here to collect their share. I don't suppose they mean great harm, but they're greedy bastards. All the same, I'd like to see them get home safe."

"And Ginni?"

"I'd like to see her safely in hell, if you want the truth."

"Everybody gets home safe," Julie said, and then laughed at what she had said; and in relief.

He grunted and took a great mouthful of tea. He wiped his mouth with the back of his hand. "How did you get onto it?"

"I took *Scarlet Night* to a man I knew who collects paintings to see what he thought of it, and the first thing he asked was if he could reframe it."

"He didn't like the frame." O'Grady was amused, or as close to it as he had been for a while: Ginni who prided herself on her taste. "It must have been quite a shock to him to discover the . . . thing."

"It was a shock to me too."

"Can you think what it would do to that poor benighted fool, Ralph Abel?"

"The almost forgotten man," Julie said.

"Isn't there a fairy tale about the little tailor who killed seven at one blow, is it?"

Julie nodded.

O'Grady said: "Suppose I blew the whistle on the whole thing and Rubinoff backed out before the last step?"

"Then I *would* have to go to the F.B.I., and the only one standing clear would be the man who was willing to pay five hundred thousand dollars for a stolen drawing."

"Six hundred thousand dollars. Does it look worth it to you? An illuminated manuscript I could understand, the Book of Kells, say . . ."

"Johnny, I was going to use the Book of Kells as an example to try and persuade you."

"If anyone laid a hand on that I'd turn Arab and chop it off. All right then. Tell me where, when, and what I'm to do."

THIRTY-NINE

Romano sat, his hands on the edge of the desk, palm to palm, as in prayer. "It was an appalling chance to take, Miss Julie. I underestimated your recklessness."

"I waited until I was sure. It helped, having his knife— and the Book of Kells for an example."

"I distrust sentimental alliances."

"I thought we agreed we might need him."

"Forgive me, dear girl, but I don't think you have any idea what or whom we may need. Furthermore, I don't believe you think so either. Or have you arrived at a modus operandi? In which case, pray, share it with Alberto and me. Unless we are to be dispensed with."

She had not expected this kind of reaction. She had rather expected to be congratulated. "It just happened, Mr. Romano. I knew I could bring him over to our side and I did it. I'm not trying to run the show. I know I couldn't if I wanted to."

The Little King ruffled his shoulders. "This is my first experience of women's liberation and I'm finding it difficult to absorb." He looked around to where the younger man, his back to them, was working at another desk. "Alberto, say something."

Alberto wasn't all that liberated either, Julie thought. Then he surprised her. "We'll be able to use him, Mr. Romano. Especially if he knows the layout of the place."

Julie wasn't about to say how limited O'Grady's knowledge of its layout was.

"You are both making an assumption I am not ready to accept: suppose Campbell is not the collector?" He pounded the desk for emphasis. "On top of failure, you commit trespass. Better the F.B.I. today."

Julie said: "I won't turn *Scarlet Night* over to Rubinoff until we're sure."

"I hope you are given that option. Do you know what I believe, Miss Julie? You find Alberto and me alien creatures. You're afraid of us, however fascinating this exotic tower of ours. Am I right?"

"In a way."

"Good! We have retained some degree of autonomy at least. But this O'Grady—is he a . . . a comfort to you?"

Julie was devastated by Romano's reprimand, the biting sarcasm, and she was tired, having slept badly. Furthermore, she was beginning to feel the strain of not being able to confide in Jeff: it was different when he was out of the country. She burst into tears. Women's Lib, oh, yes.

"Alberto!" Romano got up and fled into the studio.

Alberto flung himself around her helplessly. He offered a paper napkin, having no handkerchief. Finally, he said: "How would you like to wash up for lunch?"

"Do I look that awful?"

He blushed. "I thought you might like to get off by yourself."

Julie smiled weakly and shook her head. She went to the studio door which Romano had left open. He was looking over a tray of bottles and containers, a tuft of cotton in his hand. "I'm sorry, Mr. Romano," she called from the doorway.

He continued with what he was doing. He turned and dabbed at a painting on an easel, then gently stroked the spot in tiny, circular motions. If it were something human standing there, you might have thought he was wiping its tears. "Is the deluge over?"

"Yes."

"Alberto is right. You had better compose yourself for lunch. I shall introduce you as my niece if that does not offend you. If Mr. Kliegman suggests that you too might sit for him, don't be adamant either way. I think it unlikely unless he is in need of money. Women are not among his more successful subjects." He dropped the cotton into a wastebasket and came toward her. "You do look peaked, my dear. Mr. O'Grady is obviously a great conversationalist to have kept you up so late."

Julie was repairing her lipstick in the guest bathroom when it occurred to her: Could it be that Romano was jealous?

Leonard Kliegman might be the most popular painter around these days, but Julie found him insufferable, an egomaniac, and a fool. Anybody who could sit there telling Romano about the gangsters whose girl friends he had done portraits of—Romano had been wrong about his painting women, or maybe he wasn't, maybe he'd seen the portraits—had to be a little short on judgment. He kept dropping mobster nicknames as if he were Jimmy Breslin. And from the minute Alberto brought in the *gazpacho* and served it from the sideboard, Kliegman played to him, talking louder when he was offstage. Romano sat in an attitude of a porcelain buddha as though time were eternally his. When Kliegman stopped in the middle of a sentence, however, and asked his host what he should call him, it was a great moment.

The Little King suggested disingenuously, "Mister Romano?"

It didn't faze Kliegman.

Julie concentrated on the food: after the *gazpacho,* filet of sole—Bolognese, Romano informed her when she asked, cooked with wine, herbs, and parmesan cheese, browned under the broiler at the last minute.

It was during the sole that Romano said: "You know G.T. Campbell, don't you, Mr. Kliegman?"

Kliegman opened his eyes a little wider. They were half closed most of the time. "I've done him, yes."

"At his home at Maiden's End?"

"I've been there. It's grotesque. He has no taste. I hope he's not a friend of yours."

"I was more interested in your opinion of his collection," Romano said.

Kliegman flopped his hand at his host. "It's an exhausting collection, absolutely debilitating."

"Because of its single theme?" Romano suggested.

"Of course. No matter how many instruments there are

in the orchestra, if they don't play a different tune now and then, we must go mad."

Romano chortled. So did Julie. Not that it mattered what she did: Kliegman really believed she was Romano's niece.

Romano said, "But you must admit, he has some good things. The Courbet, for example."

"Yes," reluctantly. "And the Tintoretto is very good. Important."

"What about his Eakins?"

"I don't like Eakins. He's so sincere."

Romano did not contradict. "Campbell has some of your things, doesn't he?"

"Abominably hung. He's a segregationist."

Julie thought she was going to have to figure that one out. But Romano got it right away. "Ah, yes. He has your *Musicians.*"

"He has my *Harlem Musketeers,* which is a masterpiece."

"Of course, of course. I'd forgotten where that was."

"Which makes my point, doesn't it?"

Romano nodded, his expression sympathetic. It was lost on the guest of honor, for Alberto had come in with the salad. Romano's and Julie's eyes met. It was an electric moment.

Romano turned a bland gaze on Kliegman and said, "I wonder if you have an opinion of his Degas?"

"Ha! In the first place, Mr. Romano, the final painting of *The Young Spartans,* even as it hangs in the National Gallery, is one of the most static pieces of art ever allowed out of a painter's *atelier.* It is small wonder he kept it to himself most of his life. And in the second place, I doubt the authenticity of Campbell's sketch."

"Interesting," Romano murmured. "But *he* believes in it?"

"Oh, utterly. He's one of those people who must believe in the authenticity of everything he owns. Otherwise, it devaluates the dollar."

Romano smiled. "I will show you my collection after lunch, and then perhaps we shall talk business." He turned to Julie: "The dessert is especially for you, my dear."

It was oranges in Grand Marnier, sprinkled with shreds of the peel and glazed.

FORTY

At three-thirty that afternoon, Friday, with Alberto at the tape recorder and Julie on the extension phone, Romano reached G. T. Campbell. He had just come in off the water.

"It must be beautiful up there this afternoon," Romano said.

"Too damn calm. Only thing moving out there is the tide and you can't fill your sails with that. Your name's Romano. Do I know you?"

"Probably not, Mr. Campbell, although, like you, I am a collector of some breadth. I have been persuaded by a young scholar friend to help him put together a Degas exhibition for Los Angeles. I understand you have one of the earliest sketches for *The Young Spartans*."

"Well, yes."

"I wonder if you would be kind enough to see Mr. Scotti this weekend. Alberto Scotti . . . If you haven't heard of him, believe me, you will."

"I think I've heard of him," Campbell said.

"He's flying on to London the first of the week. Otherwise I wouldn't press him on you over the weekend. Is Sunday evening possible?"

"Definitely not, Mr. Scotti."

"Romano. It's Mr. Scotti I'm sending to see you."

"Sunday's out from, say, noon on. No. Let's say Sunday's out, period."

"Perhaps you would suggest a convenient hour?"

"Is he an early riser?"

Romano, off the telephone: "Are you an early riser, Scotti?" Then: "Any time convenient for you, Mr. Campbell."

"How's eight-thirty breakfast tomorrow morning? Put

161

him on the phone so's I can tell him how to get in here. I keep this place pretty well locked up."

Julie counted the clicks to be sure Campbell had rung off before she hung up the extension. She returned to the office. Romano was chuckling in self-satisfaction. He said: "Now I am able to believe." He looked up at Julie. "So, my dear, our fantasy has come true: His Degas is a *Young Spartans* sketch pedigreed by Edmund Schoen. And Mr. Campbell does seem to want his name in a catalogue."

"And Sunday's out," Julie said. "That's the day he expects to fork over six hundred thousand in cash for *Scarlet Night*. Wow."

Alberto said: "Mr. Romano, I don't know very much about Degas and I never studied at the Actors Forum. Isn't there somebody else you could send up there tomorrow morning?"

"Certainly not. You look the part, by which I mean—you know what I mean. And there is a tape of my conversation with the curator who gave *me* an education on Degas. You will memorize that transcription. What is of equal importance, we must get hold of Andy Davis again and have him instruct you on the preliminaries at least of organizing this exhibit. You should probably go equipped to impress him with the names of, say, a half-dozen private collectors whose paintings you expect to have in the show. I shall provide those for you."

"Thanks," Alberto said as though for not much. "And what if Rubinoff shows up for breakfast with us?"

"I can almost certainly assure you that he won't. But if he does, he will discourage Campbell's loaning his *Young Spartans*, not wanting its provenance questioned too closely. But the grounds on which he will object will concern reliability of the sponsors, transport, insurance, etcetera. Which is why we must get you to Andy Davis at once. The weekend is upon us. And I don't suppose we should overlook the real purpose for which you are going: to put it in the vernacular, to case the joint. If I have faith in you, Alberto, why have you so little in yourself?"

"Because I know what I don't know."

"Believe me, that is the best place to start. Do you realize that not having even laid eyes on you, Mr. Campbell provided us with the most important information of all: how to get on the estate whether or not the watchman is on duty? I was touched at so much trust." He sat in silent musing for a few seconds. "Six hundred thousand dollars. I wonder what denominations . . . and what sort of transport Rubinoff will be using. Your Irishman may prove of some worth in that matter, Miss Julie."

Julie said, "Mr. Romano, isn't it time I called Rubinoff?"

"Yes." Slowly but emphatically.

In the silence they could all but hear one another's heartbeats. They were about to set the countercaper rolling.

"The Maude Sloan Gallery would close at five on Sunday. Shall I tell him to come to my house at five?"

Romano rocked back and forth gently and nodded.

"I suppose I'd better ask him for five hundred dollars even though I only paid a hundred."

"In cash, Miss Julie. Otherwise, he is likely to stop payment on the check Monday morning."

"I can't do that. That would make him suspicious."

"I understand. But it's a pity."

Julie made the call from the studio.

"I'll see if he's in," the secretary said. "He may have left for the weekend."

Rubinoff was not far. "Mrs. Hayes," he said as though trying to remember. "Ah, yes. *Scarlet Night*. I wondered if I'd hear from you again."

"Are you still interested in it?"

"Oh, yes," he said, but the tone was casual. "Unless of course you are thinking of making money on it."

Julie was much too uptight to play games. "Five hundred dollars, Mr. Rubinoff. You can have it Sunday, if you want to come to my home for it about five or so."

"That is inconvenient, Mrs. Hayes. Why not bring it over here this afternoon? Or tomorrow. The gallery will be open even if I'm away."

"Because I made up my mind to keep Ralph's painting either until I heard from him—which I haven't . . ." She had to catch a little breath . . . "Or until the show would have closed in the normal course of events."

"Really," he said.

She hated him and it helped. "But if you want to let it

go for a week or two, that's all right with me. Only I'll be away next week."

"Make it at six on Sunday and I'll be there. The address, please?"

She gave him the address on Sixteenth Street.

She put the phone down carefully and wiped her palms, one hand in the other.

Romano stood in the doorway. "Bravo!"

"Now I've got to call Ginni and play it straight all the way, invite her for a drink and a last look at *Scarlet Night*."

"*Bravissimo.*"

FORTY-ONE

Ginni arrived at O'Grady's at six-thirty. Steph and Tommy groveled when she wafted through the door. And she was a vision, O'Grady admitted, for them who could stand the light. She wore a shimmery gown of bluish-gray fluff with silver slippers and a purse to match. He suspected the earrings were genuine sapphire. What would keep her from harm in this neighborhood: they wouldn't know her kind from a whofe. Beneath the makeup was the first scratching of crowsfeet at the corners of her eyes. In time she would surely look like her mother and O'Grady wished it on her at the earliest possible moment. She draped herself on the daybed, the boys at her feet dramatizing their experiences in New York.

She turned to O'Grady and translated something of her own choice: "You left them alone last night, Johnny."

"They're not children. I had an engagement of my own."

"With whom?" She smiled coyly, as though she could persuade him now that she was jealous.

"Tell me where you were and I'll tell you," he said, having a story ready that he hoped not to tell.

"I danced all night," she said and didn't want to know about him at all. "Has Rubinoff ever been here before?"

"Never. It'll tickle that delicate nose of his coming up the stairs."

"You used to be such a good sport, Johnny. What's happened to the pixie in you?"

"He's become an old dwarf. I've aged with this caper, that's the truth."

"Poor darling." She leaped from the couch and came to him. "I should never have given you all that responsibility." She cradled his face in her scented hands.

He caught one of them and held it to his mouth while he twirled his tongue around its palm.

She let him have the other hand across his face, a resounding whack which put everything into proper perspective.

Rubinoff arrived, breathless from climbing the stairs—or from holding his breath while he climbed them. He kissed Ginni on both cheeks. What a sugarplum of a fellow, O'Grady thought. A ripe olive would be more like it. He shook hands with the boys and O'Grady and they all adjourned to the kitchen where there were a table and four chairs. O'Grady went into the bedroom and swept a pile of dirty clothes from the chair and carried it into the kitchen. Ginni had taken the head of the table, Rubinoff the other end, and the boys one side.

"Get the beer, Tommy," O'Grady said. Tommy jumped up and went to the refrigerator. Steph brought glasses from the cupboard.

"They're not your servants, you know," Ginni said to him.

"Nor I yours, madam." He sat.

Rubinoff was craning his neck to look the place over. "I think this is the room we had better use. Those window shades will have to be drawn all the way, which means the windows must be closed."

"We'll suffocate," Ginni said.

"Maybe we should go to your mother's," O'Grady said.

"Very funny."

Rubinoff said, "Johnny, why don't you rent an air conditioner? Perhaps you will want to buy one? You'll be able to afford it."

"I will, won't I?" He chuckled and that seemed to provoke the mirth in all of them. Everyone around the table chortled for a second or two in pleasurable anticipation of their approaching affluence. Ginni reached for his hand

and squeezed it and O'Grady felt terrible although he kept on laughing.

Rubinoff explained that neither his office nor his apartment provided sufficient privacy, with the security people at one and the doorman at the other.

"I understand," O'Grady said. He had never before appreciated the privacy of a West Side tenement.

"I should arrive here sometime between nine and ten on Sunday night. But you must not worry if I'm a little late. There may be social amenities I will have to observe."

Ginni translated the date and the hour for the boys. That glint returned that he had seen in their eyes when she spoke of the money on the day of their arrival. Not a thought of the treasure they had stolen from a country where the people were even poorer than the Irish. O'Grady's peace with himself was restored.

"I shall have four suitcases," Rubinoff went on. "And I can't be expected to manage getting them up here myself."

"Will they fit in the Porsche?"

"I've rented a station wagon for the weekend. I have to deliver pictures out on the Island tomorrow."

"You'd better let me have the make and license number to be watching for it."

"D-A-S 320, a dark red Buick."

"D-A-S," O'Grady repeated. "It's SAD, spelt backwards."

"I wish you hadn't said that. I am superstitious."

"Things like that run to opposites, Rubin," O'Grady reassured him. "I'll make it my job to be on the street watching out for you. I spend hours down there sometimes, hanging around just. I can whistle up for the boys if you have trouble parking."

"That rings true," Ginni said. She was great at evaluating things by the sound of them. "Let's get to the nitty-gritty, the money itself."

"It will be perfectly safe money. Some of it will be bills which have been in circulation; there will be a few packets of twenties. Otherwise, it's all fifties and hundreds. I'm not going to insult my client by counting it there." He paused and cleared his throat. "I believe I've found a courier for you."

"A courier for what?" O'Grady said, taken by surprise.

Ginni said, "Johnny, to bring our money over." She then set about soothing his pride. "You really shouldn't have to do that. You've done so much already."

"You don't trust me."

"I thought you'd be relieved."

"Oh, I am. And I'm sure you are. You'll be the sooner done with me entirely."

"You're so damned right," she said, and tossed her head impatiently.

He had misplayed her again, forgetting for the moment that it didn't matter.

Rubinoff said quietly, "It will cost you twenty percent, Ginni."

"Jesus Christ!"

O'Grady laughed.

Rubinoff looked at him. "I understood you would want to transfer your funds overseas also."

"I'll find my own means of transfer. Here's one boyo who's not going into business with the Mafia."

"Is it the Mafia?" Ginni wanted to know.

"I wouldn't say that. But it's not a question one asks directly under the circumstances."

Without missing a beat she turned to O'Grady. "I don't know. What do you think, Johnny? Is it all that dangerous for you?"

He threw back his head and laughed at the brazenness of her. She gave him her shy, wistful, little-girl smile which, to use a saying of his mother's, would melt the heart of a wheelbarrow.

Rubinoff said, "Why don't you let my man handle half? That will make it worth his while and at the same time reduce the risk for you."

"How do I know he'll ever show up?" Ginni said.

"Mr. Schoen and I have used him before," Rubinoff said mournfully as though his own honor had been questioned. "And I'll be sending money abroad myself for further investment. Perhaps you and I shall do business again?"

"How lovely," Ginni said.

He took a sip of beer and made a face. It was not his beverage. He looked at his watch. "Can we go over the details of our arrangements now? Then I can run you down to Sixteenth Street. I'll wait in the car until you come out. I should like to be perfectly sure."

O'Grady went downstairs with them a few minutes later and watched them drive off in the red station wagon. He called Julie Hayes from the public phone on the corner and told her they were on their way. He started to give her the gist of their plans. She stopped him and gave him a number at which to call her after nine-thirty. "We'd better have a code name for you in case you call me," he said. "The boys are getting smarter by the hour. How about 'Dolly'?"

FORTY-TWO

Julie pushed the buzzer and watched from the door, where she caught her first glimpse of Ginni as she came running up the stairs, her auburn hair flying.

"Hello!" Ginni cried and gave Julie her hand. "It's darling of you to do this. I'm a sentimental slob."

"I don't mind," Julie murmured.

Scarlet Night was visible the instant you walked through the door where Julie had hung it in the dining alcove.

"There you are!" Ginni said, addressing herself to the painting. She cast a surreptitious glance around the rest of the apartment. Julie knew what was going through her mind: *Scarlet Night* in the tiny half-room. It pushed out like a fat woman in an elevator.

"I'll show you where I intended to hang it in a minute," Julie said. "What will you have to drink?"

"Vermouth?"

"I'm not very good at this," Julie said from the bar in the foyer. "Dry or sweet? Or both?"

"Both. You *are* good to know that. On ice if you don't mind." Ginni was running her hand around the frame. Boldly. Lovingly. "Poor Ralph," she said. "He had such high hopes when we were putting his show together. He really deserved better, don't you think?"

"I think so."

"Of course you do. Otherwise . . ." She met Julie face on as she brought the vermouth and her own Perrier. "Why are you giving it up to Rubinoff, Mrs. Hayes?"

"You'll see," Julie said without batting an eye. She led the way into the living room and stood beneath the mantel wall. "This is where I had in mind for it—at first."

Ginni sipped her vermouth and made a slow turn to survey the entire room. She had style, Julie thought, high style, something she greatly admired while not aspiring to it herself. "It is a perfect room," Ginni said, "and you have decided rightly on the mirror." Which still lay on the floor.

"I got carried away by Mr. Abel," Julie said. "And I do like *Scarlet Night*. And we were considering a painting for this wall, but . . ."

"You don't have to tell me," Ginni said. "My father is a collector, but he thinks true art came to an end with the Impressionists, whom he abominates. I bring home things that I wind up hiding in the closet until I can sell them back—or find someone who wants them. . . . You are coming tomorrow night?"

"Yes, though Jeff's away. . . ."

"Come anyway. I'll bet you don't like mob scenes."

"I don't much."

"Then I'll be especially flattered. And there's bound to be somebody there you'll like. I must go. I hope I haven't interfered with your evening? I'd have come earlier, but Mother doesn't want to let me out of her sight when I come to New York."

"I don't blame her," Julie said.

Ginni smiled like a Botticelli madonna. Demure. Beatific. "Bless you." She floated out of the room. She set her glass on the table beneath *Scarlet Night*. "I helped Ralph frame the show," she said. "The framing ought to have been lighter, but I think he had in mind those solid Midwestern farmhouses with oak furniture and roast beef every Sunday and Saturday-night blues." She picked up the glass again and toasted: "*Arrivederci!*"

Julie sat for a while after Ginni left before getting the chicken out of the refrigerator. She held her hand up in front of her: not a tremor. Romano had said that it would not be wise under the developing circumstances for Alberto to accompany her to the party at Maude Sloan's. She didn't want to go alone, but she didn't want to drop out either, not at this point. Then she had an idea. She called the Alexanders.

"Hello." It was Tony, growling.

"This is Julie Hayes, Tony. I got the interview with Sweets Romano."

"I'll be damned. Did he open up?"

"I've been with him every day for the past week."

"His life story, is that it? Once these underworld characters get the right audience—when they trust you . . . I can get you a book contract on it, Julie. You can make some real money."

"Tony, the reason I called tonight: Jeff's in West Virginia and there's a party I want to go to. I wondered if you and Fran are free for an hour or so tomorrow night, would you go with me?" She explained who Maude Sloan was and that the party was for her daughter by an Italian count.

"Has it anything to do with the Romano story?"

"I wouldn't tell you if it did right now, Tony. But you really mustn't mention his name, I mean at Maude Sloan's."

"I shall be delighted to escort you, darling, after which you and I will go on the town and give Gotham something new to talk about. Fran is visiting our daughter this weekend."

Finally Julie ate a few bites of food and then called Jeff before returning to Romano's. It felt very good to tell him what Tony had said. "Even if nothing comes of it," she added.

"Something is bound to come of it," Jeff said emphatically.

FORTY-THREE

Julie arrived at Romano's in time to take the call from Sean O'Grady. It went on the tape and Romano played it instantly. He sat chortling at the part about the Mafia courier, and O'Grady's comment to Julie: "Amn't I glad you got me out of the clutches of that!"

Romano said: "We must arrange to have all his calls come here now so that we'll have the record. And we can use a bit of comic relief."

"In a way he's pathetic."

"I hope so. Obviously you've not spoken of me in generic terms."

"He doesn't know your name even. Only that you've got lots of clout and money, and that you are not the F.B.I. or any police affiliate."

"Did you mention the C.I.A.?"

She didn't think an answer was required.

"Now for the maps. I'm sorry you didn't have dinner with us. There was a touch of garlic in the veal. I hope you won't find it offensive. I've decided we must keep our main forces in the rear to follow as close upon Rubinoff as can be done discreetly. On the chance there may be someone between him and Campbell or another place of rendezvous. I cannot believe it would be on the water, not with four suitcases of money. Too much has been made of that situation in the films. We have maps of the city and the parkways. Michael will refine them in terms of roadway and other hazards. He has driven under stressful circumstances. He will be our principal driver. And here is a walking map of the Palisades Park system. So far as I can judge, it is beautiful in its detail of Maiden's End. I have several copies. By Sunday morning we must have a master copy that is perfect. There will be a list of information we must have—turnabouts, dead ends—of which there seem to be a number—and so forth. We must have information about police surveillance in the

area. I suspect it is impressive. We also need to know
Campbell's security system. It must connect directly with
police headquarters in the area. We shall also want to
know conditions of light. If Rubinoff proposes to be back
in New York as early as nine o'clock it means the whole
tarantella will be taking place in twilight. Which can be
both an advantage and a disadvantage. There is also the
matter of Sunday traffic returning to the city.

"I can think of no better assignment for your O-Johnny-
O than with the police themselves. I have in mind his
going to the township headquarters in the morning and
getting their advice. He can say that he's about to apply
for a job as guard on the Campbell estate. Do you think
he can carry that off?"

"He's a good talker," Julie said.

"Yes, I rather thought he must be," Romano said dryly.
"Have him outside his building at ten minutes to five
tomorrow morning. Or at a place arranged between the
two of you. Michael will pick you up first, then him. I
want everyone in this room at five."

"Five A.M."

"Do you remember what Campbell looks like, Miss
Julie?"

"It's crazy, but I don't. I think he's tall, but all I really
remember is his ankles. You know, no socks."

"No conversation with him, not even 'It's nice to have
met you, Mrs. Hayes'?"

"No."

"Then he wouldn't remember you either?"

"I don't think he'd even remember Jeff."

"Good. And since your Irish protégé assures us that
Rubinoff will be going off in a different direction tomorrow, I suggest that a little bigamy won't hurt you for a
day. Alberto will take his wife along and take for granted
that she was invited."

FORTY-FOUR

How well did she know Jeff, when you came right down to it? And she'd been married to him for over four years. Julie glanced across the seat at Alberto, who seemed to be staring at the back of Michael's head. Michael looked a lot different in the driver's seat of a rented Oldsmobile. For one thing, you got to see his face in the mirror now and then. Which wasn't exactly a treat. Squinty eyes and a white scar on his cheek. He looked like a mug shot.

"Julie Scotti," she said aloud. "It doesn't sound bad."

Alberto looked at her and smiled forlornly.

"Hey, didn't you ever want to be an actor?" He really looked like one, playing a professor—dark suit, white shirt, striped tie. Actually, he looked like a priest.

"Doesn't everyone at some time?"

"All right," Julie said. "This is our big audition. We'll let him do most of the talking. I've got a feeling he does talk a lot."

"Hey, you two," Michael said, looking at them through the mirror, "get together back there. You're practically newlyweds. Although from my point of view, as far as the caper goes, it was better the way it was. This Bonnie-and-Clyde stuff, forget it. It don't work that way. They couldn't've pulled off half the jobs if they stopped to shmooze along the way like that."

"Where did we get married?" Alberto wanted to know.

"Some place we've both been."

"Take Atlantic City," Michael said. "Nobody's going to ask you about Atlantic City." Then: "Remember, you got to get me in the house. Give me an hour outdoors, then get me in. I don't want no forget-me-nots. Amateurs forget the little things. The big things they remember."

"You're not a little thing, Michael," Julie said.

"Let him take you out on his yacht. Relax. Enjoy yourselves." And a few minutes later: "Here we are, Exit

173

Four. Right on time. Don't give me directions, Mrs. Scotti. I got to know I can do it myself."

He could have driven the labyrinth. At the intercom box he announced: "Mr. and Mrs. Scotti."

Giving their host time to set another place at the breakfast table.

The wrought-iron gate opened at the middle. "Jeez," Michael said. "Just like Sing Sing."

They drove between two vast lawns sparsely populated by magnificent trees which nobody in the car could identify. Except Michael of the pines: "Them's all different kinds of Christmas trees." A huge, wide-spanned tree with coppery leaves and a massive trunk had sent some of its branches back into the ground as though for balance. The house ahead was picture-book Shakespeare, timbers and plaster.

"Or Burgundian," Alberto said. "I've seen such houses in that part of France."

"Eight entries on the first floor. Want to bet?" Michael said. "Maybe he's got a nice fat lady cook in the kitchen, and when yous all go out, she'll take me on a tour of the place." Michael's fantasy. "A house like this has got to have a female cook, know what I mean?"

"I agree," Julie said.

"Ever notice? When the men in this country started doing the cooking, it's been downhill ever since."

Julie realized he was chattering now to keep them loose.

As they neared the house, he said, "Here comes the man with all the money." Campbell was coming around the side of the house to meet them. "He's walking barefoot. Wouldn't you think he could afford shoes?"

"Please shut up, Michael," Julie said.

She did remember Campbell, seeing him. It was over three years ago that they had met, and she was glad that in those days she'd been wearing her hair much shorter and had had a tendency in the kind of company she was with that night to fold up in the deepest chair in the room and let her eyes do the socializing.

Campbell opened the car door on Julie's side and gave her his hand. "Well, now, it's just damn nice of you folks to come out this early in the morning." He gave her a good strong assist out of the car. "Best part of the day, of course." He was tall and lean, with a small head, a lot of laugh wrinkles, and very keen blue eyes; his hair was cut short and sunbleached. You could almost smell the obsession with health. Not in a million years could she imagine this man doing business with Rubinoff. The thought hit her: what if he didn't?

"I've seen you before," he said, smiling and poking a finger in Julie's direction. "You a movie actress?"

"I used to be a model," Julie said. One of the few things she had never tried. Lie Number One.

Alberto was coming around the car.

"I always read the ads," their host said, "especially for department stores. Down home we got Neiman-Marcus. Ever hear of it?"

"Of course."

Campbell offered his hand to Alberto. "Nice to meet you, Mr. Scotti. When I was a kid they called me Scotty, my ancestors being Scotch. My father made a great issue of that, his father coming over from Scotland and starting the business. Named my brother Andrew—after Andrew Carnegie."

Michael had gotten out to open the door for Alberto.

Campbell said: "Driver, why don't you go around through the courtyard and park by the garage? Then you go in the kitchen and introduce yourself to my Nellie. She'll give you a real down-home breakfast."

Oh God, Julie thought. She liked him.

"I should've told you all to come informal," he said, leading the way to the river side of the house. Julie was pretty informal, white slacks and a black-and-white-striped blouse. "You're going on some place from here, right?"

"We have plenty of time, Mr. Campbell," Alberto said and took off his tie, folded it, and put it in his pocket.

"Just call me G.T. Everybody does. I hardly know myself what it stands for. I'll bet when you say L.B.J. these days, you got to stop and think. Let me have your coat, Mr. Scotti."

"Al or Albert," Alberto said.

Julie did have to stop and think. Campbell, grinning, turned and poked his finger at her. "Lyndon Baines. Say now, how would the two of you like to have a nice swim before breakfast? Can't you see the pool from here, not supposed to, not from anywhere. I don't like swimsuits.

Just run on down and I'll be waiting for you when you come up. You'll see the towels down there."

"I'd love to," Julie said, "but Alberto mustn't. He's got some infection the doctor says he mustn't swim with." She knew Alberto would blush at the thought of the skinny-dip.

"You never know what you're going to pick up when you travel," Campbell said. "I got myself the doggonedest set of scabs from a Frog barber a few years ago."

Oh-oh. "You mean in France?" Julie said.

"Paris, France, yes, ma'am. The land of Louis Pasteur."

Alberto said, "Why don't we have a look at your Degas, G.T., while Julie swims? You don't mind, my dear?"

Julie took off down the path through a garden of rose bushes, more kinds of roses than she knew existed. She had a lot of looking to do while they discussed that Frog painter Degas. A steep drop in the land did indeed shut the house from sight. The pool was Olympic size, the river view and the view from the river blocked out by a dense wall of shrubbery. Julie dropped her clothes at the edge of the pool and slipped into silken warm water. She swam several lengths and would have given a lot to stay in longer.

She dressed and walked down the steps from the pool to the dock. There were carriage lanterns on either side of the walk, which were the lights she and O'Grady had seen reflected in the water. On the opposite shore houses that looked like castles stood adjacent to industrial sprawl. Then in the quiet, a clear ringing of church bells came from across the water. There were small boats moving on the river, and a barge in tow to a tug a tenth its size.

Campbell's dock went out perhaps a hundred feet. Two dinghies drifted on a pulley arrangement. A cabin cruiser lay at anchor to the south, an unrigged sailboat to the north, and beyond there was a vast spread of green marshes; above that, landside, rose the golden clearing which she and O'Grady had explored Thursday night. The fence came well out into the water. She noted these things because that was what she was there for. Romano wanted the entire picture. It would include a tide table for Sunday. To the south and not very distant the Palisades rose in majestic splendor.

As Julie was starting up the steps, a big Irish setter waddled down to meet her. He nuzzled her hand. She kept the fence in view all the way up. With its two strands of barbed wire tilted toward the park, the only thing likely to climb it was the roses. There were no breaks, no gates except the one she and O'Grady had come to by way of the park.

Approaching the house she saw Michael limping around the terrace from one door to the next, as though he were lost and trying to find his way in. The instant the dog saw him it charged, its ears out like a bat's wings and the promise of fangs in its bark. Julie whistled and called, "Here, Champ. Here, boy." The dog reversed itself and trotted back to her. "Champ" was the name of a dog in her childhood.

Michael moved off toward the service wing of the building.

The dog led Julie through the open French doors and trotted across the large sitting room. He disappeared into a room alongside which the stairs went up to the second landing. The Courbet was over the mantel, and across the room, under a light, was a life-size bullfight. The blood streaming down the beast's neck looked warm. Along the paneled staircase wall were the unmistakable flashy athletes of Leonard Kliegman.

Julie stuck her head through the doorway of a small study. The scene shook her. The two men were examining a folio on the desk, but beyond them a walk-in vault stood wide open.

"Hello," Julie said.

They straightened as though she had caught them at something obscene. Dirty pictures? Surely not.

"You're back!" Alberto said.

Campbell made ready to close the folio if she came nearer.

Not for anything would she have taken another step forward. "I wonder if I could use a bathroom, Mr. Campbell?"

"They're all over the place. Top of the stairs is the closest." They didn't even ask if she had enjoyed her swim.

When Julie returned they were waiting for her outside the study door. She glimpsed a floor-to-ceiling painting of a juggler which now camouflaged the vault door.

On the way out to the terrace where the table was set beneath a red-and-white-striped awning, Campbell said, "Your husband tells me you'd enjoy a little run upriver this morning. It's the best time of day to see the cliffs. We'll go to Bear Mountain and back. How's that?"

"Lovely."

Campbell held a chair for Julie. The honeydew melon was gorgeous. But it wasn't quite so sweet when Campbell picked up on previous conversation between him and Alberto. He said, "If I ever caught that little Jew clown ripping me off, you better believe I'd be his last rip-off."

A little pulse beat showed at Alberto's temple. He said, "You're wrong, G.T., if you think I'm questioning the work. It would take me much more time than I have today to arrive at a positive opinion."

"Do you know this dealer, Schoen?"

"Not personally."

"Careful fellow, aren't you?"

"It's the nature of my work."

"I'm going to be interested in Rubin's reaction when I tell him about loaning the Degas."

Alberto shook his head.

Campbell said, "I know, I know. You haven't said for sure yet that you want it. I just want to try it on him. He's got a way of drooping his eyelids if something isn't kosher. Mind you, I trust the man. I *do*. And I'll tell you why: money. My old man taught me one thing: never trust a man you can't buy and pay for, and when you can't afford him any longer, get rid of him, because you ain't going to be able to trust him any longer. I understand Rubinoff. He's American. It's this international operator, Schoen. He's smart. But maybe he's too smart."

Campbell scraped the bottom of his melon. He pushed the plate aside. "It's not just the Degas I'm talking about."

Julie avoided looking at Alberto.

A handsome young black woman cleared the table and brought Eggs Benedict from a cart. Campbell brightened up. Julie caught an exchange of looks between him and the girl that was pure lechery.

"I've been doing something interesting lately," Campbell started, on another tack. "It's a kind of speculation— like drilling for offshore oil. As you can see from my collection, I'm a sports freak—anything to do with athletics . . ." To Alberto he repeated: "I said anything, Al."

Alberto laughed obediently. From the throat up. They *had* been looking at dirty pictures! Rare and priceless, no doubt. But why show them to Alberto? Ah, but of course, a friend of Romano, whom Campbell would have checked out immediately after the phone call from him. But why wouldn't he have checked out Alberto? Simple, Julie. Because he figured Romano owned Alberto the way he owned Rubinoff. . . . And did he?

"I've been assigning living painters to do subjects I find interesting. Only they got to paint them the way I want to see them."

"Ghost painters," Julie said, and could have bitten her tongue.

Campbell looked at her as though she'd spat up on the tablecloth. "Anything wrong with that?"

Alberto, a husband of infinite patience, said: "My dear, that's how it was with some of the greatest painters —and musicians—they composed to the specifications of their patrons." He was a better actor than she was.

"Exactly," Campbell said.

Julie stabbed the yolk of an egg. She certainly looked forward to that trip up the Hudson.

FORTY-FIVE

The desk sergeant introduced O'Grady to Patrolman Donnelly, and explained, "He's applying for a guard job over at the Campbell estate."

Donnelly was a young officer with plump rosy cheeks, a dimpled chin, and the handclasp of an orangutan.

"No reason he can't ride with you this morning, is there?" the sergeant said.

"Be glad of the company."

"I'm much obliged to you," O'Grady said to the senior officer, who had been cordiality itself. "Maybe some day I'll be able to do you a good turn."

"That's what we're counting on, my friend. He's got our boys running their asses off with that security system of his. Sometimes I think he short-circuits on purpose."

"We can't complain, Sarge. He's given us and the Fire Company more damn athletic equipment—you'd think we were going in for the Olympic games."

In the car, Donnelly said: "You know anything about the Gimpel Burglar Alarm System?"

"Not much."

"Remind me when we get back and I'll give you a copy of the manual. I don't know how much good it's going to do you. These electronic things are tricky. He's got a vault in the house and every once in a while when he opens it, he trips the gate system. But the way that's timed, if somebody doesn't pass through the eye in fifty seconds, it closes itself, but at the same time it sets off the alert at headquarters, and we have to check it out. Understand what I'm saying?"

"I do and I don't. I'll catch on from the book." He felt himself lucky to be able to read the points of a compass. "Why doesn't Campbell read the book himself?"

Donnelly laughed. "I wouldn't ask him that if I were you."

"He's that kind, is he?"

"You don't cross him. As long as you say yes to him you'll be all right. You'd think I knew him to hear me talking. I only saw him once in my life, the day they found the dynamite. I'll tell you about that in a minute."

Donnelly paused to respond to a radio signal. He continued over the chatter on the police band: "There wasn't much publicity about it. They're a great lot at Maiden's End for protecting their privacy. Anyway, the state police got a call a couple of weeks back from a man identifying himself as a priest. He'd been told there was some two hundred sticks of dynamite buried three years ago in the woods not far from Campbell's gate, the stuff vented and the place marked. But by now it was nitroglycerine, see, and volatile as hell. They got the Army Ordnance experts out and they dealt with it. I'll show you the place when we pass there. We had the whole area cordoned off, evacuated every house. Two companies of fire apparatus stood by. It turned out to be a hell of a good party. The firemen's auxiliary brought sandwiches and somebody thought to bring out a couple of bottles of vodka. But what I started to tell you, right in the middle of the operation, Campbell drove up in his limousine, got out, and started to give orders. Two state troopers took him by the elbows and marched him back to his car and told him not to leave it. Everybody standing around with cups in their hands gave a cheer for the troopers. But I'm going to tell you, it was a damned frightening business and nobody'd want to go through it again."

"Did they find out what it was there for?"

"They found out where it came from—stolen from a sewage project upstate. But nobody seems to know who stole it, or what they intended to do with it, or why they left it there till now. You don't know with these radical groups. There's a new one in the papers every day."

"The dynamite was all in one place, was it?" O'Grady said.

"What was found was all in one place. Whether or not they found all that was stolen back then—that could be something else."

O'Grady thought about it. He thought about Julie Hayes and himself cavorting around the skirts of the estate. "By God," he said, "I'd hate to put my foot in a pothole like that."

FORTY-SIX

Romano sat at the head of the table and beamed with pleasure. "I can hardly believe that every man and lady of you has done so well. And may I say to a nautical man, welcome aboard, O'Grady."

"Thank you, sir. I've never been aboard anything like it before in my life."

"Think of the Cause, dear man. Think of the Cause."

"Oh, I am. But I'm also thinking of the dynamite. That was a perishing bit of information to come by—and the place where they destroyed it: as bald as an ice rink."

Michael said, "Let me give you a little inside information, Johnny. If you're going to hide dynamite in two batches, you ain't going to put them side by side like tombstones. You're going to put them in two different cemeteries, so if they find one, they ain't going to find the other just by looking around where the first one was. Right?"

O'Grady thought it through and nodded agreement. Throughout the meeting, he cast a sidelong glance at Michael now and then: for the life of him, he could not make the connection between the man translating for him at the restaurant that night and the one beside him now.

Michael returned to the Gimpel Security System manual which he had been studying. "What I think I better do, boss, is get in touch with a friend of mine, you know who I mean—Hard Luck Louis? After his accident he got to be an expert on how to open things the right way."

"Take Alberto along. He's an engineer and he will be working inside with you."

"I have a feeling we won't need that information," Alberto said. "Not if our timing is right."

"You must be prepared," Romano said. "You have no idea the things that can go wrong. It would destroy me to think of anything happening to that Chinese folio."

Tsin Dynasty pornography. It had taken Julie half the trip home to get that information out of Alberto.

"And you seen the money sitting in there in the vault?" Michael said to Alberto.

"I saw four pieces of luggage, plaid airplane luggage. I couldn't very well say, 'What's in that luggage?' could I?"

"You did splendidly," Romano soothed. "It would be the plaid of the Campbell clan, no doubt."

Michael shook his head. "I don't trust all this cooperation, Mr. Romano."

"And you are quite right not to do so," Romano said.

"You will want two roads of egress," he went on. "Can you manage the park gate, O'Grady? And the padlock at the entrance to the park?"

"I can, sir. I have a pair of cutters that'd go through the chain of a ship's anchor."

"Can you think of any further information you

haven't given us?" Each of them had separately accounted on tape his assignment of the day, but O'Grady had been self-conscious discovering his voice was being recorded.

"Not at the moment, sir."

It was interesting, Julie thought: from the instant of their meeting, O'Grady had called Romano sir. Instinct. His response to the environment and Romano's manners. She was sure he had no idea who Romano was.

"If anything does occur to you, call Alberto. Now tell me what it is you are to bring me in the morning."

"The full names and the passport numbers of the boys."

Romano smiled as though a child had given the correct answer. It irked Julie, although she wasn't sure why—something to do with her own pride. Crazy. Not so crazy.

"You may leave now, O'Grady. Be here at ten in the morning. Do you have enough money?"

"It'll do, sir." Julie could have cheered him for that.

He got up from the table and Alberto with him to see him down. They were now using the service elevator.

Julie said, "I'd like to go too—unless you want me to stay."

"Of course, Miss Julie. You must rest and dress for the party. I have the distinct feeling you did not enjoy your work today."

"It's a day I'd just as soon forget."

He waited in silence. Michael got up and limped out after O'Grady and Alberto.

"He dropped anchor and chased me around a bit. That's all."

Romano made a noise of distress. "Aren't men the most extraordinary egotists?"

"Yeah . . . most of them."

"You seem to have been called upon to give a great deal . . . for the Cause."

Julie met those deep-seeing eyes which she had once so feared.

He looked down at his hands and folded one over the other. Then he looked at her again, blinking brightly. "Enjoy your evening, my dear. We shall have our plans complete when you arrive in the morning."

SCARLET NIGHT

FORTY-SEVEN

Tony gave the cab driver Maude Sloan's address and
settled back. There was a whistle to his breathing that
was drowned out when the cab started moving. Julie had
invited him upstairs for a martini and the last of the
caviar she and Jeff had bought at Orly airport. What she
had really invited him upstairs for was to see *Scarlet
Night* before it ended its residency. If she were going to
tell the story some day, she wanted an available witness.

Tony groped for her hand and held it on the seat between them. His was a big, soft mitten. "I can't think of
any nicer way for an old cocker like me to spend a Saturday night than taking out his best friend's wife. How old
are you, Julie?"

"Twenty-five going on twenty-six."

"Tell me something . . ."

"Almost anything, Tony."

"What in hell is an oil painting doing hanging over the
kitchen table?"

"It's on its way out," Julie said.

"Don't let Jeff do that to you. If you like it, keep it."

"Yeah."

Tony gave her hand a squeeze. "Want to sell it to me?"

"No!"

"I thought I might be doing you a favor."

"Besides, what would Fran say?"

"I had in mind taking it down to the office, if you want
the truth."

Julie said, "I just realized something. The truth is
pretty repetitious."

"Julie, my pet, at my time of life—so are the lies."

The party had reached the upper decibels. Wall-to-wall
people, as was said of parties given by a friend of Julie's.
Tony Alexander was recognized at once. A lot of people
hustled him until Maude Sloan fought her way through to

him and Julie. "How nice of you to come, Mrs. Hayes."

"I'm sorry Jeff is out of town." Not at all sorry. Nor would Jeff be with this crowd. "Do you know Tony Alexander? . . . Mrs. Sloan, Tony." A crazy notion—probably the result of a week of tape recordings—Julie felt she hadn't said the words at all. Somebody'd pushed a button and they came out.

Tony raised his voice and pointed to the ceiling while he shouted: "That's a gorgeous stretch of tin." Embossed scroll work, the whole length of the loft; it was an enormous room at the far end of which, if they ever got there, Julie supposed they would find a kitchen and a bedroom. There was a lavatory in the hall next to the elevator out of which wafted still the not-so-gentle reek of sweatshop days.

"But a disaster in acoustics," Maude Sloan shouted back. "There's a bar at either end." Then to Julie: "You'll recognize Ginni—long auburn hair." Ginni hadn't mentioned their visit. "Or she'll find you," she added. "She has a surprise for you."

Oh, boy.

Tony, propelling Julie toward the nearest bar, growled, "She should have hired Roseland."

It was at the bar that Ginni caught up with them. She kissed Julie on either cheek and pretended not to notice Tony at all. Tony somehow looked ten years younger when he presented himself for introduction.

Ginni took hold of Julie's hand to make sure of her attention. "Ralph sends his love."

Ralph. "Mmmm," she said, waking up. "Where is he?"

"He's husking corn at the Iowa State Fair. Can you believe it?"

"Can't be," Tony said. "It's too early."

Ginni cast him a reproachful look. "Maybe he's just practicing for it." To Julie: "I called that shop he used to own and his cousin found him for me."

Why, Julie wondered, had she tracked him down? To make sure where he was? That he wouldn't stumble into the middle of the caper?

"I didn't want him to hold it against me that things went wrong when he got back to this country. He's one of the nicest boys I ever met. Mother liked him too."

"She did, didn't she?" Julie said, trying to get hold of reality.

"Didn't you?" Ginni said, wide-eyed and full of guile.

"Oh, yes," Julie said, and it was true.

"I lied to him, Julie. I told him that I'd gone to visit you and saw *Scarlet Night*. I said it was just beautiful where you had it hanging over the mantel in the living room."

"Thanks," Julie said. "It's going to be great if he comes back to see it himself."

"I didn't tell him you were giving it to that Rubinoff. I didn't mention Rubinoff at all. He won't come, Julie. Not for years and years. Maybe when he's got a string of tow-headed youngsters he wants to show New York to."

"Tow-headed," Tony said, finally having a martini in hand. "Where did you ever pick up a word like that?"

"From Ralph Abel, the man we're talking about. I invited him to come back to Naples to the commune and start over, but he kept talking about a silver thimble somebody gave him. He'll be a tailor just like his father, Julie, whom he really loved. All we'll be to him are beautiful memories."

"Both of us?"

Ginni laughed and gave her hand a squeeze before releasing it. "I love you," she said. "I hope next time you're on the Continent you'll come and visit me in Naples."

She gave them a flash of teeth and drifted off.

Julie said, "I'm ready to go when you are, Tony." Miss Page had always said a lady never sweats. Wrong. Or else . . .

Tony looked at his watch. "How about the first show at The Bottom Line?"

"Great."

In the clanking, rasping elevator that went down by leaps and halts, Tony said, "She don't know much about corn, but I'll bet she's great in the hay."

FORTY-EIGHT

Julie cleaned house again on Sunday afternoon. Compulsively. Her instructions from Romano were the simplest of anybody's. She would go downstairs with Rubinoff as though going out on a date of her own. When Rubinoff drove away, Alberto would pick her up in a white Mustang, and they would try to keep Rubinoff in view. If they lost him it would not be critical. Michael, the more experienced driver, would hold closer to him, Michael now driving a green Pontiac station wagon. She and Alberto would pick up O'Grady at Forty-third Street and Twelfth Avenue. They would all rendezvous at the golf range near Maiden's End.

Under Romano's eye, O'Grady had composed a note to leave with the boys for Ginni: it said he had to go to the clinic at six-thirty for a treatment. (Disease unspecified, but painful.) They were not to worry. He had a first-floor lookout on the street and he'd be there in plenty of time. Whether or not she believed him was not greatly important once Rubinoff was on the road. He had kept faith with his client, to the best of his knowledge: Ginni had no idea who or where the client was. She had no choice but to wait.

On the estate grounds, Julie's only assignment was to pacify the dog. And to obey Michael in an emergency. Michael and O'Grady had gone out that morning for a walk in the woods: they watched the whole Campbell staff depart at noon, a mini-bus load of them dressed in their Sunday best.

Michael's plan called for O'Grady to take over the wheel of the Pontiac at the golf-range parking area where they would leave the Mustang and all go on in the one car. O'Grady would wait with the car outside Campbell's main gate, careful to stop short of the electronic eye, while Julie, Michael, and Alberto walked along the fence and entered the estate from the park. He calculated that it

187

would take them twelve to fifteen minutes to get inside the house.

Campbell would have deactivated the alarm on one door, likely the front one, to admit Rubinoff: they would know that from where Rubinoff parked his car. It wouldn't matter that Campbell could reactivate it, for Michael proposed to enter the building himself by an entry not on the system: the dog door. (He had given a fascinating demonstration of what looked like a collapse of his shoulders, and Romano had to restrain him from recounting the spectacular entries he had made in his day.) Once inside, he would deactivate and unlock the kitchen door for Alberto and whatever other door or doors the operation required.

He planned to handcuff Rubinoff and Campbell together, back to back. . . . Romano, sensitive to Julie's presence, had suggested that only Michael and Alberto needed to know precise details. The vault was bound to be off the alarm system until such time as Campbell closed it 'for the night and the signal went through to police headquarters. If the information became necessary, Alberto knew the desk drawer where Campbell had gone in his presence to refresh his memory of the vault combination. He had had it changed within the week.

An intercom box and a release button for the main gate were in a lovely antique cabinet on the wall of the front vestibule. When they were ready for O'Grady, Alberto would open the gate to him. It would close itself when he had driven through. They planned to leave by way of the park and drop off Julie and Alberto to pick up the Mustang.

Julie decided to phone Jeff at midafternoon to be sure he would not call while Rubinoff was there. Or to be sure he wasn't on his way home. Then she decided not to. She was too nervous to sound natural. Besides, she ought not to tie up the phone in case Romano tried to reach her.

would take them twelve to fifteen minutes to get inside the
house.
Cogley would have to set off a store on the

FORTY-NINE

O'Grady wondered for a long time what in hell the boys
were doing in the bedroom. Not that he wasn't glad to be
out of their sight for a while. His nerves were not a working team at the moment. He had shaved a second time
that day; his face was raw. He was carving anchors and
chains in the kitchen table with the thin blade of his knife,
having, before that, whittled his fingernails to the quick.

The phone rang in the living room and he raced
Tommy for it. They'd taken to answering the phone on
him. They were learning English a lot faster than he
would ever learn Italian. As though ever again in his life
he would want to learn it.

Tommy got to the phone first. "Ginni," he announced.
"For me."

And welcome to each other. The palaver began in Italian. O'Grady started back to the kitchen and then stopped
in his tracks when he heard Tommy say, "Plaza. Hotel
Plaza ..."

O'Grady strode to the bedroom door and looked in on
Steph. They were packing, their suitcases open on Ma's
bed. Of course they were! With the money coming in,
they were going to move to the Plaza. A suite, no doubt
the bridal suite, and Ginni astride the both of them.

With an hour and a half to wait, he left the house. He
had a beer at McGowan's, having made sure the old lady
wasn't there ahead of him. He walked down Forty-fourth
Street toward Julie's shop although he knew she was at
home nursing nerves as unraveled as his own. And there
coming toward him was the Rodriguez family, the mother
and daughter hand in hand and the little bantam cock of
a man strutting a pace ahead of them. He was so puffed
up with vanity, he wouldn't know horns from a halo.

O'Grady crossed the street to avoid them and at the
corner turned up Eighth Avenue. It was Sunday. He went
to the five o'clock Mass at St. Malachy's.

FIFTY

The doorbell rang at twenty minutes to six, which gave Julie a start. It was not that she wasn't ready, but she wondered if everybody else was.

"Rubinoff . . ." The name floated musically over the house phone.

Julie pushed the buzzer and went into the hall. There wasn't much hair on his head seen from the top. Oh, God. As though she cared where his hair grew. Or whether he sprouted lilies in his navel.

"You're early," she said.

"I hope you don't mind. After all, you suggested five."

"It's fine." She preceded him into the foyer. "I'll get some wrapping paper and string." That could take time.

"Not necessary. It isn't raining and I don't have far to go tonight. What a lovely apartment! I'd hoped to meet your husband. I greatly admire him."

"I'll tell him," Julie said.

Scarlet Night was leaning against the frame of the dining arcade just off the foyer. Rubinoff gazed at it and then said, "Well, it hasn't changed much, has it?"

"Would you like a drink—or a cup of tea?"

"That's very kind of you, but I mustn't stop. I made the check out to Julie Hayes." He spelled the first name aloud.

"That's it."

He gave her the check. "You've been very gracious in an awkward situation."

"If you'll wait a minute, I'll go downstairs with you." Julie got her purse and stuck the check into it. She turned on a light to leave burning in Jeff's study, stretching time by seconds. "Let me make sure I turned off the gas. I am absentminded."

Rubinoff was standing in the hall, *Scarlet Night* under his arm.

"Thank you for waiting." She got out her keys and had

deliberate trouble with the second lock. "The light's not very good out here."

She had just put her keys into her purse when the doorbell rang within the apartment—one long ring and two short. Jesus Christ. "That's Jeff now," she said, and galloped past Rubinoff to be down the stairs before Jeff could make it up. "How nice. You'll get to meet him."

They all converged in the downstairs hallway.

"Jeff, this is Mr. Rubinoff. I may have spoken to you about him."

"How do you do?" Jeff put down his bag.

Rubinoff shifted *Scarlet Night* so that he could shake hands. "It's an honor, sir. I've just told your wife how much I admire your column."

"Thank you. Well! Are you two going some place or can you come back upstairs for a drink?"

Rubinoff blinked his eyes and said regretfully, "I wish I could, but I have a cab waiting." A cab. Not a dark red Buick station wagon, license D-A-S 320. He offered Julie his hand. "Good-bye, Mrs. Hayes."

And out he went like a sloe-eyed bat.

"Jeff . . ." Julie finally kissed him. "Call Tony. He'll explain. I'll be back sometime tonight."

She waited in the outside vestibule until the cab pulled away. Jeff waited with her, either stumped for the right questions or having the sense not to ask them. She kissed him again and ran down the steps when Alberto pulled up in the white Mustang. Just before she got in she called back to Jeff: "There's cold chicken in the refrigerator."

Alberto said aloud the license number of the cab. Julie repeated it while she got out a pencil and wrote it down. "What does it mean?"

"He's parked somewhere else, that's all. Michael will pick him up there."

"He's early," Julie said.

"Not much. The trouble is O'Grady may be late."

Traffic was light. They were making much too good time. They had supposed, counting on the station wagon, that Rubinoff might go on to Twelfth Street and along beneath the highway to the next ramp. He turned up Eleventh. Alberto did not turn. "It's better that we let him go in case he saw us. The last thing we want to do is scare him off."

"Hey, you're good at this."

Alberto glanced at her. "I don't think I'm going to make it my life's work."

There was no sign of O'Grady as they approached the diner. But when they got there he emerged from the red Volkswagen parked in the corner. "Jesus," he said. "I just saw Rubin in a cab."

"Did he see you?"

"It wouldn't matter if he did. It's where I keep the little car."

"But from now on it will matter," Alberto said. "You'd better both get in the back." The rear window was strongly tinted.

As they drove up the ramp O'Grady said, "Do you know what the two acrobats are doing back in my apartment? They're packing their clothes to move to the Plaza."

"My favorite hotel," Julie said.

"Hers too." He could not bring himself to say Ginni's name. He took the metal cutter from his pocket and laid it on the seat between them. "I'd better not forget this," he said.

Or drop it, Julie almost said but didn't. "Are you sure it will work?"

"I am. I already used it on the back gate this morning."

They rode on, all three in silence. The northbound traffic continued light. The southbound traffic was heavy. Delays at all the exits. "We'll be coming back in traffic like that," Alberto said.

"As long as it's not in a basket," O'Grady said cheerfully.

Alberto kept watching through both side mirrors. Suddenly he said, "He's coming up on the left. Cover your faces."

O'Grady threw his arm around Julie and kissed her cheek, his hand a shield between their faces and the traffic on the left.

"All clear," Alberto said over his shoulder.

"I might never have such an opportunity again," O'Grady said when Julie pulled away.

"Here's Michael coming up on the other side," Alberto said.

The green Pontiac wagon overtook and passed them. Michael looked right at them but gave no sign of recognition. In the left lane, the red wagon, D-A-S 320, was beginning to pick up speed.

Michael was waiting when they reached the driving range. He stood alongside the green wagon smoking impatiently. He climbed into the back. Julie followed him. Alberto rode in front with O'Grady now at the wheel. He had the gears screaming before they got out of the lot.

"I thought you said you could drive," Michael roared at him.

"I'll have the hang of it in a minute. I'm used to the foreign shift." All the way back to the traffic light O'Grady talked to the Pontiac.

Michael said: "You get another job, Miss Julie. I want you to let the air out of Rubinoff's front tires. Can you handle that?"

"You bet."

They turned into Maiden's End. People were playing croquet on a lawn and youngsters were riding bicycles, and a man and woman, jogging, waved at them, mistaking them for friends. Julie wanted to scream, "Let me out! Pick me up at . . ." She couldn't even remember who it was Jeff and she had visited.

It was darker in the woods. Lights were beginning to come on in the houses. Twilight. They passed through the stone gates marked Private, and Michael ordered O'Grady to stop. They changed places and Michael himself drove up to within a couple of feet of the electronic eye. He wasn't taking a chance now; one lurch of the car in front of the box would alert Campbell. "It's in your hands now, Irishman. You know what to do when the gate opens."

"Drive through in a hurry."

"Drive through natural. And park on the lawn when you get near the house. Stay clear of Rubinoff's car. Anybody coming by here while you're waiting, speak nice to them like a chauffeur, waiting for your boss."

"Godspeed," O'Grady said.

They walked, Indian file, Michael ahead along the path into the woods. The fence was in sight all the way. They wore dark clothes, Julie a brown sweater and slacks, her purse under her left arm, the strap slung over her right shoulder. Sneakers. Coming from that direction, they reached the overgrown but passable drive and turned onto it before reaching the clearing. The moon was rising over Tarrytown, a tumult of clouds swelling around it. Michael slipped the chain from the gate. Alberto opened it wide.

"You first now," Michael said to Julie.

The dog. Julie wasn't sure she could get her lips together for a whistle.

The lights within the house, at this twilight hour, had the quality of candles. They burned softly throughout the building. Rubinoff's station wagon was under the portico, blocking the drive as Michael had foreseen. They approached a roadway of fine gravel which led to the four-car garage some fifty yards from the house. Campbell's assorted Jags and Cadillacs were at rest there.

They proceeded in the grass alongside the driveway until they were opposite the kitchen. At Michael's signal they stopped. He removed his coat and gave it to Alberto, who had been instructed how to carry it, the pockets loaded.

Michael stepped onto the drive and scuffled his feet in the gravel. Out through the dog door came the setter. Julie whistled and opened her arms to him. He gave one brief rattle of barks before discovering Julie. Then he was all over her, a slobber of joy. She drew him away from the house, the dog prancing and tugging at the leather strap of her shoulder bag which she gave him to pull on. It was one thing to snatch a man's money, but she hated to corrupt his dog.

Julie watched from the distance until she saw the kitchen door open and Alberto disappear. Then she moved back toward the house and around to the main entrance where the Buick wagon was parked.

She could see through window after window into an eerily empty house. The only room in which the draperies were drawn was the small study where, she felt, they must now be undressing *Scarlet Night*. She removed the cap on the tire valve of the wheel furthest from the house and pressed her thumbnail on the valve. The hiss sounded lethal. The dog licked her face. It kept him busy.

Every step toward the wheel on the house side made breathing more difficult. One flat tire ought to be enough. But Michael had said two. Then, through the small window alongside the front door and through the glass of the vestibule door, she saw the two figures across the vast living room. The one with the limp was Michael. There was the glint of metal in his hand. The two figures disappeared from her sight on the far side of the open study door. They would be alongside the stairway.

The tire was never going to be flatter. A plane motor sounded overhead. But no sound from within the house. She waited in the shadows and watched through the window. She smothered the dog with affection. Time: the thump of her heart, the whoosh of the dog's tail, the tick of her watch when she held it to her ear. Someone came into the vestibule. It was Rubinoff. He brought two suitcases. Julie fled to the shield of the nearest bushes, but he did not come out. She saw movement again there presently, but from that distance could only surmise that it was Rubinoff again with the other two suitcases. She had trouble now keeping the dog with her. He ran off finally and did not return at her whistle. He could well be going in the dog door unless Michael had blocked it from inside. She counted slowly to one hundred and then back down to one. Not a sound came to her from the house. She left the bushes and approached the car again, staying on the far side of it.

A bright light came on in the vestibule and she saw Alberto.

O'Grady tried to take his mind off the fact that he had to urinate. He knew the trouble was with his nerves, not his bladder. But the more he tried, the more painful the condition. The girl and the two of them had been gone twenty minutes. It seemed much longer. He was sure Michael had underestimated the time it would take them to get into the house. There was no telling how much longer it would take them. He had to take a chance and do it quickly.

He started the car motor, left it running, and left the car door open while he went to the edge of the woods. For all his urgency, he couldn't get started, his mind and his eyes on the gate. He turned his back to it. In time to see two bicyclists come around the curve in the drive. Youngsters, their bikes pint-size. The devils kept coming and would not turn back. Boys. With the car door open and the light on, they would want a look inside. Let them. He'd go out and speak to them, and if they were like himself at their age, they'd know damn well what he'd been doing. Finished, he stepped out of the woods. But at that instant, the gate started to open and he had to make a run for the car to get it in the grounds before the gate closed on him again. Fifty seconds. He glanced back to see that the kids had abandoned their bikes and taken to their heels down the road.

Julie had watched Alberto open the cabinet and press the switch that opened the gate to O'Grady. He unbolted and opened the front door and came out to watch for the approaching car. Julie went to him. "Is it all right?"

His eyes were wild. He went back and pressed the gate signal again. Julie looked down the road. The car lights came on. Then she heard the motor. O'Grady was on his way in. The four suitcases stood where Rubinoff had left them. Without a word to Julie, Alberto returned to the study.

The dog came racing out of the semi-darkness and leaped over the suitcases into the house. There was no use pretending she was any less involved by staying outdoors. Julie went inside and, at the study door, saw Rubinoff and Campbell standing with hands to the wall alongside the open vault. Michael held a gun on them. The dog was leaping up on Campbell, trying to get attention. He tried Rubinoff, then noticed Michael.

Julie hardly knew what happened to her: a bolt of rage when she heard a click she knew to be Michael's release of the safety catch on his gun. She felt the scream in her throat while she plunged in front of Michael and grabbed the dog. She got hold of his collar and dragged him away. The two men at the wall may have moved. Michael shouted at them. She didn't know or care, only that she was pulling the dog to safety. She looped the strap of her bag into the collar. Alberto was with her. She hauled the dog outdoors where Alberto opened the door to Rubinoff's car. The dog got in when she did. Julie managed to get out again and left him confined there. She was shaking badly.

Alberto put his arms around her awkwardly and held her for a moment. "I don't think he'd have done it."

Julie knew differently, but she got hold of herself.

O'Grady stood gaping at them. "What the hell's happened?"

"It's all right," Julie said.

"The suitcases are in the hall," Alberto told him. "Better load them quickly."

They were all three on the steps when the sirens began to wail in the distance.

"Jesus, Mary, and Joseph," O'Grady said and grabbed two of the suitcases.

Alberto returned to the study, Julie paused at the door.

Michael ordered: "You, fat boy, put your hands behind your back. Do it slow."

Poor, quivering Rubinoff took his hands from the wall, clasped them over his head like a clown in a ballet, and brought them down as far as he could behind his neck.

"For Christ sake, put your hands on your rump," Michael shouted at him. He handed Alberto a set of handcuffs.

The sirens persisted.

The phone on the desk started to ring as Alberto put the cuffs on Rubinoff. It kept ringing, four, five, six, seven . . .

"Where's O'Grady?" Michael wanted to know.

"Loading the car," Julie said.

"You get out of here, miss," Michael said. "Get in the car and stay there." To Alberto he said, "What's the sirens about?"

Campbell answered him. "They're coming for you, man. You'll never make it."

"Shut up, you." To Alberto, about to give him the other set of handcuffs, Michael said: "Answer that phone like you were a servant or something."

Alberto picked up the phone: "Mr. Campbell's residence."

The message was cryptic. No questions. Alberto said, "Yes, sir," a couple of times.

O'Grady came up to where Julie lingered in the doorway.

Alberto hung up the phone and said, "The police want the grounds evacuated. They suggest by boat instead of using cars. They want to keep the road open for emergency equipment. There may be more dynamite."

Silence.

Then O'Grady said, "Oh, Jesus Christ." In his mind's eye he saw the two youngsters running, as for their lives, past the spot of the previous demolition. "It'd be a false alarm, I think," he said, his voice a croak. "I was taking a pee and some kids saw me run for the car when the gate opened. I scared the hell out of them."

Campbell's hands slipped on the wall as his shoulders heaved. The man was laughing.

"I wouldn't laugh, mister. Get in the vault," Michael said. "O'Grady, get him in there. See if you can do *that* right."

Alberto got out of the way, coming out to Julie. "Nobody's going to get hurt," he said.

Julie shook her head. What in hell had she expected?

There were other sirens now, coming closer. But anyone trying to get through the main gate would have trouble until someone opened it from within the grounds.

O'Grady and Michael came out of the study. "You're supposed to take orders, Miss Julie."

Julie glanced into the study. The room was empty, the vault closed. She said, "Michael, where's the painting?"

The scar all but disappeared when his face went white.

Julie said, "You and O'Grady go. We can make it by the river. Please, Michael. I know what I'm doing. We'll meet at the penthouse."

Michael offered his revolver to Alberto. "Do you want this?"

Julie answered for him. "No."

Michael limped out after O'Grady and a few seconds later the Pontiac took off for the park.

Alberto found the vault combination in the desk drawer.

"I hope it works," Julie said, but she had more in mind what she intended to say to Campbell.

Alberto repeated the combination aloud as he twisted the dials with trembling fingers. He pulled the great door open. The light inside lit automatically when the door opened. Campbell came out blinking, Rubinoff after him, his hands still cuffed behind him.

"Please stand where you are and listen to me," Julie said. "We want to take *Scarlet Night* and the drawing with us. If we can do that, Mr. Campbell, and borrow your boat to get away in, nobody will ever know that G. T. Campbell intended to pay six hundred thousand dollars for a stolen Leonardo da Vinci. The drawing will go back where it came from in Italy."

Campbell pulled at an ear while he thought about it. He glanced at Rubinoff, hunched beside him. The sweat had plastered his hair down, exposing the bald spot. To Julie he looked like a tonsured monk. Campbell said, "What do I get for my six hundred thousand?"

"A live dog."

FIFTY-ONE

Michael drove as though the woods would explode behind him.

"I keep telling you it's a false alarm," O'Grady shouted. The car would collapse beneath them if he kept it up. "And they'll be stopping back by the stone gates maybe, waiting for the explosives experts. It's a terrible thing I've put them through for nothing."

Michael said, "You want to stop by police headquarters and tell them all about it?"

O'Grady looked at him by the light of the dashboard.

"You don't have to be so damned sarcastic. If the girl and him don't get the picture, where'll we be then?"

"Costa Rica," Michael said, slowing down a bit. "The boss won't monkey around."

"Mr. Romano?"

"Yeah, Sweets Romano. Did you never hear of Sweets Romano?"

"Holy God. Is that who he is?" You couldn't grow up on the west side of New York without having heard the name. He might even own the building O'Grady lived in.

At a curve in the road they came in sight of the highway. It was jammed, cars bumper to bumper, with the whirligig lights of police cars flashing over their roofs. Michael stopped and put out the car lights while he thought for a moment. "What we've got to do, Johnny, is cooperate with the police. Tell them Campbell opened the back gate for their emergency vehicles. Tell them they can get through that way. You can say we work for him. Isn't that what you went to them for in the first place?"

"Don't rush me, Michael. I'm a slow learner, but I keep what I know. What about the girl and him back there?"

"It's better them than us with what we got in the back seat."

And him with a gun, O'Grady thought. "What'll we say's in the suitcases if the police look in and ask?"

"Papers! Important papers Campbell doesn't want around with this dynamite business again. You're an Irishman. The cops'll believe you."

"Drive on," O'Grady said. "I'll be better able to talk to them than to you, sure."

They pulled up to the pole at the park entrance. Dead ahead, on the other side of the barrier, an officer was standing outside his patrol car.

"Get the gate open," Michael said to O'Grady. He beeped his horn at the cop, motioning him to move the car.

O'Grady hopped out, turned his back on the officer, and with one hard twist of the cutter nipped the hasp through which the padlock hung. He pocketed the cutters and hauled the pole out of the way.

The cop moved his car and Michael drove out. A fire truck, crawling along the shoulder on the wrong side of the road, pulled alongside the Pontiac. O'Grady spoke to the cop and the fireman who jumped off the truck. "You can go back through the park there and get in by the Campbell gate. He's ordered the place opened up to you."

"That's all I wanted to know," the fireman said, "as long as we can get through there." He ran back and instructed his engineer.

"You work for Campbell?" the cop wanted to know.

"Aye. We're taking out some papers he wants safe in New York."

"You're better off using the Tappan Zee bridge than trying to get through this way."

"Why are all the cars backed up?" O'Grady said.

"There's a jam at the traffic light. We're trying to pull everybody out of Maiden's End till the Ordnance boys go through the woods back there."

"What if it's a hoax?"

"Better safe than sorry, wouldn't you say?"

"Oh, I agree. Much better." O'Grady got into the car and Michael drove north, the road wide open in that direction. O'Grady remembered the Mustang they had left in the driving-range lot. "What about the other car, Michael?"

"You got a key for it?"

"I don't. Alberto would have it."

"I'll tell you what I got the key for," Michael said. "The handcuffs on that Rubinoff fella."

FIFTY-TWO

Campbell did not loan them the cruiser. He took them downriver himself and put them ashore at the Seventy-ninth Street marina. Julie stepped onto the dock first. They had reassembled *Scarlet Night* in the cabin. Alberto handed it up to her.

It was more of a problem landing Rubinoff, his hands still cuffed behind his back, but hidden beneath a raincoat of Campbell's. The coat was buttoned at his throat and, on him, ankle length. "I wouldn't care if you dropped him overboard," Campbell said, "if it wasn't for the publicity."

Before casting off, Campbell spoke to Julie. "You know, little lady, I got to hand it to you. I'm just a country boy from Texas and you slickered me proper."

While Alberto watched for a cab, Julie called Romano.

He had just heard from Michael. They had made it across the Tappan Zee bridge.

"You do have *Scarlet Night?*" Romano said.

"You bet."

"You had better bring Rubinoff along. Michael will be able to liberate him."

"Mr. Romano, we had to leave the Mustang at the driving range."

"So Michael said. You do seem to have come home in bits and pieces. I shall arrange for the rental company to pick it up. Good-bye, Miss Julie."

In the cab, riding the jump seat, Rubinoff whimpered all the way across town, "Ruined, ruined, ruined."

FIFTY-THREE

It was a quarter to ten when O'Grady went up the stairs to his apartment, where Ginni greeted him a little less than tenderly.

"There was a mix-up," he said. "We're to meet somewhere else for the distribution of funds."

"No," Ginni said.

"Yes, God damn it. The money's down there in the car. Come on now before it's hijacked."

That moved her. If only he'd known how to speak to her before, it might all have been different. She lined up the boys. They had already transported their luggage to the Plaza.

O'Grady opened the car door when they reached the street. "You'll have to sit three across," he said. "I'll ride with the driver."

"Where's Rubinoff?"

"He's waiting."

"I'm going back to Mother's until I hear from him."

"You'll wait a long time then," O'Grady said. "Come here, my darling." He took her rudely by the arm and led her to the back of the station wagon where he lifted the hatch door. The light went on. After looking up and down the street, he flattened one of the bags and unzipped it far enough to turn back the flap. It gave him a turn himself to see one eye of Benjamin Franklin staring up at him from a packet of hundreds.

"*Lacrima Cristi*," Ginni said, and went around and crawled in alongside the boys.

The boys helped load the suitcases into the freight elevator at Romano's.

Alberto opened the door to them, and conducted them through, money and all, to the office. He diverted Michael to the kitchen to free and fetch Rubinoff. Julie and Romano were waiting in the office. Ginni balked at the door, but O'Grady put one arm around her and the other

202

under her flailing legs and carried her over the threshold. He put her down in one of the chairs that had been set out in a half circle. The boys sat on either side of her. Romano waited for Michael and Rubinoff, to whom, when he came in rubbing his wrists, he murmured, "I'm so glad you could join us."

The Little King took his time. Then he said: "I am Romano and you are my guests. I will not say you are welcome, but you will not be detained long. I understand you were looking for a courier. So am I." He took three envelopes from the desk. "You will distribute these, Alberto."

Alberto gave an envelope each to Ginni and the boys.

"You needn't open them now," Romano said. "There is enough money in each to cover your expenses for the duration of your stay in America and your plane reservations for ten-forty-five tomorrow morning." He repeated what he had just said in what sounded to Julie like beautiful Italian. He took a folded sheet of paper from his other pocket and gave it to Alberto to pass on. "I would ask that you sign this, Miss Julie. It is a bill of sale made out to Miss Bordonelli for a painting called *Scarlet Night*. A modest sum, one hundred dollars.

"You will take the painting back to Italy with you, Miss Bordonelli. I don't think Customs in either country will trouble you, the daughter of Count Bordonelli. But it is a chance you must take.

"I expect to hear in not later than forty-eight hours that a work of art stolen from the Italian people in Venice last March has been safely recovered. Otherwise . . . Ah, but there won't be any otherwise."

Julie signed the prepared document. Her hand wasn't very steady, but neither was Ginni's when she accepted it from Alberto.

"There is one last bit of business and then we can adjourn, some of us to meet another day. Please follow."

Romano moved lightly ahead into the studio which was ablaze with lights. *Scarlet Night* was on the easel, where Romano had put it when Alberto and Julie arrived a scant few minutes before Ginni and the others.

"Alberto, please remove the frame, gently, gently."

Everyone watched in silence.

The frame removed, Romano turned the canvas around himself, took a palette knife and removed the drawing.

He offered it to Rubinoff. "Perhaps you, sir, would like to have this as a souvenir?"

Rubinoff backed away as though this were the greatest horror of his day.

"Come now. Didn't you notice? Perhaps not with such other weighty matters on your mind. And of course your client wouldn't, his excess of trust surpassed only by his ignorance. . . . And it is a very good reproduction of a Michelangelo. It may be that Leonardo himself copied it, but alas, Alberto and I could find no reproduction of the Leonardo. You will understand now, Miss Julie, why we could not risk your going that day to the F.B.I." He tossed the reproduction into a bin. "Now, Alberto, dear boy, shall we put our unworthy hands to the real thing?"

Alberto went to the case where the Leonardo had been placed on the day Romano revealed its presence to Julie. It had been there ever since.

Romano said, "Miss Bordonelli, you did it once so expertly. Perhaps you will assist again in the preparation of our treasure for international travel?"

"I can't do it," Ginni said, probably for the first time in her life.

"Then we must manage, Alberto . . . Miss Julie."

FIFTY-FOUR

One long ring and two short. Julie waited in the vestibule, her legs still shaky. She did not want to scrabble for the keys in her purse if she didn't have to.

The buzzer sounded, releasing the lock, a mocking answer-back—one long buzz and two short. Two fairly drunken men were waiting for her when she got upstairs. Not sloppy drunk, not Jeff ever. Hilariously drunk.

"Is there a book in it?" Tony wanted to know the minute she came in. And to Jeff: "Listen to me, friend. Your wife is a book writer. That's the whole problem. She needs space—not a goddamned pica-measured newspaper column. There's a book in it. Right, Julie?"

She nodded and kissed the top of Jeff's head. If she'd bent any lower she would have collapsed.

"What do you think would be an appropriate advance?"

Julie counted on her fingers: Romano, Alberto, Michael, O'Grady, and . . . Julie. Five. "About a hundred and twenty thousand dollars," she said.

Leonardo Drawing Recovered

Special to The New York Times

ROME, July 29—Acting on an anonymous telephone call, the Rome police today recovered a priceless drawing by Leonardo da Vinci from a storage locker at the Rome airport. The drawing had been stolen from the Venice Institute of Art last March. It was unharmed except for a slight discoloration on the back where a small amount of adhesive had been applied. The police speculate the thieves had intended to smuggle the drawing out of Italy but abandoned the scheme in view of recent security improvements.